THE WALL

PETER VANSITTART

THE WALL

A Novel

PETER OWEN · LONDON

PETER OWEN PUBLISHERS
73 Kenway Road London SW5 0RE

First published in Great Britain 1990
© Peter Vansittart 1990

British Library Cataloguing in Publication Data
Vansittart, Peter, *1920* –
The wall.
I. Title
823.914 [F]

ISBN 0 7206 0784 1

Typesetting by Action Typesetting Gloucester
Printed in Great Britain by Billings of Worcester

TO

T.W. OWENS
PERHAPS OF ABERGELE, ONCE OF EPWORTH

To be ignorant of what happened before you were born is always to live the life of a child.

Cicero

For, in a citizenry as large as ours, there is a multitude of people fearful of the penalties attached to crimes of which they know they are guilty, and who therefore strive for political confusion and revolution; others are stricken with inbred madness, driving them to gorge on civil conflict and rebellion; others too, whose private affairs are in such tumult that, rather than die alone, they prefer to pull down the entire state in one general conflagration.

Cicero

The armed forces stationed to attack the state outnumber its defenders, for only a nod is required to inflame the reckless and desperate – indeed these, of their own impulse, incite themselves against society.

Cicero

PREFACE

For those unfamiliar with third-century Europe, I am including the following outline, to avoid tedious explanations in the narrative. For place-names I am inconsistent, using Latin or English as the case may be, whichever I think is the more familiar – for example, Milan for Mediolanum and Strasbourg for Argentoratum.

Between the murder of Emperor Domitian, 'Lord and God', in AD 96, and the death of Emperor Marcus Aurelius, in AD 180, the Roman Empire was ruled by the five remarkable Antonines: Nerva, Trajan, Hadrian, Antoninus Pius and Marcus Aurelius. The thoughts of the last, a Stoic, haunted Europe for a thousand years:

> Let your constant care be to do thoroughly whatever your hand finds necessary, in the way of a man and a Roman – with care, unpretentious dignity, humanity, freedom, justice.

> It is man's peculiar duty to love even those who injure him.

> A man should be upright, not *kept* upright.

> A wrongdoer is often he who has left something undone, not always he who has done something.

Foreign predators had been subdued, commerce prospered, internal order was maintained. The succession, however, of Marcus's useless son, Commodus, initiated almost a century of misrule, civil corruption, violent usurpations and invasion, with only such an occasional exception as Septimius Severus emerging as temporary saviour. Emperors elected by fickle

9

guards and troops, often without sanction from Rome, emerged with bewildering rapidity. Trajan was Spanish, Septimius Severus African, while Philip was Arab, Maximinus Thracian, and Claudius II, Aurelian and Diocletian were from Illyricum (Yugoslavia), 'barbarian' to Roman conservatives.

Commodus was strangled in AD 193. The Emperor was not the Princeps, First Citizen, which in doubtful sincerity Augustus styled himself, but too often a mere commander enthroned not for military or administrative flair, but as a source of payment, blackmail discharged by the fearful ruler. The brutal Praetorian Guard, the Emperor's personal retinue, largely Germanic as a precaution against local factions, murdered Pertinax the same year, then auctioned the Empire, selling it to Didius Julianus before killing him too. Niger was slain by his rival, the hard, efficient, Septimius Severus, in 194. Caracalla, cruel and extravagant fratricide, who granted Roman citizenship to all save slaves, was murdered by the Praetorian commander in 222. The excellent Alexander, victorious over Persia, succumbed to mutiny in 235, as did the vicious Maximinus in 238. Becoming Emperor aged eighty, the intelligent Gordianus committed suicide after the death in battle of his son and co-ruler, Gordianus II, in 238. The same year, after the murders of the shadowy Pupienus and Balbinus, his twelve-year-old grandson, Gordianus III, was enthroned by the legions, to be assassinated in 244. Philip perished in battle, perhaps from fighting, perhaps by murder, while combating the Pannonian Decius, persecutor of Christianity, who died with his son, withstanding the Goths in Danubian marshes in 251. The appeaser Gallus was slaughtered by his troops in 254, suspected of having fatally betrayed Decius. He had certainly bought Gothic peace through paying tribute and allowing pillage. Worse occurred under the vain Valerian who, fighting Sapor I of Persia, was enticed to a feigned peace conference and captured, never to return. His memory lingered as a spectral scapegoat, humiliating reminder of Roman disaster. Anarchy followed. Proclaiming independence, Isauria reverted to mob rule and human sacrifice: Alexandria suffered over a decade of civil conflict precipitated by a dispute between a soldier and a civilian over a pair of shoes. Valerian's son was Gallienus, fitfully brilliant, with a certain charismatic flair but insufficient moral stamina to resist the temptations of power. His reign, during which he was increasingly indolent after his success against the Teutonic Alemanni invading North Italy, proved catastrophic, the entire Empire almost collapsing from an eruption of pretenders, some of them able and responsible, but all dying bloodily. One general and senator, the forceful conqueror Odenanthus, husband of Zenobia of Palmyra, he acknowledged as co-Emperor, ruling in the East. Of Gallienus, Gibbon wrote:

> In every art that he attempted his lively genius enabled him to succeed; and as his genius was destitute of judgment, he attempted every art except the important ones of war and government. He was a master of several curious but useless sciences, a leading orator and elegant poet, a skilful gardener, an excellent cook, and most contemptible prince.

This paragon was killed by his soldiers in 268, while besieging Milan. His son had been abducted and killed by a commander, Postumus, who had grabbed much of Gaul before sharing Gallienus's fate in 267.

Alongside local pretenders, Alemanni invaded Italy and Gaul, Goths pillaged Roman Asia and Greece, pushed up through the Balkans and sacked Ephesus in 273, including Diana's great shrine. Trajan's conquest, Dacia, was to be permanently abandoned by Aurelian. Franks broke into Spain, Quadi and Sarmatians ravaged Pannonia, Parthians seized Mesopotamia and plundered Syria. Exhausted populations tended to welcome conflict as a solution for imperial incompetence, debt, slavery. A few usurpers were to show some substance. Tetricus regained Britain, Gaul and Spain, less for 'Rome' than for himself, before being defeated by Aurelian in 274.

Before Aurelian, the débâcle of Gallienus had made room for the peasant, Emperor Claudius II, remembered as 'Gothicus' for his Gothic conquests. Appointed by the dying Gallienus, Claudius wrote, or is said to have written, to the Roman Senate: 'If I conquer, your gratitude will reward me. If I fail, remember I inherited my job from Gallienus. The whole Republic is worn out, worn to the very bone. We lack javelins, spears and shields. We shall bear ourselves magnificently.' He routed the invaders, but two years later, in 270, died of plague. For a few days a soldier, Quintilius, held the purple until ejected by a peasant ex-ranker, now the victorious cavalry general Aurelian, Consul of Rome under Gallienus, successful against Goths and Vandals and personal rivals, and then looking eastwards towards Palmyra, which was always endangered by Rome, by the Great King of Persia. Currently it was ruled by Zenobia, widow of the murdered Odenanthus, Augustus, King of Kings, who had deserted the Empire, and, with his wife, defeated a Roman army in Syria and threatened Egypt. Ruling alone, Zenobia unwisely taunted and challenged Aurelian, claiming descent from Rome's enemy, the hated Cleopatra. She professed rule over much of Syria and took Egypt, so essential for Rome's grain supplies and naval strategy. Palestine, Arabia, Babylon and Asia Minor acknowledged her. From Antioch and Alexandria she issued coins displaying her head alone, a power hostile to Rome and on a Persian scale, though her underestimation of Aurelian served to demolish her pretensions.

Rome, however potent a symbol, was ceasing to be the pivot of imperial administration, though the Senate retained powers, sometimes little more than nominal. The Emperor was perforce too often in camp, against rivals, restless provinces, and defending the frontiers, notably the Danube and Rhine, against Teutonic and Gothic peoples, and, in Asia, the Persians. With Italy now far less productive, the defence of Mediterranean trade routes was also vital.

Behind the Goths were the fearful Huns, periodically encroaching on Gothic lands, compelling the inhabitants to push into the Empire. Also, by AD 200, the Goths had crushed the remarkable Scythians and Sarmatians. Rome's old enemy,

12

Parthia, had sunk between Persian and Kush, with rich chances for Sapor I, who swiftly overcame Peshawar, then, striking through Roman Asia, captured Antioch and built a city to house his Roman captives, jeeringly calling it 'Sapor, City Superior to Antioch'. Claudius II, Aurelian and Diocletian had ample reason to seek redress from Persia, and to learn from their 'barbarian' enemies, most of whom respected and wished to imitate Roman ways. The powerful Gothic cavalry had finally to be copied by the defeated Romans, who had hitherto relied most on infantry. In bribery, appeasement and shrewd clemency, Goths and Teutons were permitted to settle within the Empire as colonists and client 'federates', often, and dangerously, entrusted with frontier defences, not least in Britain, a policy perhaps originating in more confident times with Augustus. Visigoths, fleeing the Huns, supplied some such colonies, with their accompanying tensions.

The third-century problems were not only military. Traditional Roman religion could no longer galvanize cities now swollen and cosmopolitan. Exotic oriental deities attracted many: warmer, more personal, with esoteric, democratic Mysteries, more explicit promises of after-life, and, save for Mithraism, attractive to women, and, to a disputable extent, to slaves. To the intellectual élites, the atomic determinism of the philosophers Democritus, Epicurus and Lucretius encouraged fortitude but scarcely a flamboyant resistance to irresponsible rulers, contracting markets, crumbling institutions. Hedging his bets, Emperor Alexander (AD 222 – 5) allegedly retained images of Abraham, Orpheus, Christ and the wonder-working sage, a sort of rival Christ, Apollonius of Tyana.

Rome itself was a parasite on the Empire, sustained by grain doles, over two hundred public holidays, degrading spectacles. Literacy had decreased since Augustus founded public libraries, and education languished, with more imitation than creation. Physics, astronomy and mathematics were degenerating into astrology, vulgar hermeticism, mysticism. Deforestation induced erosion and malaria. The Italian population was decreasing, a worsening economic situation encouraging

13

traditional infanticide, while Italians seemed more susceptible to plague, often introduced by soldiers returning from the East, than Jews, Egyptians, Teutons. Compact, self-sufficing cities and autonomous client states had been undermined, the small continuously absorbed by the big, authority becoming too remote for its subjects, the ever-enlarging, corrupt bureaucracy clogging the works. Huge, unwieldy central government headed for mindlessness, at the expense of local pride and purpose. Productivity, singularity lapsed into over-reliance on the State, which, by Aurelian's day, was greedily requisitioning men, goods, animals and land from the classes hitherto most productive – artisans, farmers, peasants, merchants – to combat invasion, trade imbalance and inflation. Local government by gentry, once a voluntary honour, had become a compulsory burden, unwilling and dispirited landowners forced to be unpaid tax-farmers and magistrates, having to remedy deficits themselves, and surrounded by the sceptical, indifferent, resentful. Tax evasion was rampant, the bureaucracy cruelly ruthless, though at least maintaining some administration beneath the hectic careers of the emperors. When the gentry rebelled, by flight, sometimes suicide, their properties could be abandoned to squatters and bandits.

Nevertheless, few could have felt that the Empire's setbacks were irreversible. Claudius Gothicus had restored morale, Aurelian promised more.

I am no specialist in Roman history and aim only at the suggestive, hoping I shall interest readers enough to encourage them to probe further. I myself often find some detail, casually observed, read, or overheard, lingering in my imagination, which slowly or suddenly I come to recognize as momentous. In such detail originated this novel. At school I read in H.G. Wells's *A Short History of the World*: 'A chill had come over the pride and confidence of Rome. In 270 – 275 Rome, which had been an open and secure city for three centuries, was fortified by the Emperor Aurelian.' Just this, but it lurked within me for fifty years and I sometimes mused over it in novels of mine set in modern times. It was reinforced by certain facts and queries

14

I found in Robert Payne's illuminating *The Roman Triumph* (1962). Finally, and all writers will understand this, I found myself, with no very conscious decision, writing *The Wall*.

I acknowledge with gratitude a bursary granted me by the Eastern Arts Association, which has greatly assisted me in preparing this book.

P.V.

I

The settlement, now a mere village three hours' ride from Rome and no longer supporting a mayor, had once, none knew when though a few pretended to, been part of a sizeable town, Optima Fortuna, valued for its harbour, now silted up, and some salt-mines in the hills above. Fallen mansions, crumbling, weed-strewn theatre, abandoned basilica, a meagre forum and rather disreputable baths mourned a lost prosperity. Burdened by a name too big for it, the residue survived on a little fishing, a few vineyards and employments at the Villa Ammianus in its woods above the bay, still occupied by one of the few surviving patrician families.

Through no love of villagers, whom he berated as lazier even than slaves, Senator Clodius Ammianus, in a speech exalted, apt, though incomprehensible to its audience, had endowed them with a library, which he could not afford and which, by now illiterate, they did not want. They would have preferred a distribution of pork. The school was no longer used. The last teacher who, Clodius Ammianus complained, had some learning but the manners of a Tuscan flautist and the morals of a Thracian goatherd, had vanished with a handsome shepherd, to the delight of the few pupils, substantiating the Senator's appraisal.

The countryside was impoverished. Mines were exhausted. Since their far-off efforts against Carthage, Corinth, and the last Republicans, ex-soldier smallholders had been crushed by absentee urban millionaire landlords, their descendants reputedly joining aboriginal Former People, contemptuously termed Oscans, supposedly masters of language but of little else. Such folk, bitter, brooding, mumbling spells, were said to haunt fens, remote valleys and stony hillsides where earth and

17

sky merged in common harshness. Other veterans had sold themselves to ambitious generals, or as slaves to the new land combines and business men, working swollen estates through harsh freedmen bailiffs and lawyers, whose chief qualification was deftness in tax evasion. Taxes were ever more savage as the expenses of army and the Officialdom redoubled yearly, by processes few could explain and even fewer dared to. The poll-tax raised against the Goths had never been rescinded despite the Gothic defeats.

Some terraced olive groves remained with the vines, bright strips above the tumbling sea: ancient arbours were tangled with rose, ilex, hydrangea, though their owners had mostly fled, illegally, dangerously, to Syracuse, Antioch and Alexandria, to avoid the onus of unpaid administrative duties, once a privilege, now an intolerable liability. One such family had been evicted for incomplete grain returns; a former governor of Thessaly been executed for falsifying accounts. Slaves too had been risking their lives after hearing a doubtful rumour that in Sicily, slaves, peasants and agitators, squatting on abandoned estates, now governed themselves. The dwelling nearest to the Villa Ammianus had been briefly occupied by renegades from a Frankish colony planted to guard the coast. By special dispensation from the Officialdom, and for a considerable payment, Senator Clodius Ammianus had been permitted to arm certain slaves.

In prosperity, Optima Fortuna had applauded the hero, Cotta Maximian Felix, for his delicacy in dying there, ensuring that his spirit could be relied on against trouble. This had been required only during the Slave Rebellion. Which rebellion? The one in which Augustus had impaled six thousand captives. Which Augustus? Hush! Meanwhile a stone Cotta, cracked, with hands missing, was still occasionally garlanded by unknown hands.

The coastal road, Herculean Way, built by Hercules himself, remained, reaching south to Naples, winding beneath the Iseum and the empty barracks, past the horses trudging round the mill, within sight of the lighthouse lately broken by African

18

pirates, then skirting the Dragonfly Field of the Ever Living, where ancestors, remote and flitting, professed gratitude for State bread and rancid wine, or were said to. Down the road, despite its holes and fissures, plodded fleabitten cowherds, sailors, salt-sellers in ancient carts, detachments of soldiery, sometimes illicit and moving furtively by night and best not investigated, labourers with oxen, fishermen with turbot and tunny fish, peasants with wheelbarrows of leeks, chestnuts and raisins. Pedlars, in groups, often with weapons, would display linen they vowed was from Tarsus, 'Antiochan' bracelets set with emerald and topaz, bags of coloured beads, offered as Trojan jewels to the ignorant, and sometimes, unprofitably, to those who had never heard of Troy. Preachers would trudge towards Rome with strange news of gods still stranger, followed by caravans bearing Gallic glass, Egyptian dyes and, on festival months, pilgrims to Isis, star of the sea, known in certain moods to illuminate the wrecked lighthouse. Hail Isis, Ever Virgin, Ever Mother.

Litters might pass, borne by slaves who, aggrieved, sometimes abandoned the occupants in inconvenient places and fled. The few children, always excited by curtained palanquins, were ready to pelt any sudden timid face.

This bustle deceived, for commerce was everywhere failing. Insurance consortiums had trebled their rates against banditry, mutiny and storm. A sheep, with a proven record, had foretold a tidal wave, confirmed by the consortiums' own astrologers, while prices soared higher than any such wave.

Daily, this week at Optima Fortuna a spring sun lay golden above the sea, rising from early bands of bluish mist like a marvellous promise. This was later remembered as the fulfilment of a pledge from Isis, though what the pledge had been remained disputable, indeed disputed. It may have been no more than the annual renewal in which blossom foamed, spots of green hung at all levels, the tiny chatter of cicadas rose from crab-grass and the sea acquired the richer texture observed by poets, though here there were none.

More obviously, painted eggs had been hidden and found, allowing a passing wiseacre to babble importantly about the egg of creation, at which an unemployed salter muttered that His Honour Orpheus had promised rebirth. 'We don't see much of him, though.'

Hare-shaped cakes had been gobbled and some ageing sheep sacrificed to Bacchus and Ceres in the old way. At the Festival of the Ambarvalia, youngsters in soiled white, with olive-leaf bandannas, had zestfully expelled demons with tinkling bells and ridden donkeys backwards while virgins or would-be virgins danced and tossed flowers for Flora. Few, however, came to watch, though presumably these included the Goddess herself.

Rites to appease the dead were performed most punctiliously at Villa Ammianus, so that no ghost, complaining, indignant, was ever seen. Actually, as the house had been built by the Senator himself, it lacked family tombs, or appeared to. A slave had once shied at an underworld presence though, returning from Rome, his Master dismissed this apparition as a swirl of leaves, a dream induced by too generous rations, or the presence of wine.

Days of golden promise now presented another apparition. A youth, bare-armed, bare-legged, slender and glistening in soft green tunic, hair dark and matted and bound by a golden thread, limped through the village bearing only a staff tipped with a bright sun-disc. He said nothing, looked neither to right nor left and, ignoring the capering children, soon left the Herculean Way and vanished into the hills, leaving all tongues clacking. Perhaps he was the god Faunus, or a messenger from the sky with hints for the future, or one of those princes apt to arrive from nowhere in particular, behave unusually in a casual manner, then depart for better things.

Long remembered, the stranger was later known to have been seen that day in districts throughout Italy. He must certainly have brought a message, though one probably incomprehensible to all save a rascal priest or quack. Such are the ways of gods and men.

20

II

Villa Ammianus, wide, sturdy, roofed with clear red and brown tiles, was too busy to notice limping strays or half-pay gods with time on their hands. The day was indeed special, but for a family reason. Now, as faint incense spiced the kitchen fumes, slaves bustled about with fresh garlands, tenant farmers were sending appropriate offerings, wreaths had been laid for Hesta, guardian of the hearth fire, not, on this warm day, actually needed, and nosegays laid for the less important though cherished domestic gods, required to be at their best. Chian wine had already been poured to the family ancestor, Mars. Also to the current ruler's favourite deity, the Unconquered Sun, and, with less conviction, to the Emperor himself, the Senator, in purple-rimmed official toga, who had survived certain criminal rulers and pretenders, intoning the formula with a scepticism veiled only because of the prevalance of spies: 'To our Lord, Restorer of Mankind, Extender of the Name and Empire of Rome, Founder of Eternal Security, Lucius Domitius Aurelian. Fortunate, Almighty, Pious, Inviolate, Most Noble, Ever Augustus.'

Privately, the Republican magnate must have reflected that the Extender of the Empire had lately abandoned Thrace, and that the Inviolate was probably fated to join those who, when provinces sprouted usurpers in job lots, had tramped noisily into history, hacked out a spell of nervous glory from scavengers and illiterates, ruled a few cities and parcels of dirt, before – dandelions turning heads to the sun – meeting the blade. Emperors of the World carted away filthy.

Raising both hands, the Senator completed the prayer, while in identical tones he touched on more everyday matters: 'Now hurry there, you dawdle like one-legged hens. At any instant he will arrive.'

An elderly slave grinned impudently, swiftly converting this grimace to a yawn. The steward hurried him and his fellows away, barking in Umbrian accents, a reminder that Former People had ruled here earlier than any Latin, when Rome was only a disreputable wood.

Not to be classed with slaves, the tutor Diomede followed more leisurely. He professed himself Greek but was probably no more than Greek-speaking, a language despised by his employer for making the serious sound ridiculous and elevating the nonsensical. He was also librarian, both here and in the village, a sinecure, so that to his chagrin he had to oversee the fish-pond and, not always behind his back, was vilified in the kitchen as His Excellency the Fishmonger. Fairish, smallish, plumpish, he often spoke of returning to his colleagues in Athens, faint alarm puckering his forehead when Clodius Ammianus suggested the easiest route. By now a family tutor was unusual, but the aristocratic descendant of Mars, a god with indefinite claims to scholarship, maintained all traditions still possible, nevertheless grumbling that pedagogues worked only because of their tax exemptions.

Unofficially the Senator was styled 'Prophet' for his habit of constantly deploring the future. A former Consul, former Governor of Cilicia, former Commissioner of Public Works, though with duties largely lapsed, he had also been elected Quaestor, supervising finances directly under the Treasury, though for some reason he never explained he had not assumed office. Allegedly he had once benefited as a favours broker, influencing sales of offices and military commissions, with ready information about the bribes requisite for interviews with the Officialdom. With questionable legality Senator for Life, Companion of Caesar, whether here or in Rome he now performed few duties save as local magistrate and tax-collector, both, he declared, ruinous to any honest gentleman. He would lament that for years the Privy Council, urban boards, the ever-growing Officialdom, the thrusting freedmen and crafty Levantines ruled unopposed, save by a few traditionalists like himself, and corporations of Equestrians, business men aggrieved at being excluded.

Heavy, grey eyed, grey skinned, grey bearded, mouth · twisted in unflinching discontent, the great man was awaiting his elder son Clodius Constantius, a staff officer returned from Aurelian's campaign against the Palmyran Conspiracy. He was stationed rather grandly in the central hall under a mosaic of Neptune Triumphant, flicks and flacks of blue, white and gold. Furnishings were spare. Family busts stared from niches, a circular marble table supported a candelabrum of simulated bronze. A saucer of warm blue salt appeased more household gods. On a shelf the Egyptian water-clock had long ceased to work: a visitor from Pisa, expert in mechanics, had listed its defects in impeccable detail, but it remained inoperable.

With heads bowed, radiating from their Master, alert for blame, wearing Phrygian caps of different hues, were slaves and freedmen, copying clerks and secretaries. One file was parting for a neighbour, an elderly magistrate nicknamed Ulysses, so withered that children mistook him for Ulysses himself, a notion encouraged by his custom of referring to himself as a sagacious general, on evidence untrustworthy. The host greeted him with his own valuation, pronouncedly condescending.

Sunlight slanted, the old men confabulated, domestics waited. Behind them, surrounded by her women, motionless on a gilded chair, sat Domitia, the consort of the Prophet, himself foretelling unpunctuality, and mother of the awaited hero. Her broad face under its myrtle chaplet, between silver ear-pendants, was calm but watchful. At her feet, clutching a rag doll but only as if this were expected of her, with an air resembling her father's as he greeted Ulysses, was the child Clodia, her large, dark eyes as if about to spread across her face, pale despite the new sun, as they watched not the adults but the doves outside circling the columbarium like soft, thrown-up silver.

Absent was Julian, the younger son. Also, Bran, the former steward, ensconced on his own farm with the best winepress in the district, from whch he supplied the family on terms far from respectful, which his former overlord disdained to question. Bran remained a slave, refusing freedom doubtless to avoid taxes. He now had his own slaves at work in substantial holdings. Years back he had travelled on Clodius Ammianus's affairs to Sicily, Africa and Gaul, but now assiduously cultivated his beets and vines, cabbages, figs and lentils, cheese and walnuts, and prospered mightily.

The weightiest prophecy can somehow fail and, very punctually, quickly tramping up the central path to the clamour of dogs, Constantius arrived, standing under an arch in full military rig, for his father, one of the hallowed College of Hercules, would have been affronted, even dishonoured, by anything less. Pointed sword, small cylindrical shield, silvery belt engraved with trefoils, leather breastplate painted to resemble metal, dark linen cloak, green feathered helm. Saluting, he waited, for to speak first in such a demesne, neo-archaic as Julian said, said indeed too often, would have been unseemly. Conversation would be a laborious acknowledgement of filial obligation though not, as it was for Julian, an incessant taking of risks.

Some thirty supper guests filled the smaller triclinia, a less numerous gathering than formerly, men and women together at three low tables, men lolling on 'neo-archaic' couches, women upright on stools. Elbow cushions had faded, but knives, goblets and toothpicks remained brilliant, though, unknown to the Senator, some were borrowed.

Clodia sat with them, her small, neatly packed face trained on her tall brother. She had eaten well, particularly of her favourite peppered carp sunk in lemon sauce and borage, to honour, she explained, Constantius. She also had a full share of lobster and oyster on asparagus, and rather more cake, though failing to contrive the appreciative belches favoured by the men and one old woman, a stack of moist flesh apparelled in imitation silk and very large pearls, bits of the moon which was beginning to crumble.

Slaves hastened with platters of pickled venison, stuffed turbot, ham baked with figs and honey, at times interrupted

24

with pewter bowls of scented water. Others strained wine into mixing jars. Lamps were starting to glow. To please their host, the men wore with some discomfort or awkwardness, as if fearing ridicule from the menials, the Curial toga, seldom displayed save on such occasions as a visit from the Emperor, itself improbable. On reaching manhood, Julian had politely excused himself from these pompous folds and bore with discreet indifference his father's dislike of the coloured cloaks and long, tasselled tunics, barbarian style, which he had always preferred.

All were ready for Constantius's adventures. They could well have seen a cheap medallion, distributed free, bearing the rough features of his commander, victor over Goths, Sarmatians, Parthians, Armenians, Burgundians, Franks, Vandals, Aurelian Germanicus Caesar – Old Sword-in-Hand, Armpit Orry, the streets and barracks preferring this nickname to World Saviour, Son of the Unconquered Sun, Liberty Restored. For such a being the earth must seem too small; he should be praised for deigning to remain on it. Aurelian, Face of the Highest, now captor of Tetricus, the Gallic usurper routed at Châlons and soon to be exhibited in seething, jeering Rome.

Plates were removed, goblets refilled, and Constantius, now on his feet, began, quiet, respectful, distinct, remembering to glance periodically at his enthralled sister, lover of stories. Everyone was very attentive, save for the Senator, who leaned back as if ready to prompt the young man in a recitation he himself had taught.

'I'd never imagined distances so long, so dry, the wide skies and great deserts. Glittering oases weren't always real. The air plays tricks. Imaginary cities would tremble on the horizon. New names. Ancyra, Tyana – where we're told a teacher had walked on water and changed it to wine. We fought hard near Antioch. The enemy expected help from the Great King, but he died suddenly. The gods were with us. We were all in good heart. Some of us were detached to Baalbek, the City of the Sun, Hadad-Heliopolis, where the Emperor's built a temple to the sun.' He smiled again at Clodia's rapt, still face. 'Yes, a city built by a demon called Eshmudi, where King Nimrod tried wrestling with a god in a sky chariot pulled by other demons, but only fell down on to a mountain. He once tried to build a tower high enough to reach Jupiter himself – Jupiter, holding whip, thunderbolt and corn sheaf, as we saw at Heliopolis.'

'What else?'

'At Byblos by the sea we picked rose-laurel for the Emperor's name-day. Red from the blood of Adonis, the young Lord, gashed by the boar. Three days after death he regained life. Every spring the women lament his agony, rejoice at his rebirth.'

'But Zenobia? Her accounts settled, eh?'

'Assuredly. We called her that, actually she's Bat-Zabdai, harder to get the tongue round. Jews called her Protector of Rabbis, and later had second thoughts.' His rather solemn face smiled. 'She spoke many tongues, treating all peoples like mere worshippers, though ready to swig wine with her officers and trudge along with the infantry. Our Emperor was curious about her, despite her bad faith. He enjoys dark beauty and had demanded her portrait. Jewelled eyes, teeth very white against skin brown as walnut. Of course he didn't want a long siege. He's an old hand. The walls of Palmyra are mountain thick, great slabs, so, in a truce, he sent her five generals with gifts, which the foolish lady accepted as tribute. She laughed at his offer of the lives of herself, children and lovers. He promised the rights of the townsfolk. He didn't only want her to surrender, he knew all about her palaces stuffed with silk and gold. She had famous mares and hounds, troops of camels. And Palmyra itself . . . wonderful. Trees and fountains, theatres, canals, finer than Corinth, grander than Athens. . . .'

Here the attentive faces affected not to hear a sound from Clodius Ammianus usually described as a snort.

'Of course she made the usual fine speeches, or was said to have.' Constantius looked grave, where his brother would have been amused. ' "Daughter of Cleopatra, death is finer than slavery", the usual thing. She mocked our generals, confident that sickness and famine would save her from battle. She was throned in the heart of a world stolen from Rome. She still had Egypt, or thought she had. But it was all cobwebs and shadows.

26

Only pantomime. Food was rotting, getting scarce. Water drained away or was made to. So did she. Desertions had begun, she abandoned her last supporters. We captured her by the Euphrates, fleeing to Persia.'

Cracked faces stirred, faintly lascivious, though Domitia revealed nothing, as if deaf. In golden wig, brows darkened, lips reddened, in her long, pale-green stole, she looked a rival queen, holding a dark-blue feather like a sceptre, purified by Rome's genius.

Constantius spoke faster. The Senator liked guests to depart early, well fed and, some would feel, unfashionably sober.

'Once in our hands she did her Cleopatra turn. Our Emperor had her brought before him unchained. I was present, in a ravaged field surrounded by the army. He never wastes many words. Why had she dishonoured her word to Rome? Her haughtiness was well staged. In black and yellow, in golden veil, jewels everywhere, gorgeous headband, she seemed a visitor from the sky. She replied in our tongue, very fluently, that in sixty years only one Roman had proved worthy of rule, and he was dead. As for the rest, the legions had shown their own thoughts. I could see Aurelian didn't like this. He has his own way of showing anger – moving a foot. But then she saw the headsman straight before her, behind the Emperor's chair. At once her scorn changed to sweetness, she announced that Aurelian alone would she respect as her superior. The troops began to threaten, shouting for her head. All imitation of Cleopatra collapsed. Tearing her veil in panic, she huddled weeping at the Emperor's feet, imploring forgiveness, blaming everything on her advisers. Foremost of these was Longinus, her celebrated thinker, and she blamed him most, glaring like an ungrateful cat. Very quiet, very erect, he listened with interest, then bowed politely to Aurelian, and, without awaiting more, waved to his friends, introduced himself to the headsman, and they walked calmly away together like old friends. In dreadful silence the thud was heard by all of us. Departing, he had allowed one glance at that wretched queen, and, imagine, it was full of compassion!'

Indistinct, outside the lamplight, Clodia recollected that Constantius often looked troubled, and now his eyes, Mother's eyes, were clouding, gazing away from the dishevelled tables and expectant faces to somewhere else, deep in pools of shadow. He had given her one of Zenobia's coins, on which the great eyes of the Queen of Sunrise gazed out at the world. He had told her in a letter of her slaves' wearing the royal pearls to keep them alive and glistening. It would be like swimming in a moonlit sea. She swiftly thought of her favourite bowl, greeny blue engraved with the slim hounds never quite catching the fleeing hare.

Constantius loomed higher, a voice from the garish East. Lights fell away, making walls mysterious, the mural of a gay, crowded harbour no more than a blot. Faces were distorted. Hairy old Decurian Martius had become a porker, Julia Antonia a sharp bird. Julian should be here, as himself. But Constantius had brought her a delicate sandalwood box containing an ivory comb engraved with streaming tritons and steep waves. Dear Constantius.

From a dull recess a gruff question: 'They tell me that, at Palmyra, the Emperor behaved like a drunken centaur.'

Sudden unease, thick with secret fears and plans, though Clodius Ammianus, wrapped in grey authority, nodded, approving either the speaker's reproach or Aurelian's conduct.

Constantius was unperturbed, a young man with the world unrolling before him.

'He packed Zenobia off to Milan, all claws clipped, replaced her with a senate, consul, one of our generals as Governor, with six hundred archers, just in case. He levied a tax, a moderate one, and took us all off to Emasa, towards the Danube, to punish the Carpi lot. None of us had stolen so much as a flagon from Palmyra. Only the royal treasures were confiscated, much of them grabbed from us. Egyptian bales, Syrian embroidery, coins, weapons. Then news came that Palmyra was in uproar, the Governor was dead, most of the archers dangling on the walls. The Emperor didn't hear the man out. His fury paralysed us, not for the first time. He hurried us back like a galley-master. Once there . . .'

The fading air tautened, touched by random gleams. Expressions were peaked with evil interest, the stone Mercury in a corner grinned knowingly. Constantius, remembering, looked very young and inexperienced despite his warlike trappings.

'Yes, back in Palmyra he rounded up all he could get hold of. Old, young, children ... women, priestesses, rich and poor. For six days killings went on, half the place was in flames, warehouses, conduits, temples, markets ... statues, parks, smashed, finished. Palmyra's dead. Aurelian was inflexible, I hadn't imagined anything like it. Then, quite suddenly, he reined in the army, crucified a few who hadn't listened. It was as if a god had warned him. Perhaps so. The Emperor had discovered a temple already in flames, another one to Belus, a local sun spirit, and saved it, rededicated it to his father in heaven, the Unconquered Sun. He was suddenly glad and human as a child.'

Again he looked down at Clodia, gentle, soothing, suspecting her sadness, obscured by a table, overlooked by all others.

'When Zenobia still wanted to reach terms with us, hoping we'd accept her theft of Egypt and the treachery of her husband, she dispatched a deputation to the goddess Astarte, at Lake Yammouneh, where she and Adonis shared an oracle. The oracle told them to throw Zenobia's offerings, the carpets, gems and brocades, into the lake. If they remained afloat, it meant divine displeasure. Sinking meant acceptance. Yet almost nothing sank – only a small bag of emeralds. I don't know what Zenobia was told. Probably not the truth, for she certainly ignored it. Her fate may depend on what the priests say about those emeralds. But now Aurelian is master of Asia, we shan't be hearing much from Persia, though he'll probably set about her too. The Senate's decreed him a Triumph. A formality, of course. All Rome's demanding it. Fate....'

Constantius ceased, nervously abrupt, overtaken by the nameless but forbidding. The Senator sat on, silent, yet the word remained on the air, inescapable, like a drumbeat far in the night.

They were soon alone, amongst scrolls, tablets, busts. The night was cold, a small brazier glowed between them, the lamps had guttered. Beyond the window glimmered a pale wall, a flimsy tree stem, leaves unshaped by the blocks of gloom, and, far away, a red spot on hill or sky. The air stirred, a moth, or, far away, a thought: then was still. Or was it the tree breathing?

At last the older man looked up. He was querulous. 'But where is our young man? What is he condescending to do?'

Both knew that Julian, too fastidious to join the Equestrian Order of financiers, contractors and speculators, too disrespectful for the aristocracy, genuine or bespoken, was a gambler, unprofessional but oddly successful, dabbling in property, commerce, the races, the combats. A Greekling, Clodius Ammianus complained. Now he would be charming creditors in Naples, forestalling a Jew over a ruined street-corner in Pisa, insinuating dubious information about a cargo due at Ravenna, or, easily bored, languidly swimming in the warm, sulphuric waters of Baiae where once the famous and notorious had strained for the attention of Nero or Hadrian, sometimes imprudently.

The Senator enjoyed his own irritability. 'He spends too much time in the South. Lounging his way into those disreputable transactions. The Empire . . . he sees it as no more than a far-fetched prospectus. Responsibility makes him turn up his nose – well, you can smell his perfume three days before he arrives. When the Treasury catches up with him he won't be envied, even by himself.'

Domitia, for all her marbled demeanour, probably preferred Julian above all of them, but Father would never condone the scents, the long, artificially curled hair, affected smile, the ornate bracelets modelled on those of the appalling Emperor Gallienus, connoisseur of cruelty, who had almost lost the Empire single-handed, Mystery initiate who had confused shadow with substance. Constantius could respect as public spirited some of those who had failed to usurp Gallienus's throne. Julian, he knew, had charm, which he himself lacked. Charm was a lucky coin dropped by the Fates, a trick of eye, mouth, voice, sometimes compensation for ugliness, weakness, lack of talent, none of which pertained to brother Julian.

Emperor Aurelian had no charm but possessed much else. Like a column he would endure. He relied on his will, divine goodwill, and those he rewarded well.

Constantius smiled, though humourlessly, recollecting an ancient law, now obsolete, which entitled a father to kill a disobedient son, forbid his marriage or divorce, prohibit him from owning property.

In the darkened space he sensed a familiar tightening of mouth and brows, heard the disparaging sigh. 'This Aurelian, your Illyrian bravo, must sometimes, in his own good time, ponder the matter of certain predecessors. To swear oaths to such creatures ... oaths are a currency thumbed too often. Once, to break an oath would have shamed one's name, sullied mankind, scandalized the gods. I call myself a virtuous citizen, entitled to certain judgements.'

Clodius Ammianus was rehearsing familiar grievances; he had a flair for constant repetition. He was a grim voice from the darkness, one hand hangman red from the brazier.

'Rome takes blood from impure stock, bedevils herself with unnatural gods. Carthage besmirched us, even in defeat planting poison in our body politic. Egypt ruined Antony, as Greece did Nero. It's what I see in the Senate. Gauls, Spaniards, Jews, even Asiatics shouting unintelligible quackeries. Showers of unpleasant saliva. Talk and ill-earned wealth destroyed the Republic. Lawyers, each man his own Cicero! They let in the soldiers, the costliest liabilities of all time.'

The Senator always registered his thoughts rather than confided them. 'And this surrender of Dacia! Explain that.'

'It follows the advice of Augustus himself, Father. That our best frontier is the south bank of the Danube.'

Constantius kept his words level. He disliked excess. The entire army knew that Fortune depended on restraint, and had extinguished Gallienus for not knowing it. Neither was Father displaying it.

From out of the night the waves hummed and toppled, the

31

beach seemed to be clearing its throat.

'Frontier! I've learned to shudder at such a word. Who defends the frontiers? Refugees quailing from Huns. Packs of hired Teutons. Pannonian, do-nothing conscripts more interested in somebody else's purse than in Roman quality! Spies and deserters from Persia, trustworthy as wasps. The only trustworthy fellows today are the money-lenders who know that their existence depends on the preservation of routine, stability, contracts. But none of that foreign pack owes us anything. Do even your own picked men know where Rome actually is? Of course not! Our own people aren't much better. There is no true people. The whole lot are strangled by idleness and debt-collectors, tied up with clever words from anonymous syndicates. Two hundred public holidays, vacation from very little! If the Goths were to reach Rome, the multitude would rush to them for deliverance. Deliverance not least from themselves!'

Behind these routine complaints there surely lurked something more, some personal plea or dilemma which such a man would never divulge, least of all to his family. Constantius remembered old, never quite disproved allegations about Father's own financial exchanges. He had also noticed that certain familiar vases were missing, and one circular table.

'Still, to return to Aurelian. From what you say, he sets his teeth against indiscipline. No nonsense in that direction. We hear that he strapped a slacker to two young trees held down by pegs. When the pegs were removed . . . hardly a spectacle for a gentleman!'

Every soldier knew that story, endlessly repeated. In such details the Senator was usually unanswerable, and Constantius, disliking his tone, seldom disputed his facts. Neither did Julian, though deriving satisfaction, even entertainment, from them.

O Julian! Jarring songs of childhood, soundless but inescapable, sharper than javelins!

He had once, though silently, disagreed with Father, over that story of Pompey. Having captured some deadly pirates, he was expected to butcher them, as Caesar had once done, fulfilling a vow ostensibly frivolous. Instead, Pompey had removed them from the coast, planted them as independent farmers, taming them for ever. A most evil precedent, Father considered.

'You and I, son ...' – these words always introduced something tedious – '... know that an army should be more than weapons. Our ancestors marched with spades also. They were builders as well as conquerors. Their spade was a true symbol of the spirit. Now they hire the nearest tramp to do the work for them.'

Gratified by his exposition he leaned further back, beyond range of the embering brazier. Constantius remained, seated as it were at attention.

'Nevertheless, Father, the armies are again advancing at will. We've got the Standards back from Persia. Valerian's disgrace.'

'I am never worried about Persia, or China for that matter, or the moon. Here at home is the real danger. Horses, now. We rather despised them, but need them now. But they are vanishing, like Romans themselves. The cities are choking with the Levantine trash your brother is so at home with. Those cursed Sicilian abortionists, worse than the average butcher! The Senate does nothing. We chatter away about street lighting and a drain or two and worthless barbers, but Privy Council and Officialdom kept the real stuff to themselves. We all see the result.'

Constantius was at once more convinced that Father, of the stuff of Brutus and Cassius, both of whom he would have strenuously disliked, was awaiting some footstep, more ominous than that of a trespasser or robber, an outburst from a night lengthier than this. He missed further words, then heard:

'Aurelian's a cavalryman himself, a cut above languid do-nothings who prefer to look into their souls than work in public service. Though do not I know that public service has become public slavery! In Rome I'm being permanently jostled by leering strangers begging, no, demanding a donation, before slouching off to toast some hero they know nothing about. As if any of us has money to throw away! The whole system depends

33

not on solid cash but wafer-thin promises. A coin's life is briefer than a candle's. Either it falls apart when you touch it, or it buys nothing when you use it. Let your Emperor scrutinize a common coin and what will he see? The face is so smudged that it could be any rank plebeian, the superscription illegible. Madame Zenobia's output was quite another matter.'

True. Even as a novice under Claudius Gothicus, Constantius had seen his men paid in salt, pigs, plots of somebody else's land, the sight of scores of tiny, misshapen coins rousing growls, jeers, threats. As for Aurelian he had only once encountered him, when, as a very young subaltern, walking too fast, he had almost stumbled into him, burly, unescorted, staring at him without expression, then with a curt, inhuman nod, ordering him aside. A dismissal exciting, truly imperial.

'And, son, do you realize that, journeying to the City, I have to pay exorbitant fees for arming some of the men, who do not know a sword from a billhook. I have to consider building a tower, then hiring a few verminous gladiators. Bandits, you understand, those squatters on the Marullus estate . . . throwaway Teutons, parading their so-called lineage, a descent from sticks and stones. As for our own gods . . .' – his voice dropped, he slumped in real or pretended weariness – '. . . well, they still comfort our little Clodia. She makes herself welcome to our neighbour, the Lady Isis. Scarcely a Roman, yet she may help keep the girl from trouble. As for this Emperor's blazing acquisition, let us hope he remains unconquered!'

He stooped towards the dim brazier, his bearded face hollower, gaunter. 'Whether gods now exist, is unimportant. But Augustus knew what he was doing when he rebuilt the temples and cracked his whip for the priests. Ceremonies, duties, maintenance of oaths, they join hands with past and future, they are your real frontiers. Always remember that. For a soldier you read too much. That blasphemer Lucretius, and so on. Leave that to your brother. His belief in disbelief is fulsome. Athens talked itself into bankruptcy, mocked itself into abject servitude. He is a word-perfect Athenian. And what is Greece herself? No more than our squalid province of Achaea. Had Xerxes pocketed the place and sent the orators about their business, the world would have been quieter. As it is, we have too many words, too few thoughts. Too many giggles. Romans no longer know how to laugh.'

Certainly, like Julian, Father did not. He had once attempted to do so when, in Mother's presence, a visitor declared that the Senate should learn sense from women. Father, too, always spoke of Julian as 'your brother', as if disowning a loss-making transaction. He had once remarked, wrongly, that 'your brother' quoted readily from books he had not read, while he, Constantius, misquoted what he had read, indeed read too often.

'The Empire, my son, is a body, a physique. Do not let it become a corpse. Feed it, drain it, punish it occasionally. Maintain its speech. For where is our Latin tongue? Words have lost depth, even meaning, put on so much fat that they can no longer be injured by garrulous aliens and obsequious demagogues. Yet. . . .'

The brazier gave a last flicker, tired yellow on faint blue, and losing rather than forgoing asperity, he relapsed again, a vague, tired heap. Legislator of an obsolete order, residue of a forgotten Republic. Abdicating authority, he addressed his son as if needing reassurance, the comfort not of ceremonies, certainly not of laughter, but of vigorous physique and imperial design.

'It is said in Rome . . . I hear it in the clubs, the baths, in the Senate, that certain books survive, containing the names of all emperors, past and to come. And . . .' – he made an attempt to rally, but spoke as if after painful coughing and affronted by it – '. . . they say further . . . the names have reached the last page.'

III

Dawn was blood-orange red under blue soft as milk, brisk with cocks and swallows and the horses shuffling in stables. Through the fresh light the fountain splash was louder, more commanding than it would be at noon; a voice, Julian had said, from the secret earth, restoring links with the departed.

The meal was soon over. A few eggs, a little honey, a loaf, a jar of mint water. All was still cool. Constantius went out with Father to inspect the fields, Mother moved about the house, supervising, reprimanding, expelling a dog, nodding at a chest within which dwelt a household spirit exercising no very obvious authority.

Clodia had to avoid bald Diomede. She disliked books and grammar, Ovid Big Nose and something called *paedeia*, which suggested that to be Greek was more dazzling than to be Roman, which would certainly offend Father. Thus to escape Diomede was to be loyal to the family: far better to stare at heroes and birds painted on a vase, always about to move, to fly away, or to remain loving her green bowl. Also, Father himself considered girls' lessons unnecessary.

She proceeded warily, informing Mother that she must take clothes to the fuller's, then swiftly sidled away, rejoicing. Mother was strong, never needing to laugh or weep, never angry, supplying each with his wants, with more care than love. She taught that without work you go mad. As for Father, he loved his Name and sometimes Constantius.

Forgoing the clothes, dodging the thought of Diomede waiting in the atrium, she ran through the kitchen, pausing to inspect Constantius's gift, fifteen polished wooden plates from Syria, cut so fine that, stacked, they seemed but one. 'That's magic,' a barrel-shaped old cook grumbled suspiciously.

She darted into freedom, the day opening in many directions, all leading to farewells, for the family was ordered to Rome for the Triumph, in which Constantius, upholding the Name, would march with the Emperor. Certain paths, trees and animals must be told to await her return.

She disliked the City, where Diomede was inescapable. She was forbidden to enter the streets without him, and direct disobedience was impossible. There, noise and dirt made voices harsher, sausage-sellers screamed after her, beggars grimaced impudently, made even ruder gestures, and, on a high red stool a barber said something incomprehensible but which turned Diomede bright red. Rome's stories were shivery. In the Great Forum Cicero's head and hands had been nailed by Emperor Augustus, Father of his People, except of course Cicero. Stilt-walkers, tall and thin, would slant towards her masked like gorgons, braying rhymes which Julian said were uncultured and needing revision. Theatres, Baths, the Games, the Tiber, were prohibited her. Trajan's Column was cruel, with its captives and killings, though she enjoyed Jason and his friends painted on Agrippa's Portico, the fleece shimmering on the wise ship's prow. If you stared long enough the ship began to move, though she was never allowed time to do so.

Rome, Father said, more than once, was unlucky, rising from a pool of blood, blood of Remus, slain by his brother Romulus for jumping over a wall. Slaves spoke of plague brought in by soldiers, perhaps in a black bag. Roman tales were darker than Bran's light, airy roll of dangerous quests, enchanted cauldrons, heart-tearing loves. Nero the Great had been dead three days, then rose and burned half the streets. In Rome, the men would kill helpless Zenobia. Ragged children, some of them blinded by the beggar-masters, yelled taunts about the rich going to be drowned in marshes. And in Rome Father was heavier because of the thick frowns always dropping on to him. More beggars, well dressed, soft spoken, filled the house daily, smiling, polite, but demanding food, and others also came, less often, tight-faced, in small, unfriendly groups, smelling of money. These were called Equestrians, though they never rode anything, and their visits turned Father's words into ice.

Julian was often in Rome but seldom bothered to please Father, who complained of his love of new clothes, cock-fighting, and of losing his money at races and in places closed to her.

In spring, all save her wished to be somewhere else – people, birds, clouds, though gods were probably too high to feel this.

She stood in a small, deserted yard awaiting more thoughts. Isis might be waiting, amongst her poplars and willows. Father disapproved of her, he belonged to Jupiter and great-grandfather Mars. Mother prayed to Juno and Minerva, Constantius to the Emperor's Unconquered Sun, today more unconquered than usual, supreme in a sky otherwise empty. Julian was friendly to all gods. Could a god have really been seen limping through the village when Constantius returned?

She disliked her name, which bound her too close to Father. Secretly she was Marianna, a daughter of Isis, and, outside the house, this was the self in whom she lived. Crossing the gardens, she saw gnats dancing around the roses, the flower Father called poison from Asia. They must have been loved by Queen Zenobia.

Feeling herself truly Marianna, she again pondered the limping stranger. He might be the hero from the sunrise who, in slaves' tales, lures children from home with ghost music, to wander in forests and hills, lost for ever. Apollo, perhaps, whose lyre had freed Troezen from rats. Where was Troezen? But questions made people frown and Mother say that she was too talkative. Yet questions were keys. That butterfly, was it drinking from a blue cup of blossom? Was it the soul of a dead villager? Surely not. Marc the Smith who had promised her a ring then, ungenerously, had died after a wounded heron had blinded him! But tread shyly, for even when most alone you seldom escape the weak, spiteful stare of the dead.

Questions. Here in the brilliant morning, within reach of the trees and under sky almost as deep as the humming sea, they were as insistent as birds, as pools, as traps. Was the dew from sky or earth, was it half rain? Was she still a child? Mother undeniably said yes, Julian appeared to say no. Secretly, by candlelight, she darkened her eyebrows with damp ash, ringed her eyes with antimonis, and from glass consulted the new face she was growing like a flower. But she was no queen of Eastern deserts. Like her name, her face was not quite her own, did not belong to Marianna. Left over mostly from Mother, her chin was too sharp, hair too black, eyes too quiet, mouth too thick, in all she had nothing to boast of. At birth she must have offended a goddess, Juno probably. Julian had called her a vixen, by no means praise. Constantius had promised that she would marry well, but nobody else did.

She danced a few impatient steps and made for the end of the garden, determined to enjoy the morning stolen from Diomede. Her favourite pig would enjoy acorns, even stories about Baalbek, the rivers and towers, huge dry suns, Zenobia the Canal Cutter. Before reaching a side-gate and the stone gods, old but usually smiling, she felt a dull gleam changing to a certain memory apt to flicker unpleasantly, as though she had swallowed a sunbeam. She forgot the sunlight, the bees, the trees awaiting her. She was Clodia again, back in the Villa. It had many rooms, mostly small, each with a face known only to her. Many were dusty, left to spiders, shrew-mice and old slaves thought to be dead but still lingering on straw in corners, the smells disgusting. Also spirits, for stores, windows, doors and hinges had guardian presences, unseen but liable to play tricks. Once, exploring an area above sunless yards and broken fountains, she had discovered Julian in a damp room under rafters, lying on the bare floor, eyes open but looking past her, blank as water. She had silently fled, realizing that he was really somewhere else, leaving his body behind with naked figures fading on walls and ceiling. She often wanted to return, examine them more closely, ask forbidden questions, but dared not do so. Somewhere the room still beckoned, dangerous and enticing, stuffy with secrets, but she had only once tried to find it again, and, failing, had begun to think she had dreamed it. She did mention it to Julian, but he had sighed as if over a dead joke, before giving a slow wink, as he had when Constantius spoke of the cruelty of the Goths.

Would Julian have saved Adonis from the boar? Sadly, she admitted that he would acquire some strange credit for leaving this to brave Constantius.

Outside the garden, again Marianna, she must seriously plan the new hour. The pig would be missing her, the mullets enjoyed feeding from her hand, the carriage mules needed inspecting, also the blind, patient mill donkeys, even the pigeons trailing silver above the roofs. But the dew, moon water, still flashed on grasses, and by moving her head she made a thousand bright points change from fiery red to pointed blue, from gold to greens sharper than any grass. This done, she decided to bid goodbye to Bran. His home, thatched and timbered, was smaller than the Villa, but warmer, its orchard, olives and barns better kept.

Beside his path the stone herm, often sly and malicious, was friendly. The air cooled as she reached elms which vines had begun to climb, the broad, flat leaves pale green, ready for the clusters to come. Bran was soon visible, his back to her, amongst olive trees cracked and twisted like himself.

He had been brought here long ago, from Gaul, where old women had trained the warriors who once fought with Rome for the World, and had sacked the City or pretended to have done so. In those times, Bran said, had lived the first Bran, who could be hurt only in his heel, and he had voyaged on seas with twelve followers, seeking a cauldron of eternal youth. Old people would plunge in, then emerge with hair like bright barley, eyes like stars, bodies like birch saplings. Bran himself, bald and lumpy, with a very ordinary heel, had no such cauldron, but implied that he did not need to, and indeed Julian had said of him that the sly would inherit the earth.

Slightly deaf, Bran did not turn, and she ignored a common slave, who bowed to her as he piled lucerne. Bran was examining a row of peas, his ruined head protruding from a long woollen cloak, very hard and polished, as if carved. From his belt hung a metal spoon with a dragon's head. Slowly, but as if he had all the time been aware of her, he looked round and, anxious about his mood, she waited. The bearded, depleted face, small eyes, often seemed to smile when he was angry, and his laugh was a growl.

'Bran, you haven't told me a story. Not for so long.' He knew more stories than an oak has leaves, and a poem about trees lamenting a dead brother, at which Diomede would lift his cold nose and be boring about Ovid, Virgil, Livy. Bran's stories hung ready to be plucked; usually she wanted the familiar. Stories of the nine bright shiners, daughters of a lost moon, of a boy who lost his soul ... a bean, web or transparent blue glow. An oracle revealed that on an island was a wolf, in the wolf a hare, in the hare a partridge, in the partridge thirteen eggs, and in the last egg, see you, was the soul. A quest, Bran usually ended, impossible but not altogether difficult.

She gazed doubtfully at the withered eyes, reddish beard, but was soon at a rough table among the herbs, listening to his half-grumbling, half-friendly voice.

'There was a boy, he might have been me, he might not have been....' Knowing what was coming she smiled delightedly, chin on clasped hands, and gazing at a grape stain on the table which was now a cloud, now a pond, now the island where the soul was found. 'The boy dreamed of a black man who frightened him. A long time later, believe it, believe it not, he must sail to New Carthage on his master's business, and there, on the ship, stepping out of the dream, was the captain, the black man, and he refused to sail with him, as well he might. A week later, that ship sank in a calm sea and all save the captain were drowned.'

This was very believable, but Bran suddenly went surly. 'You'll be going back to Rome. This Triumph. A slippery business!'

Puzzled, she nodded, but said nothing. He watched her as, head high, she departed down the white path to myrtle and chestnut, oak and fern, pausing to wave back, though he had already vanished.

Dangers would have fled at cockcrow, perhaps to the hills where lay a stone camp, mysteriously abandoned, uncanny, like the Neuri people who, Constantius said, could change into wolves. Here in lights and shadows, golds and greens, safe, she reminded herself of Bran's talk of dwellers behind the north wind. To reach them you must pass the lands of the Cyclops, the griffins who protect gold, then, wrapped against iced gales, you reach Apollo's temple by some distant sea.

In the wood, messages were frequent as stories. On that tree someone had tied a dead tongue to help it speak, on another a nightingale might sing. Yesterday she had seen a mother thrush diving at a cat to protect her babies. At home, no one spoke of birds or music, though sometimes alone Mother might sing, at first very softly, slow and sad. Doubtless she did not believe herself alone. From kitchen gossip, once from barely heard words from Bran, Clodia knew of another girl, her younger sister, destroyed at birth. She could never speak of it, but the girl might have been marked by the sign which made certain women avoided, ravaged by magic.

She shook herself free of such thoughts. Green branches did not darken the sky, a cloud drifted across like a cloak, which perhaps it was. Scents of wild mint, wild celery, sweetened the thickening heat. She was happy, Marianna among friends. At the wood's edge sunlight rushed over her, showing an old square well-head knobbed with mossy faces, some crumbling to no more than a lip, an eye. Often the rim was decorated with fresh flowers, though today there were none. She dropped in a scrap of mint, with a prayer for her brothers, who would scarcely need it, then for Zenobia, who would. O incline the Emperor's heart to mercy! The well reached to the underworld. Passing the family boundary stone she straightened it – a nearby village had disappeared when bandits removed its stones.

Climbing a rough hill she saw the Old Town swing into view, derelict place of ghosts, curses, bats, the vagrant and venomous. A boy had died in the amphitheatre, exhausted from screaming. Beneath it, in the village street, plebeian children were playing catchball, their cries distinct and raucous. She was glad to avoid them. They filled dogs with wine and jeered at their bewildered helplessness, stoned birds and were said, for a wager, to have drowned a tinker's boy.

42

Surrounded by its fellows, the hill narrowed above her, matted dark green, rock in places showing through: the sea was opening, a wide blue and white fan, now flat, now shuffled. She rested on a boulder chipped with unknown markings, content to gaze down at the lulling water. Even when apparently empty, no ship visible, no pale white limb flashing beneath surge, much might be astir. Bran knew of unseen crystal halls and watery fields, declaring that gods and mortals had begun in the sea. A Lord Manannon walked the sea, at his foot waves became a meadow, spray hardened to blossom, fish flew up as birds. Diomede repeated, too often, that when Aeneas's ship reached Italy, the Former People had begun shrinking to dwarfs, frightened of future Rome. A Marianna does not revere Aeneas, even Rome, preferring the soft and sparkling, the sea children. Her favourite floor picture, daily trodden and unnoticed, was of foam transforming to a lion under flakes of moonlight, or perhaps a lion becoming foam. The Oscans, defeated and tiny, might also love it. Diomede, for once interesting, had mentioned that Oscan letters remained on old rocks, tombs, posts, though they were no longer understandable. She had begged for more but he only looked angry, as though he had said something perilous.

Sunlight had reached a house on a far-out island, glittering, complete, as if fresh from the depths. She had never landed there, never believed it quite real. The island merged into a dream in which a ship swayed into a forum; without warning a tree pushed out of a barren mine. Such a morning as this, when light drank the darkness as if for ever, Manannon might yet come, blue-green Neptune, shell-crusted, magicking waves not to lions but flowers.

Through a hot valley, seen as if through gauze, were the curves and squares and blue, airy spaces of the Iseum, and she stooped for a daisy to hold towards Isis. Its gold held the goddess's love, its white was her dazzling soul. Here, amongst the daisies, solitary yet watched, the small girl saw without surprise white smoke rising in response from the sacred grove, slowly waving like a sash.

IV

Roma Dea. Dedicated to Jupiter and birthplace of warriors, the City, like Victory, is nevertheless a goddess, more ruthless than the Father with his wayward thunderbolts and genial caprices, outcome of Creation, not Creation itself. Division lunges throughout Rome's history: goddess and god, patrician and plebeian, slave and free, Republic and Empire, Senate and Army. Incessant conflict. The goddess works surreptitiously, nagging, agitating, barely controlled. More ostentatiously, though rulers may be on distant frontiers, Rome, in destiny and name, remains an emperor's capital. Though less dependable, grain ships still arrive from Egypt, Boeotia, Gaul; Ostian warehouses are sufficiently stored with pepper, copper, linen, imports harvested by many, planted by few. Nevertheless the Palatine, once resplendent with palaces, patrician mansions and trim parks, is now raddled, half abandoned to unpaid clerks, scheming freedmen with secrets to exploit and penniless families claiming ancient lineage. Below, the pale marble of Augustus's Mausoleum is lichened and fissured, statues mutilated, terraces uneven, in places collapsing, only the bronze Princeps still brooding and lofty against the sky. Of the sacred poplars mere stumps remain after illicit maraudings for firewood, and carpenters complain in a dozen languages and fifty dialects that pines, even beyond Volturno, long ravaged, have not been replanted. Squalid grass covers many alleys, one ivy-tangled aqueduct choked several years back remains untended, forcing an entire Section to use a fetid ditch. Regularly the deputy Aedile, parasite from heaven knows where, orders its repair, but though the workless and work-shy number thousands, none consents to volunteer. A stagnant pool oozes over the Horatian Way, cloudy with venomous insects.

Many live underground, straining upwards to colossal arch, soaring portico or some image forgotten or wrongly remembered yet lurking like an unredeemed pledge. A vast pyramid is thrust hard upon the Empire, the peak usually lost in the empyrean, residue of some incorporeal substance, far higher than Trajan's Column, too steep to be attempted by any save barbarians with gladiatorial instincts and no manners. Like, for instance . . . but hush! Crowds stumble aimlessly against each other, faceless even in sunlight, yearning for more than high air and fresh winds, though either not daring to name it, or naming it too violently. An apathy almost blind alternates with recklessness, savagely erupting when least expected, lightning flashes in which a god or pretender is acclaimed, before half-heartedly dissolving. Hordes drift, drift: to bet on horses at the Circus Maximus, on the Blue or Green chariot champions at the Campus Martius, to stare at naked athletes oiling themselves after ball-throwing, hoop-trundling, wrestling; to meander round puppeteers, comedians, snake-charmers, striving for some spasm of sensation. For such hordes, without work or responsibility, gratification must be instant, lusts satisfied in a single plunge, goods grabbed, money spent, prayers answered before completed.

Others stand in groups, to jeer, threaten, even vote, usually illegally, at Assemblies. They hunt bodies, pray in corners, clamour for Nilic bread, Cappodocian lettuce, Nomentium apples, honeycake (ah, honeycake!), steal from markets, dream up lascivious deities, flock to theatrical spectacles ever more extravagant, or slink to the latest Mystery promoted in a dubious temple and promising freedoms barely conceivable, nakedness even more naked, heights and depths for which no words exist. Fervid for doles of corn, salt, oil, to which Aurelian has added pork, they offer votes, loins, voices, on the open market. Libraries are empty, the cosmopolitan multitudes are noisy but illiterate, the past has been snapped off. None remembers Cato or Cicero. Raw hill-dwellers and cave families invent unlikely tales of the garlanded heroes and submissive chiefs decorating

45

Trajan's Column, the cavalcades and sacrifices, imagining spendthrift orgasms at the world's beginning, the sky splitting apart, the birth of gods and wild days of return. Trajan? Who knows? A centaur who invented ice, Time glinting through burned air, the father of Jupiter? Thronging street and arcade are alien predators, criminals, the pretty, the shrewd: patient, sandalled Boeotians, woolly Libyans, Numidians clotted with dark semen, hucksters in Gallic trousers, Pannonians with closed, arrogant faces, Ephesian refugees still harassed by Gothic atrocities; Britons, Galicians, Bithynians, preyed upon by fraudulent guides and interpreters, smiling whores, noseless beggars, diseased children.

Public buildings, vulnerable, even frail, despite grandiosity and legends of being born from stone demigods, are guarded by armed Teutons, a double ring round the Mint, often troubled by strikes and violence. Terminus, god of boundaries, has long been expelled by the purloinings of speculative combines, rich from subjugated kingdoms, client states and bankrupt cities, so that sky is blocked by tenements, huge but hastily erected from materials second rate or carelessly acquired, fine tiles and mouldings clamped on mouldy but ornate façades already rotting and now patched here with cheap plaster, there with a slab of best Tuscan marble. Such places, with upper floors degenerating to cheap plywood, are apt to sway; they topple, in gales from the sea or the Apennines, burying hundreds in the rubble. Last week in the Subura, such a building, unwieldy, ominously suspended over crooked lanes and cobbled squares, crashed on a windless day, the deaths inciting a fruitless riot. Fires are common, a brazier upset by a child, malicious slave, a dog, can swiftly ignite a street thick with rubbish, the firemen, usually unpaid for weeks, mutinous, indifferent, demanding bribes while dicing in cellars, the red gale enveloping half a Section. Blessing Prometheus, arsonists prosper like abortionists, and star-guided Chaldeans, for a sesterce, will date the world itself ending in flame. 'But, for just one more little payment....' When this cataclysm scorches the sky and rips the universe, crowds may still be too listless to part for 'little bucketers' trying to avert divine wrath with a flurry of water.

Sensation, after centuries of gratification, is jaded. The Marcellus Theatre is often barely filled, as animals are stabbed, guts hooked out, Blue and Green chariots collide screaming. Beasts must be as exotic as the Hesperides, in vulgar melodrama boys and girls parade swollen, artificial genitals. Unconventional couplings, a boy with a goat, a girl impaled on a bull, a pretty slave, no longer guarantee thrills. For a stage killing, a condemned convict must be crucified or torn. Who governs? Privy Councillors are mostly as anonymous as the omnipresent Officialdom, multiplying, ordaining, prying, threatening. Generals appear, with outlandish names – one, imagine it, called 'Satyr'. Emperors can be no more than a rumour. The great Claudius Gothicus, but three years dead, is already blurred or denounced as a scoundrel Goth. Dates are mostly forgotten, though in any father's youth a single summer witnessed six rivals hacking for the throne, exercises in personal relationships unconducive to sensible administration. Tax farmers, generals, nondescript freedmen, Illyrians, Pannonians, emperors all, have fled Goth and Teuton, the barbarian fury; have masqueraded on public stages as apes, ballet dancers, indecent goddesses; have raped a Vestal Virgin, imitated Jovian thunder, replaced Olympian effigies with their own. Sighs are drawn for those rulers, antique or imaginary, who once raised glistening corn from the moist womb of the Earth Mother, controlled unsullied water, walked with gods. In Hadrian's Parthenon you can circle red and white pillars beneath the huge intact dome and inspect gods and heroes, then trudge towards Trajan aching aloft on the spiralled panoply of his conquests, impervious to the tumult beneath, the tiered marts, stalls and plinths, colonnades and rubbish piles, the smells, the jabber from money-lenders' tables.

Censors with spies and informers still progress to supervise public behaviour and opinions but, while retaining roseate salaries, they have been virtually superseded by Treasury agents and imperial secret police. Before suicide the opulent merchant, T. Cornelius Necritus, wrote his own epitaph: *Fleeced by the State*. That last word is replacing *Republic* and even *Empire*.

Venerable senators confer lengthily, though with little to say and less to manage. Behind bolted doors Equestrian bankers, monopolists, middlemen swaddle money in the grand tradition of those celebrated usurers, Brutus and Seneca. Such men dress unobstrusively, drive in shrouded palanquins, demand no Triumph, win plaudits only for underwriting some blood-drenched display, for a stupendous distribution of alms, for sponsorship of some Circus champion.

Money is the new Mystery, exploited by initiates. It abounds, even slaves' purses jingle, yet secures less and less. Refulgent emporiums can be empty for weeks, arcades abandoned to whores and sneak-thieves, consignments arrive under armed escort, but promptly vanish, presumably grabbed by the escort. The Emperor, fancying himself a plain man's economist, is said to be wanting to meddle with the coinage, Equestrian financiers prudently concealing their scorn. In temple porches or by the Capena Gate under the titanic Marcian Aqueduct, better-class prostitutes and workless dancers inexpertly hold small Syrian harps, the get-rich-quick squat over dice or draughts, ignore the traffic endlessly rubbing against itself, getting jammed in arches, breaking down, to general curses and looting: the riders, litters, handcarts, oxen wagons crammed with furniture, vegetables, sheep and goats entangled in nets, ramshackle sledges piled with milk vats wedged amongst crates of honey, wine and oil. Supplies of Puteoli and Bilbilis iron are escorted by soldiery. Gaudier carts transport whores and actresses from Ravenna, Milan and Pisa under ribboned canopies, forcing the gamblers to look up, whistle, joke, then resume quarrelsome deliberations.

Daytime hubbub is incessant, legal restrictions on early morning traffic are ignored. By night it subsides to a subterranean murmur, ceasing only at such news as the troops stamping out smiling, wilful Gallienus, slave unrest, or a rumour *moratorium on debts,* creating a stillness uncanny as Colchis, an uncanny grip on the throat.

Graffiti bestrew all walls: on an imperial palace, astrologer's cavern, barber's cubby-hole, abortionist's kitchen. *Julio, where roams thy cock! I am Gaius. I wish I were Maximus. Her cunt is a prison. I want to do time.* Daubed on houses, troughs, damp arches, filtering through dreams, implied by back-street oracles, is the crude outline of a youth, no emperor, naked or in simple tunic, rustic, innocent yet also mysteriously knowing. He remains vague, premonition of a divine messenger or perhaps only a gibe at high-flown authority. He will not yet deter Treasury vultures who ransack even temples for jewels and minerals. Also, from the high-class booths along the Argiletium, the weighty basilicas of lawcourts and counting-houses of the Forum Romanorum to the flimsiest riverside cat-house roam agents, informers, killers hired by landlords and debt-collectors; not to mention prominent officers and jurists, ignored by annalists but stealthily manipulating the City.

Newcomers usually avoid the native temples, flocking to the Eastern upstarts born of doubtful fathers and lascivious mothers: leering dog-heads, winged serpents, gods with lions' haunches, from infernal realms of poison and treachery. Gods dying cruelly, sinking to underworlds, rising to rekindle the world's hope. Isis, in the Campus Martius, Lady of Alexandria, glory of Women, Lighthouse Mother and, attracting bawdy witticisms from masseuses and bath-loungers, Star of Sailors. Orpheus on the Vatican, neighbour of Attis, Shepherd of Stars in lolling, zodiac-spangled cap, dying castrated under a tree, a disreputable ending, though resurrection followed. Adonis, lover of Venus – Astarte, of erotic wiles. Serapis, then Cybele, ruthless Thracian Great Mother, imported against Hannibal. Secluded on the Aventine is the cave of the Good Goddess, her name known only to women. Surviving despite hoary prohibitions is the gilded image of evil Cleopatra, deposited by Julius Caesar on the altar of Venus Genetrix, Mother of Aeneas. Installed on the Capitoline, preserve of Jupiter, is Mithras, Light of the World, a soldier's darling, Persian bull-slayer, doubtless a spy of the Great King. Stand outside the Mithraeum and listen. *You who saved us, having shed your blood, give us Eternity.* His devotees, like the Stoics, await universal conflagration, a discouraging prospect. Nevertheless, speak softly, for World Saviour Aurelian reveres the Unconquered Sun, some substance of Mithras, and has led armies flaunting a sun mitre. The Sun, his courtiers jabber, grandly eternal, sees all, exemplifies order, a phenomenon verily imperial. Did not the Sun beget Aesculapius, healer of nations? Already, erected with inspired, headlong swiftness, flanked by victory chariots under eagles golden, or gilded, gleams Aurelian's temple to the Unconquered, within which a huge orb glows at midnight and crouching figures leap up to dance to the sun, by no means a shrine for storing goods or renting fancy buttocks on easy terms.

No Roman *gravitas* lights on Serapis, Anubis, Astarte. Such creatures have long been feared by the magistrates as tempters, deceivers, warlocks. Cybele's temple is known to harbour masked, whirling dancers; the poor, imbecile, ill-favoured, sacrifice their balls for a few coppers, screeching gratitude to the Mother of All. Corrupt love-feasts to crazed, orgiastic flutes, pipes, drums are celebrated in barely legal temples of Attis and Bacchus. Had not the corrupt Marc Antony hailed himself Bacchus? As for old Roman deities, the sacred flame still lights Vesta's sanctuary. High-nosed jurists brief advocates and exchange documents in Diana's cloisters, but magistrates are protesting against valuable meat being consumed in sacrifices. Near the temple of Jupiter, thunder-cloud on the Capitoline is that of Minerva where, for a fee, you sit between two sacrificial joints, which absorb your ague, failure blamed on your own impiety. On a Tiber islet, Aesculapius performs cures more unusual, more expensive. North of the Julian Basilica, Venus shelters wealthy courtesans; in Augustus's New Forum half-pay veterans grumble on Mars's steps, though higher, on the Quirinal, dwells the more sedate Mars Romulus. The theology can be left to scholars hunched in Apollo's Palatine Library.

Crowds listlessly divide for manifold religious processions: noisy priests of Mars, with double-circled shields, white-garbed shavelings, eunuchs of Cybele or Attis with castanets and cymbals, intoning Phrygian hymns, provoking gibes at best sacrilegious, Diana's virgins in groups of five, their gliding aloofness spectral even in dusty sunlight. Youths taunt the pale women of Ceres, mostly plain, though dedicated to fertility. Preceded by torch-bearers, Jovian flamens in round, spiked caps descend the stately Capitoline into stench and uproar, disdainful of market-place philosophers and Jewish rabbis proclaiming themselves sons of God or brawling with killjoy Galileans. These, mostly gentrified landowners, Hellenized freedmen, profiteering Equestrians and indolent scribblers, are unpopular. Honest fellows avoid military service without making a noise about it, but Galileans flourish disloyalty like a badge of divine favour. Pouting at the Unconquered Sun as if to extinguish it, they quote learned unreadables and apparently eat children. To punish their curse on Rome, Emperor Decius tried to extirpate them. Indignantly they promised him ruin, which befell. A tricky lot. Their god is a failed magician with abstruse notions of spiritual and physical freedoms which he practised on naked youths.

The accumulation of so much godhead has not sustained Roman virtues, either in Subura slums or under the cool Caelian cypresses, though, withdrawn from yells, threats, curses at the price of pork or the mouldiness of the bread dole, a few genuine philosophers mope over Seneca's words, that God lives within each virtuous man, though which god is unknown. Also, that he who is everywhere is nowhere, a statement today easily construed as treason.

Half-way to heaven, above seething, flammable streets, feigning unawareness of cess fuming from open drains, ladies, fashionable, would-be fashionable or merely opulent recline on the decaying Esquiline, gossip on Belvedere terraces, regaled with scandal and intrigue, while within, men's faces pucker over reports from mine or shipyard, murex deliveries or falling shares, before the hour to belch over quails and Falernian, pile up coarse jokes like counters, be inspected by marriage brokers, perhaps sicken from fish supplied by lying purveyors from the polluted Tiber. Applauded or cursed by crop-head buffoons, more ladies traverse the City secluded in palanquins or swaying imperiously in litters or high chairs, wrapped in rainbow tints,

51

silken transparencies deplored by moralists. They make for the forums, not always the most illustrious, to linger over Arabian myrrh and gum, Cappadocian incense and cinnamon, a stone charred in Hades, the dried eye of a Cyclops useful against gout, live frogs necessary for magic, British alabaster, Spanish ironware. Of more substantial offerings, the observer will notice that little is manufactured in Italy, though connoisseurs avoid copper and silver confections sold as African, Syrian or Cretan, as they do 'Diana's charmlets salvaged from sacked Ephesus', honey 'guaranteed Attic', 'Baalbek garlic Zenobia-style', 'Indian coral'. Polyglot mongrels are exhibited as noblest British and Pannonian hunters 'cherished by Hercules *himself*'. Blocks of petrified wax are sold to gooseheads as finest Carrara marble. Meaner streets are jammed with soothsayers promising a giant ant from the Red Sea, barbers ply scissors and razors, are jostled by tailors, perfumers, conjurers, acrobats, flautists, dainty-footed taverners with jars or smoking platters on their heads; by rope-walkers, bird imitators. Cobblers' trestles are thick not only with slippers but phallic *olisbas*, dildos, 'fresh from Miletus', for unsatisfied women, and combs 'licensed by Diogenes' despite his baldness. Beneath dirty awnings ink-makers lean over gums and lampblack, public letter-writers wave styluses, ready to address the moon, oracles, mothers-in-law. Moorish quacks sell teeth of the hanged, bound in threes, remedy for bone-fever and 'nostril trance' which none had suffered and all wished to escape: a cheapjack is castigated for attempting to fly, breaking his neck for using hens' feathers instead of eagle pinions. 'Not cheap but by no means expensive' guarantees gimcrack saws, billhooks, jars, votive statuettes, mirrors 'consecrated in Delphi' to trap spirits fleeing death-beds, rattles to expel ghosts, formulas to avert the Evil Eye, painted maps of the underworld, descriptions of life on the sun. Vets and canine philosophers swarm amongst singing masters, preachers, muleteers, herbalists, disputes rising like starlings. 'Cowherd! ... Betrayer of thresholds ... swindler!' The swaggering, the disfigured, the humble, the crafty. Off the Sacred Way, whores, cheeks red-ochred, legs bare, ankles bangled, ogle from fornices scooped from haughty walls. Certain doctors sit guarded by ex-boxers or gladiators, professing protection from plague, the one-eyed hag on a donkey. Soldiers hustle felons and runaway slaves to the Mamertine Prison.

The new and the obsolete are inextricably entwined. The howls in the blood-swamped Flavian Amphitheatre had long ago hailed Sulla's political killings, or the desperate human sacrifices to repel Hannibal. Houses reveal the layers of Rome; the lower floors, their balconies combating street filth with potted lavender, belong to the rich, while the higher are successively dingier, more fetid, with dispirited faces at broken windows cajoling water-carriers, or night-soilers, then bawling to children playing *morra* round a dried-up fountain or opening hands as a litter passes. Hints of a mightier Rome may still haunt lanes darkened by garbage, birds, dogs, pigs, hints from a plundered arcade, pediment deserted by its god, Venus on her scallop shell, Prometheus with flaming crucifix, a gracious arch festooned with delicate stone foliage overlooking a pauper cemetery heavy with carrion smells and but a step away from luscious gardens slanted on the Esquiline. Such remnants resemble a Ciceronian advocate attempting success with elaborately crafted digressions, slyly introduced irrelevancies, dazzling sleights and misleading similes. Mendacious guides gull strangers into believing a pile of stones to be residue of the Pons Sublicius where Horatius defied the Etruscans: in queer, uncoiling movements, beggars move towards you, with information of how to reach the bleached altar of Our Lady of Fevers. Legends maunder on about Nero's Golden House, burned years ago: its banqueting hall with ceiling on which mobile, gemmed constellations imitated the sky patterns, of supernatural encounters in its wooded gardens now bedraggled between the Palatine and Esquiline. Some blackened wall survives amid nettle and thistle covering fallen masonry, much of it pillaged to reinforce patrician tombs on the highway, where ghosts abound.

Night is dangerous. Vague streets under ill-tended sconces meander through withered air, a sudden torch illuminating pimps and petty criminals flitting towards windows, lurking in shadows, concealed under wooden buttresses of gimcrack buildings. More obvious are 'the Clubs', the Weavers, Patriots, the Band of Love, Fraternal Cobblers, Sons of Bacchus, armed gangs named from the guilds, drinking associations, mutual aid societies, temple devotees, of earlier times. They include declassed younger sons now at one with runaway slaves, fallen racecourse champions and prize-fighters, who retain their gloves of oxhide or metal, sometimes spiked. Also, professional perjurers, dismissed servants and parasites, the slum Catiline and Spartacus, dream figures of our time.

Rivalling these in violence, usually with one member blind, or blinded, to extract more cash from alms-givers or as mascot against the evil eye, are children's gangs, crazily dancing, stealing, offering themselves to rivermen and soldiers, spitting at officials, assaulting the old, publicly masturbating each other, begging, darting forward like a dim dust-cloud to rob or stab, abruptly vanishing. One such lot, partial to throwing babies into the Tiber, styles itself 'The Goths', revering those hordes who, during the Troubles of Gallienus, had, within ear-shot of Rome, sacrificed captives to their warrior god Odinus. He stabs himself nine times every nine years and chooses the warriors to die fighting the Empire. With Rome endangered, Minerva's priestess grows a beard; she must have worked overtime under Gallienus.

The Clubs stake themselves bastions in the desolate terrain of wild cat and vulture, where the City peters out into bramble and wreckage before reaching the Pontine Marshes. Here, in depopulated suburban villages, saplings push through once busy forums, ivy smothers fallen statues, swarthy streams choked with rubble, bits of furniture, dead pigs, donkeys, babies, mostly girls. Atrocious smells rise from flesh spread over lost cellars or decomposing in shallow earth. Rats' haven, carrion land. Slow, heavy birds flap above madmen, exhibitionists, maggoty-eyed scarecrows, manic conspirators, outcast harbingers of disaster, easy meat for Club stalwarts. Here 'The Goths' encircle a prone Hercules crucified on a sun-wheel or a

Venus at the mercy of obscene fingers. Quite close, Tiber masts strain to discoloured clouds and traffic grinds down highways with hallowed names and forgotten heroes: Flaminian, Cassian, Appian ... to Naples, Capua, Turin, Brundisium ... to everywhere and nowhere, radiating from the bronze column in the greatest forum.

Likewise, packs of dogs speed wildly down streets, over walls, into cellars, towards babies and the aged. To feed them is forbidden, though they are visibly self-reliant. Last defence against plague, fire, gangsters, officials, is the Emperor. The amorphous populace cleaves to two rulers. One, the live Aurelian Augustus, saviour from the witch Zenobia, Custodian of Order, more vulgarly Old Sword-in-Hand; the other, more mysterious, a figment compounded of all those previous leaders, lustreless dream spirits seeking their lost powers. In tavern and catacomb, stew and dungeon voices haggle over Valerian, now a Persian slave presenting his neck as stirrup for the Great King. 'No, my friend, he's starved hisself for shame. They flayed him, stuffed him with hay, hung him up, at Persepolis.' 'But you're wrong. He's kept as a professional traitor, to advise on Roman strategies. Ugh!'

Outraged by a Valerian, a Gallienus, who so smudge the Genius of the City, the old gods may have withdrawn, leaving the Empire less to Mithras and Anubis than to the visible Emperor, empurpled, enthroned, guarded by silver spears topped with golden eagles, his generals ranged behind him on glossy steeds, under a cloud hung with the rigid, bloodshot eyes of Mars the Avenger. Emperor, pole of desire, fiery top of necessity. When such a figure sighs, the world's heart chokes. His Triumph approaches, Valerian's Standards, lost, now redeemed, will be rededicated to Victory spreading her wings, obsidian sharp, behind the bronze doors of the Curia. Rome is again Rome, stamping on catamite kings and eunuch-ridden courts, on atrocious queens and vile pretenders. In the Senate the Enrolled Fathers laboriously recite Virgil: 'The defeated can be saved only by recognizing that rescue is now impossible.' Not all the vats of the South can contain the blood lost to invincible Aurelian. Boards are already up, depicting him receiving abject Alemmani, spurning vainglorious Tetricus, trapping wily Zenobia. *Unconditional Surrender.* Of her, scented package of Asia, rumours are swapped like kisses. Pregnant by Odenanthus, she rounded up handsome adolescents to infect her baby with their loveliness. Yet the Gods are ironic, he was born ugly. Secret prayers may have assisted, for envy seeks all, refuses even sleep to humanity. Some say she bore a toad, or nothing at all, she herself being a man in a metal wig.

V

In the ante-rooms of Senator Clodius Ammianus the jostle was
almost as lively as in his days as Consul, as Governor. Daily,
clients, petitioners, and better-class parasites, mingling with
importunate clerks with wrinkled eyes and dirty fingers, Gallic
doctors dangling small scarlet bags, almost all seeking recom-
mendations, market information, openings towards a legacy
from some childless old widow or widower, magnate or freedman, though ostensibly only anxious to enquire after the
Senator's health, while the humblest meekly bore *sportulae* at
their waists to be filled with whatever could be acquired.
Greeted by the steward with smiles expertly graded between
deference, disdain and odium, they stood in small groups,
eyeing each other, concealing anxieties under nervy chatter or
prolonged, meditative silences through which they respectfully
contemplated an ancestral mask or wall painting – a green and
blue river scene of ducks, crocodiles, egrets, leaves, a battle in
which Marius on horseback routed Numidians, a harbour of
polished ships sailing past lighthouse and pier over slapping
waves. Specially favoured by the steward with small goblets of
second-best wine and plates of honeycake were a few Hellenized
lawyers, each in a long decorated byrrus, primed with some
florid speech to be delivered later in the Julian Basilica, talking
with several senators. More loudly assertive were freedmen
enriched by vast landholdings, slave exchanges, Ostian ship
insurance, Baltic amber; several, perhaps most, were Galileans.

This morning, however, the routine was upset. Some Equestrian notables entered, without courteous preliminaries, pushing past the uneasy steward, barely acknowledging Domitia
stationed in the second room, each taking as his due her grave,

formal smile. Long ago this class, rich enough to afford a horse, had manned the scanty Roman cavalry, but now it was far from field and beast. These men were stout, indeed cumbersome, with quick, raking eyes in faces jowled, surly, rigid, pursed as if in pain. Their hands shone with gold rings, crimson hems adorning their thin cloaks. They swiftly vanished into the inner sanctum, leaving an atmosphere of grievance and speculation.

Watching from the stairs, Constantius frowned. He had seen them before, and hoped that his father's legal training had not wholly rusted. He glanced at his mother, very composed in her grey cloak, miniver bordered with green silk woven with narcissus and orange blossom. Guarding the home rather than welcoming the guests, she would not have been pleased by the latest intrusion. Of genuine patrician stock, she resented those with more wealth than manners.

Ignoring the gabbling petitioners, he bowed to her and withdrew to the empty, sunlit loggia. He fretted, always mistrusting the unexpected. All should be clear-cut as an athlete. Thankfully, after the Triumph, his furlough in this city of brooding death and despairing licence would end, the Emperor perhaps returning East.

He paced the warm paving, in an effort to thrust off disquiet aroused by the Equestrians doubtless now ringing his father with hard demands. They had the relentless tread of creditors, and he wondered how much Domitia knew of the Senator's business dealings. Unhurriedly, calmly, she spoke to him only on domestic matters, in which she was methodical, capable, just.

A sudden scent of early summer struggled through the stench and dust of the City, provoking early recollections, before withdrawn as if at an order. A shadow thickened under a sprawling fig tree. Sparrows were safe, for Clodius Ammianus had all cats killed, and the eagles circling the Capitol never deigned to swoop here.

He resumed his pacing. Thoughts of the East revived his secret hopes, of another Empire, purer, more secure than the mouldering Rome so palpably sinking to the underworld. A new Rome, lit by a star not quite visible: Hercules reborn from himself. Then, as he stared into a low tank within which mauve fish stirred lazily beneath thick, splayed fronds, Clodia approached, slight, in short green jacket, dark-brown eyes glowing under her black fringe.

'What will happen to her?'

His brief silence was oppressive, with images best kept from her, before he answered, telling no more than that Zenobia would grace the Triumph in the usual train of captives. She need not know the customary sequel, in which illustrious prisoners, having stalked in ceremonial attire through murderous, scoffing Rome, were hustled out of the sunlight, stripped, then lowered down a dark hole to be strangled or starved in the stinking Tullian dungeon under the Mamertine.

'I don't know . . . but I'll tell you a story about Zenobia. She told a courtier to arrange a bowl of flowers. He was new to court ways, so, though he mixed the flowers very carefully, very gracefully, he did not understand that for the Queen and her friends all flowers are symbols, of love, death, knowledge, that sort of thing. So he arranged them ignorantly, and when everyone assembled, they stared at the flowers, and interpreted them as a message that Zenobia was to betray them all to the Great King of Persia, in exchange for seven loads of copper vases. She saw their horror, glanced at the flowers, understood at once, but, in a merciful mood, rather rare, I'm told, laughed, and merely ordered the courtier to eat the flowers.'

Clodia, standing in decorous silence above the fish, appeared content, and he told her more. At Palmyra the huge sun temple had stone avenues so tall that they seemed to be lost in the sky, taller even than the columns at Heliopolis, City of the Sun. She smiled, gave a small sudden hop, kissed her hand to him and darted away, turning swiftly like the fish.

Later, delaying his departure, dismissing the entourage of clients, petitioners, hangers-on, so anxious to escort him to the Senate, the Baths, to wherever his mighty will directed, Clodius Ammianus joined him, tufted brows frowning, voice irritable. Though he said nothing of his late visitors, the conference must have gone badly. They sat opposite each other in a silence tense as that of a surgeon's waiting-room.

The Senator never retreated. Rome always marches forward, while Etruria, Carthage, Corinth, Egypt, reel away, lie prostrated. The laws, principles, arguments of his youth he still repeated, regularly, monotonous as a frog. Had Domitia, Constantius wondered, ever seen him youthful, attentive, loving? He felt uncomfortable. Had she even seen him naked? Father had been old before his time, solemn, but – disloyalty tried to check his thoughts – but not wise, though he could quote wise maxims and indeed continually did so.

He did not do so now. The words broke out testily from the grey, parched face, bearded like a retired Jove.

'This Triumph ... it is more your affair than mine, though in my position I must of course grace it. I've seen it before, I may never see it again. I feel ashamed of such manifestations. Rome herself I can no longer feel is very real. Giant shadows, gigantic piles of litter, cracks everywhere. The great consuls and lawgivers ruled as they breathed, walked, slept, going about their business like ordinary mortals. Government, I am saying, so listen well, was a natural function, not a matter of debate, philosophy, juggling with words empty as sucked-out oranges. Fellows gazing into the sky and falling into the ditch. Minerva kept appetites in proportion, bridled extravagant spirits. No doubt you'll all put on a spectacle, but spectacles fill no treasuries, pay no more debts than a halibut.'

Constantius lowered his head dutifully, acknowledged gratitude for the old man's insights. But the house, Rome itself, packed and clamorous under the disordered hills, was too small, stifling the blood. Alone again, he returned to the loggia. Sunlight had hardened, the fish were hidden, then, as he stood irresolute, the shadow moved under the fig tree and out of it, like a pantomime mimic eager to astonish the mob with lewd grimace, irreverent quip, slightly on tiptoe, face half concealed by an absurd blue floppy cap currently fashionable, stepped Julian.

60

VI

The clamour harshened – sharp voices, unoiled wheels, rising to a shriek, sinking to a discordant hum, but never ceasing, though sometimes at night, in a brief, suspended instant, a single cry could be heard, a threat or curse, or, ominously distinct, a whisper noted, before again submerging in the general inescapable movement of the times.

One summer morning people awoke long before dawn, aroused less by a new sound than a new momentum, a grinding, a scraping, mingling with thuds, clangs, exclamations in unknown tongues. Afterwards many claimed to remember sullen troops of unkempt, polyglot diggers, masons, carpenters, African cement mixers, Sicilian quarrymen, Calabrian transport captains, Capuan surveyors, Spanish engineers borrowed from the legions, roller-men from Ostia. Some were convinced that stone caryatids had been released, on the Emperor's orders, from the huge, tragic weights piled on them, then set to work on the mysterious project. Nevertheless, nothing unusual was spelled out from the Acta Diurna, the senatorial reports daily displayed in the Forum Romanorum for those concerned. Very few.

Yet, agog for something novel, multitudes found themselves hastening, thick-eyed and apprehensive, to the outlying Sections, to discover, puzzled, hundreds of workers, supervised by armed soldiers, in curved, irregular lines, demolishing houses, pushing aside the frantic owners, ignoring complaints, threats, lamentations, ripping down fences, unloading hard blocks of granite from gigantic, almost supernatural drays, stacking bags of cement, thousands of bricks, bundles of coarse-grained larch supports. Kilns were smoking, cranes swung across the sky, pulleys strained and rasped, mules dragged mortar vats up ramps. Plasterers awaited orders, men with mallets and trowels streamed away to areas already cleared, slaves carting away rubble often damaging whatever properties survived, while others dug wide pits to receive it. Blocking both ends of the horizon were tall platforms, from which naked giants hauled up more cement, bricks, water. An entire army seemed at work, encircling the City: calloused flatteners, hooded riveters, lithe blacks with shovels, mattocks, spades, a conscript assemblage, ruthless and ashine, of wedges and gabions, staples and fascines, temporary stanchions, hawsers, bollards, winches. Lashed, groaning bodies heaved at a consignment of Platean iron; others improvised shelters from the coarse, unremitting glare under the cranes. More carts and handbarrows rolled forward with planks, boards, buckets, and from far away echoed the work of destruction, the gapers endlessly speculating about whatever was intended. A prison for Zenobia, another palace for the Emperor, a temple, or, more likely, a barracks mightier than fabled Babylon, or perhaps mighty pillars to withstand a comet whirling towards earth with incalculable speed.

Again, barely articulated, as if from a queer noonday darkness, there glimmered some broken dream of the earliest Rome, slowly spreading from the Capitol on which, grimly concealed, remained the sacred cavern where the founding brothers had been suckled by a wolf, or, the usual mockers sniggered, a harlot. Romans knew of Aulus's head, still bleeding, under the Capitoline Hill where once Tuscan acrobats had struggled with sacred bulls, mastering life itself, blood strengthening the earth, uniting the tribes. Aulus? Nothing was known of him, but many felt in their own blood that, beneath the columns, terraces and monuments dominating the City on behalf of the divine Trinity, Jupiter, Minerva, Juno, that head still miraculously dripped, in dim compact with the unseen.

Crowds regathered daily, breeding new inventions. Skeletons from charnel-houses had been purged in bone-fires, then thrown into the foundations, to appease the baleful three-eyed Hag who dogs all peoples. The usual omens were recollected: a baby born with two heads at Rimini; a fish making a ribald remark from the Rubicon. Astrologers prospered, with deep talk of conjunctions, astral confluences, wavering convergences, auric gleams. A very fashionable seer, the Chaldean Grand Master, now sported a velvet cap to restrain the blue magnetic powers gushing from his head, and, on the Esquiline, the Elder Brother of Orpheus, though invisible, attracted respected congregations awaiting some 'configuration of etheric reality substance', which did not come.

After seven days trumpets sounded from outside the Senate House and the populace gathered for the Censor's proclamation. A Wall had been ordained to surround the entire City, of kiln-baked brick faced with cement and stone. Imagine it! A new wall with nearly four hundred towers with outlying bastions, sixteen gates flanked by rounded watch-towers, the first such defences since at least the Gallic danger of who knows when. Here was ominous acknowledgement of that dark pageant imperilling Rome: Goths and Vandals, Alans, Alemmani, Franks, Burgundians.... The Wall would soar, irresistible, invulnerable. From the steps of the venerable temple of Vesta a celebrated rhetorician intoned Pindar to a concourse briefly hushed.

'Man is a shadow's dream. But when, god-inspired,
    brightness settles on earth,
A bright gleam flickers amongst men,
    a mild age comes to birth.'

Elation swept over roof and statue, square and bridge, palace and slum, a brilliant banner unfurling. The Wall would be wider than the Spanish Via Plata, loftier than the Segovian Aqueduct or the Rhodian Apollo. The least of its shadows would consume the Caracallan Baths and all memory of the Golden House.

Children, many still flushed from gutter fever, squawked excitedly, as if before a new game. In a sudden quarrel, one

63

child knifed another for insufficient delight at the prospect of the Wall. Would the Wall, people wondered, entail a new god, or would the old god suffice? Who was he? Romulus, Murus, Julius Caesar? Undeniably he must now work harder; in dilapidated Rome he had lately been idling.

VII

Exhilaration whirled like dust devils, wavered, then collapsed. Nervy as a breeze, the City was baked by summer, though low, swarthy clouds buried the sun and a harsh wind periodically gusted from hill and fever plain. The Sons of Bacchus, levying dues on shops and markets for protection against themselves, terrorized entire Sections, and after a spectacular murder had mutilated noble statues in the Augustan Forum and hung them with insulting epithets. New rumours, perhaps little more substantiated than washerwomen's cackle, agitated louder than street gangs and alley warfare, one pervading tavern, brothel, latrine and cellar, that the secret purpose of the Wall was not to repel barbarians but to prevent citizens leaving the City.

'We'll be penned in like sheep.'

'But remember, safe from the wolves.'

'Or staked for the wolves – remember that too!'

Strangers confessed shamefacedly to each other disquieting dreams and daytime imaginings. 'You wouldn't believe it, my dear friend, I scarcely believe it myself, but I distinctly saw a gap opening in the Alban Hills. Black! Stygian! When I approached again, nervously, I admit – well, it wasn't there, not there at all. Yet, you'll see for yourself, the hills have shrunk. It's alarming.'

Others maintained that sea defences had been ransacked for stones to erect the Wall, so that whole coastlines were endangered. Should a great wave be dispatched, it could swamp Rome herself, drowning whole provinces on the way. Yet another rumour was swiftly about, that the Wall, rising in such headlong haste, was indeed intended to repel a gigantic wave that had already extinguished the land of Denos, of which, until now, no one had heard.

All agreed that ceaseless turmoil, trundle of wheels, clank of soldiery and convicts had altered sound itself. But they themselves had done so, listening more acutely, more apprehensively, seeking to overhear, discerning angles of being, alerted by a distant but menacing note expressed in uncanny silence. A recent thunderstorm was held to have been Jupiter's anger at the Wall, as if accused of powerlessness to defend his own city. Others thought it the wrath of the divine Trajan, outraged by surrender of Dacia. The old story sidled into forum and tavern, into temple, mansion, tenement, drifted through tiny chinks of half-forgotten childhood and the lore of eel vendor and fried meat cook, of that primitive wall, low and crude, dripping with blood, as in pique, or in sacrifice, one brother slew another. The killer, Romulus, son of Mars the Avenger, had himself vanished in the Goat Marsh during an eclipse. Some believed he had ascended in a cloud to join the gods but others held that he had been smitten by an angry thunderbolt.

Affected by this dawn memory, few repeated the latest rumour in public, but all knew of it.

'They say ... they say ... a child's been killed.' Young blood, warm and lively, smeared over foundations to give them life, an injection of spirit for the Wall to outlast time and Goth.

Clodius Ammianus was not considering any child. He lay more or less naked on a massage slab amongst familiars at a once exclusive club within the Baths of Sallust, on the Palatine. From outside, din seethed as hucksters bellowed the splendours of Cremona sausage and urchins dangling melons had encroached almost to the great doors where donkeys were tethered and no-goods clustered to gibe at great ones on their way to the tubs.

The Senator, wincing at the attentions of the Moroccan masseur, had to speak louder. 'It's outrageous! A surrender! A wall round Rome! What a confession, a retreat to eras of swamp and rapine! To primal existence! And who's to pay for it? Tell me that.'

None of the moist, puffed faces bothered to answer, but several turned morosely towards the far end of the massage hall, where, under a statue of the goddess Hygeia and red and white tiled walls, fully at ease, swathed in warmed towels, reclined members of the tax-collecting syndicate whose profits were sufficiently bloated to risk lending to provincial cities at a rate at which even the assassin Brutus would have jibbed, though not for long. Most had bought themselves into patrician families, or, by formal adoption, had acquired distinguished names, Appius, Agrippa, Flavius, which adorned very loosely these faces mostly originating no nearer Rome than Antioch or New Carthage. That fellow Frobenius, ex-Aedile, sleek as a seal, who made millions from swindling the public over a grain contract, was whispering to a so-called Caius Antonius, once a wealthy costumier's parasite, who had then outstepped his patron, grabbing his farms.

At this instant, both these toads now looked up and nodded at him, Clodius Ammianus, former Consul, with something like compassion. Motioning the masseur to desist, he thought rapidly. Had they by mischance heard of his recent dealings? Betrayal was rife everywhere. Despite notable services he was a stranger in his own city. Yesterday a vile immigrant had shouted that there were too many of his sort about. He now forced himself into cumbrous acknowledgement, and the Moroccan resumed his nudges and slaps, in tune with his fellows assiduously manipulating the grunting, complaining bodies of ageing gentlemen, not one of whom the Senator could respect. They spoke incessantly, but with nothing to say. Earlier, in the steam-room, he had had to endure thick lips releasing only reports of the latest degenerate farce, ballet, an exceptional sea bass and unusual sauce, a round table with ivory legs auctioned for a million. 'Lucrine oysters,' Frobenius had repeated, like a proclamation of victory, his accent thick enough to clog a drain. 'Things of the past.' Though he would not have recognized one if he were given it, or, more probably, had snatched it. Such creatures were alien predators, ignorant of age-old rites and manners which preserved the unique Genius of the City.

The Senator was at once infuriated by a wink passing from

the masseur to a latrine attendant, lowest of the low, of bestial lineage, a repellent Jew or Levantine, whose circumcised nakedness insulted human kind, whose mouth reeked with garlic, and dyed, tawdry hair dripped cassia. Shocked by the insolence, the Senator yet felt powerless. He had to sound persuasive, pleading even.

'Softer, man . . . more gently . . . I'm not made of wax!'

His rheumatic leg was being rubbed with damp Ancion sulphur, the black hands viciously determined to knock all bones together and crush the intervening flesh. From beyond, water gurgled. The supply was haphazard, accompanied by inadequate heating because of wood shortages. The steamroom had a complex hypocaust mechanism, now cracked, and the repair money had been deflected to, of all things, a hydraulic organ, requested by a bunch of young fops. On the tessellated floors, sandals were seldom necessary against the heat.

Nearby an obese Cretan banker lay prone on a raised and faded mattress, two naked hirelings oiling him with the 'ointment of youth' compound of barley mead, honey, eggs and narcissus roots, guaranteed to resist old age. The coils of fat oozing on a belly flaking from age and luxury did not improve any right man's disposition. He wanted to turn away, but the banker was gasping out some customary nonsense. 'Things periodically improve . . . only last year. . . .'

'You may believe that, if you discredit the obvious. Our Empire has suffered absolute decline for over a century. Please refrain from informing me about periodical improvements. In the Senate they are termed "readjustments". Just look around you, at the schemers, scavengers, improvident and shamelessly lazy.'

Indeed, body-scrapers and depilators, neglecting their duties, studiously ignoring indignant complaints, had congregated by the central column, moulded with indifferently executed riders and jumpers, heads slanted together as if conspiring. Spies, of course, were always here, noting and overhearing, amassing evidence for the Officialdom, not least for the Treasury.

Clodius Ammianus contemplated another opulent figure, and did his best, scarcely distinguishable from his worst, to conceal resentment. With his oozing paunch and prawn-like fingers, he had been one of those pushing Equestrian oligarchs who, a few mornings back, had intruded uninvited into the Senator's home. The deliberations, adroitly swayed by this grandson of a Neapolitan scullion crawling above his station, had not won the favour of a descendant of Mars. All Neapolitans, Julian for once had said something sensible, made mendacity an applied art. This one must have grossly pro-fiteered from secret contracts involving the Wall, which would probably collapse with the first autumn storms. In a spasm of lingering hope, the Senator allowed him a reluctant smile, looked away, but only to encounter once again the obsequious eye of the Cretan banker.

Refusing a peck of Indian ginger, perfunctorily offered, the Senator resumed, in a tone he assumed was conversational, though actually, trained for domestic use, it was lecturing and harsh.

'The Scythians once invaded Cimmeria, so my elder son tells me, an army officer. The Cimmerians fled, but their leaders did not lack spirit and resolved to die, I might say perish, in their own lands under the eyes of their tribal gods. Thus they divided themselves into two clans and fought each other to the death. An example to our young men, though I have seldom met any barbarian to whom death does much harm.'

The pinkish flesh opposite stirred laboriously, porcine eyes blinking through swollen casings. He could have measured himself for the honour of being Chief Eunuch to the Great King. Vile! 'But, Senator, pardon my presumption . . .' – the schoolboy sarcasm was insufferable – '. . . would they not have done better to turn their blades, so to speak, on . . . did you say, the Scythians?'

He was not granted a reply, to which he might not have listened. Moved by Constantius's story, Clodius Ammianus was wondering where young Romans actually were. They were not amongst these prone bodies, the sighs of discomfort, the indignities of maltreated flesh. Youth had deserted Rome, but to where? They were not with those southern types exercising in the gymnasium or throwing a ball in the colonnades, but more likely reading lewd Greek fables in the upstairs library or crowding the gambling cells. Estates were lost on the fall of a knuckle-bone, a forest surrendered. They would be conferring with some tittering, flute-voiced merchant over the price of a boy, or being toyed with by sniggering girls, or yelling at bribed, ruffianly charioteers in the Circus Maximus, where a carelessly nailed wheel might win the favours of the most celebrated courtesan from some Bithynian taphouse.

Two rough-spoken Lusitanians were approaching, inclining courteously at the Senator, then passed on, probably chuckling. Each was scarcely superior to a bargee overseer yet possessed unending letters of credit and bills of exchange: the sort who overloads a ship and fattens on the insurance paid out by a competitor after his own company captain adroitly sinks her.

Suddenly the Senator felt ambushed. Here, in the capital's foremost baths, the most powerful dignitaries and magnates, most of them trash, were trussed in thin wrappings, powerless, at the mercy of slaves. The cord at the masseur's waist was immediately menacing, even a silver toothpick glinted unpleasantly, and the suggestion that he should now present his back to be rubbed made him hesitate. In a lower-class of baths a man had been emasculated after a quarrel about a tip.

The thought of spies returned. Political concern exposed one to suspicion of treason: each attendance at the Senate was secretly recorded, each speech, each demeanour, to underlings shrouded in secret rooms, the nameless men of power linked not only to the Emperor but to the Praetorian Prefect, unpredictable in his loyalties, against whom upright men were more essential than ever before. Even if Hercules had never existed, the conservative College of Hercules was as indispensable as Standards, Vestal Virgins, the more respectable gods.

Drawing around him an invisible toga, the last upright man of Rome stared about him defiantly, looking tomorrow in the face.

70

VIII

'Father is angry!'

Indistinct in a room shuttered against glare, Julian seemed to smile before murmuring lines from Martial:

'Wealthy men feign wrath – useful plan –
It's far cheaper to hate than assist a man.'

At Constantius's manly smile he added, 'But is Father wealthy? Is he even in funds? That Agrippa dogs him without signs of reverence, actually like a Nemesis more or less male. A mishap of a fellow! His descent from a goose is by no means wholly unconfirmed. Perhaps, of course, one of those that allegedly saved us from tiresome Gauls. We can suppose Father has his private reasons for wanting to suppress him? One needs initiative, of course. Remember the easiest fortune ever made? Numerius Atticus reaped a million sesterces for reporting he had seen dead Augustus ascending to heaven!'

Constantius remained silent. Disliking discussion of his father, he had nevertheless recently dreamed of him defending himself from bears with weapons swollen, too heavy.

Like a harp waiting to be plucked, the silence lay between the brothers, divisive, keen. Julian was seated in a blurred corner of the vestibule, half concealed by an ancestral bust. Despite his light tone, gay sandals, brilliant sleeves decorated with small, lustful centaurs, he was a wintry presence, teasing as Mercury.

Constantius could barely remember a life without Julian smiling mischievously, pointing at what others wished to avoid, or staring at a closed door, darkening grove, blue pool, with peculiar, unexplained intensity. When absent, he was indistinct, recollected as if under lamplight. Not once in their life together had he begged for his elder's protection.

With neat, scented head, beard trim and pointed, tinged somewhat darker than the rest of his oiled, crisp hair, and as if fixed on, as disguise or imitation of some comedian, Julian had style neither patrician nor plebeian but singularly his own, at one with the pale, clever smiles, rings of sapphire and garnet, fashionable cloaks and manicured hands. He had always been Domitia's favourite, though she betrayed no sign of it. Within a family such feelings are part of the air. As a boy he preferred chuckling with Diomede to playing with other boys, and the two must have shared secrets which Father would have condemned as foully Asiatic. Diomede had referred to Julian as courteously unteachable, leaving himself, Constantius, a ready pupil, feeling inferior. He had obediently composed heroic declamations for long dead Fabius, Scipio, Sulla, odes to Apollo and Ceres, while Julian listened superciliously, periodically slipping Diomede a tablet scratched with an indecent epigram or abstruse love quatrain. At twelve, doubtless primed by the Greek, Julian had let himself be seduced by some older boy, here in Rome. For this he professed gratitude, and was inclined to boast. Father had been furious until learning that the culprit was of a vintage Palatine family, and then convincing himself, not implausibly, that the seducer had been Julian.

Women bear children, Father would say, too often, but men create heroes. They did not always do so and, in Julian, had rather markedly refrained. A natural civilian, he had, like an Official, a gift for transforming mishaps to personal advantage, sniffing profits from earthquake, defeat, an emperor's murder. Earlier, Father's beatings seemed to make him rejoice in unique wrongs, and at a measured rebuke from Domitia he smiled like a proud lover. He had enjoyed throwing coins into long grass, spending a morning in search of them and chuckling when he failed. He would still tell Clodia stories that were preposterous but related them in convincing tones, affecting perplexity at her trusting admiration.

Once, as boys, discussing the future, Constantius had chosen to be a senator. Julian grimaced fastidiously as if at a latrine witticism. 'I'll be a house. A very expensive one.' He had also desired nine sisters, all very rich and recently widowed.

They had always disagreed, Constantius sometimes hating his brother, though never for long. His own praise of Claudius Gothicus induced Julian's fulsome respect for Gallienus, ignoble creature who found pleasure and disaster identical, who shrugged away rivals, indifferent even when slain by his own followers, by men well respected in the army for undertaking a duty so patriotic.

After a quarrel, Julian always silken and pert, Constantius, even when tearful with indignation, too often yearned to embrace him, a furtive inclination that Julian must nevertheless notice and despise. With his dapper attire, frivolous gossip, successful dealings, Julian, at twenty-three, might appear the elder, gazing at the physique and panoply of a rising officer, a survivor of battle, as mere toys too big for those absurd enough to possess them.

The brothers remained silent. Flies buzzed in the distance between them, the general stir continued from street and forum. Mosquitoes were back, whirring in from the dank pools of the Campagna which spread, torpid and malodorous, as the trees vanished. Constantius scratched a wrist, an ankle, annoyed at Julian's unconcern. He wondered what Clodia was doing. Earlier, she had plucked a dark-red flower, studied it with the fixity that Julian awarded his stones, then, very gravely, eaten it.

At last he mentioned the Wall, but Julian's expression suggested that the mighty project must rely not on imperial engineers but on his own approval. 'Ah, yes!' His voice was idle. 'Another trial! First we had to endure, indeed subsidize that Unconquered Sun nuisance. Now this rhetorical and rather too noisy defence of the indefensible, even the insupportable. What an opportunity for a master graffitist in that grandiose collection of bricks! A Venus with raging tits, to annoy your Emperor. But it's tempting Fate, surely! You, my good sibling, believe in Fate, destiny of Rome, that branch of thought, and

73

with commendably fewer words than our worthy parent. Less prattle. I myself, of course, am disposed to respect luck, chance, the whimsical caprices of sheer muddle, reinforced by a whiff of corruption. Not too much, but sufficient to keep the wheel turning. Someone should have told Livy to look into this. Doesn't muddle deserve a temple? Has corruption a stool on Olympus? They've some voice in our mortal world, though annalists and poets turn their backs.'

Lounging away from the fierce sunlight as though it affronted him as it strained at his face through a cracked shutter, he closed his eyes, slowly, as if delicately swooning, his lips, thin, faintly carmined, glowing in the insistent flake of light. 'You, most solemn Constantius, get your thrills from obedience, obedience to death itself. You cherish discipline as we cherish flesh.' His smile was a drawl made visible, though in truth, at an imperial dismissal, Julian, at dire risk, might have courteously stood his ground. Scarcely admirable, not absolutely deplorable. Forced to admit it, Constantius breathed faster. 'To sneer is really to confess oneself subordinate.'

'Just so. I enjoy those who are obviously wrong-headed, so that I should get on with Father, our Prophet, better than I actually do. Though I suspect he needs it, he won't accept my tainted money. Immoral earnings, threat to Roman integrity! But he'll grandly drive creditors into the ditch for trusting his Name, trusting too well. Few enjoy consigning their goods to the tumbling waves. Nor do the fish appreciate it. Father's out of the stock comedy of Terence and Plautus, though less comic of course. He enjoys possessions. Comedy is struck from the suspicion I've already mentioned that, to the observant, he owns very little, despite high-falutin' title-deeds. He once complained of dreaming that he'd gone blind. I could scarcely tell him that this was an admission that he'd been morally unaware since birth. Well, a Prophet should foresee his own end, or at least its nature.'

Constantius had few possessions – some favourite weapons, a dozen book rolls, but no jewels, slaves, dogs, fine robes, no money deposited in the temple of Mercury. Julian too, despite his exchanges, bargains, contracts, owned no dwelling and seemed to cherish only a collection of small, common stones.

'As for you, Brother,' Julian's smile, a mere crease, was not repeated in his indeterminate eyes, 'you'd make a valiant hunter. Of unicorns, mind.'

Constantius strove for the good temper that usually eluded him during such talk. 'Father probably shows judgement in suspecting these cults you're always discovering. He believes the Galileans conspire against Rome. Certainly in the army we prefer to fight simple northerners than the East with its teeming, slippery gods. I've heard Galileans treat slaves badly, but pretend otherwise.'

Julian's smile, edging between the shadows of his oiled, immaculate beard, glinting like a new trowel, politely included the bust above them. The Senator had dismissed Chrestus as a Jewish felon organizing a cannibal cult to impair the pork industry.

'Father', Julian spoke as if of a mangy bird, 'thinks of Chrestus grubbing in a very greasy trough. As for Galileans, I meet a few in Alexandria. An unwholesome lot. The men guard their cocks like treasure sacks, which of course they are. They take rather perfunctory vows against spreading their spunk around, and yes, do rather pose as being sexless as aphids. They indulge in marriage, mostly to rich widows who don't miss carnality or haven't much choice, and are apt to turn pious, not much liking the prospect of death. In business, Galileans drive hard bargains. I deal with them but don't care to dine with them. Too opinionated, too smug. If anyone's to be smug it must be me, and I'm not! Gallienus's wife, Salonina, was one of them. It didn't help anyone. About Chrestus, though, I haven't found much that's reliable. Father's probably correct in believing he never cared a jot for the Empire, the frontiers, and all the fine excuses for the almighty defence tax. He didn't condemn them, merely ignored them. Rather refreshing! I gather he wanted strangers respected. Not easy. Actually very novel, save in Naples of course, for deplorable reasons. We must both admit, however, that novelty in behaviour, as in art,

75

often produces lunacy or rubbish. Yet you yourself are probably about to remind me that novelty never occurs, and you may be right.'

His tone flickered with amusement. Knowing that Constantius hated being teased, he continued, as though in casual afterthought.

'Chrestus never affected not enjoying his wine-jars, setting us an example. His own home was called after Bacchus, the House of the Vine. But he saddled himself with the Jewish god, which causes trouble. That divinity's a ruffianly prude who camps on a mountain, even cruder than Vulcan. He'd have sued Achilles for being late returning a mousetrap. Jews say he created man, then, thinking further, woman, then raged at both for some nonsense about an apple. A number of interpretations of that! The apple might have been Babylonian. The Jews were said, though by Pompey, to worship a donkey.'

Whether or not he was joking was, as so often, uncertain.

'Curses flew about like crows over that apple. Then another god appeared, from nowhere in particular, more amiable, and, impressed by Jupiter sending down his fancy son Hercules to repair damage, he sired Chrestus to do the same. The older god was angry, released evil stratagems, but Chrestus must have learned a thing or two from Orpheus and Attis about side-stepping death. He got done in on a cross as a public nuisance but had become adept at walking on water, all the tricks of the trade. Before execution he roundly cursed his father, which, for my money, makes him less of a tall story than Attis or Adonis. He despaired of all but his dog, and he wasn't too sure of him. That too is unusual. Anyway, in one story, after crucifixion, he trotted down to Hades to chat with the lost, and, after a few pointed words with the ruffian god, got some released. But at Antioch, when I was inspecting an empty site after a dish of quite tolerable venison and Syrian pears, I heard another version. The crucifixion was only a pretence. He'd done some deal with the Romans, who liked to spite the Jews, and escaped. My informant had gone half shares over a consignment of fish, though his eating habits made me doubt if he'd survive to enjoy the profit. He was nothing but belly, his girl nothing but tongue.

'As for Chrestus, he seems a considerable joker, though his laughter was cutting. If he simply becomes another Olympian, he'll lose his essence. In Alexandria his cross is regarded as a symbol of stillness, physical and moral equilibrium, reconciliation of opposites, the usual jargon which you understand better than I. He wasn't exactly grandson of a comet, nor a client of the sapient dolphin that always turns up when needed. But, unlike many others, he actually taught something. He preached some sort of mirror kingdom either within or beyond mortal life, in which all is reversed. Slaves deferred to, masters downgraded, opulence out of the question. A rather specialized goodwill. If he's now a god, you'll remember that gods are idealized possibilities, irregularly measured gropings.'

Constantius did not so remember and shifted uneasily. Julian, filling the air with edges, irritated one like a street-corner buffoon. The quiet room itself was fidgety, from the swooping shadows of pigeons, while Julian resumed as if graciously granting a favour too long demanded.

'Despite his wife, Gallienus was bored by beliefs. If he'd tried to shock Chrestus, he'd probably have failed. Chrestus shrugged off most beliefs, enjoyed getting a higher sense of being, through various procedures of hypnosis, of himself and, I dare say, of others. We hear that blessed Aurelian, the Triumph-monger, is getting impatient with Galileans. Chrestus didn't stop at roundly castigating family life as an obstruction to reality. He also spoke of lawyers, priests and magistrates, in no very exalted way. Hated professionalism. Brisk with moral invective, with a high opinion of his own status. His credentials, it is said, are respectable enough. Like Mithras, to whom you soldiers like doffing your headgear, he was born in midwinter, under interesting relations of Ox, Ass and Virgin.'

The elder brother had felt no god's touch but could believe that what Julian termed luck could occasionally be divine intervention. 'But Julian, Chrestus could have been only one more provincial failure.'

'Yes. More than likely. That's what interests me. I enjoy failures, without intending to be one myself. Chrestus seems to have been betrayed to a disagreeable Jerusalem gang by a devoted follower anxious to save him from haughty delusions. Most gods, it's now fairly clear, need our help rather more than we need theirs. But unlike our undraped, handsome Olympians, so very enticing, Chrestus needed to query convention. Quite likely he wasn't a real god but a fakir with some scholarship, a pinch of insight, and bad temper. Thus without the boring symmetry of Apollo, Diana or Venus. A mountebank called Cyril thought him the ugliest of all sons of men. That, you'll agree, makes excellent sense. People were to admire his spirit, not his beauty. So, scowling and cursing, he could have been no pretty sight. In matters of lust, you may know more than I, and I know nothing. Near his home his magic always failed. But that's the nature of magic.'

'What is?'

But Julian only smiled, and briefly Constantius had lost attention. The mention of Aurelian reminded him that, though known to the Emperor, he was outside his councils and held no very senior rank. Contact with Galileans must be avoided. None of the senior staff worried over such notions that Julian had gathered and which were indeed un-Roman, as Father had insisted.

'There's more.' Julian was playing the generous uncle, his pocket filled with treats. 'Though not very impressive. Chrestus believed that the whole world was about to end, so he wasted some time devising techniques to deal with the last days. In the light of universal catastrophe, there was no obvious need to resist nastiness, refuse to share clothes, give honey to enemies, even deny taxes to Rome. All would soon be transformed. The labyrinth of existence. I suspect he rated improvised and crafty humility higher than reasoned philosophy. Like a money-lender. Meek and lowly he was not. Like Socrates. A great actor, he may have fooled even himself. Mithras is nicer, simpler, but not morally braver. Attractive to boys, of course, but presenting a certain quotient of boredom. Chrestus, though, was as unpredictable as a donkey in July.'

'But the world hasn't ended.'

'Can you prove it?'

Constantius suspected a cheap joke but, with an air of finality, his brother added: 'It may not have ended as he wished. We destroyed Jerusalem and scattered the Jews – I meet them everywhere. The Emperor's supposed to have consulted them about his almighty Wall. But I shouldn't look too closely into that.'

Constantius had begun to throb with his customary impatience, though noting that, mentioning the Wall, Julian had looked slightly disconsolate. Ever the officer, Constantius thought of his most trusted military tribune, Manilius, declassed landowner bankrupted by taxes, who followed Mithras, Light of the World. He spoke briefly of Manilius's beliefs. Training for salvation by personal virtue. Purification by baptism in blood. Struggle against darkness: darkness of night, darkness of ignorance.

'Logical enough, but still too easy and somewhat prim. An improvement on Apollo – a very cold sun. I suppose your great man, Saviour Aurelian.... Like all people....'

He stopped, placing a finger to his lips, ostentatiously peering around for spies, before reaching to pick up and fondle a Nilic vase inscribed with grapes and a grinning, Panlike face.

'People are themselves.' Constantius was still considering trustworthy Manilius restarting his career without rancour.

'They should of course be rather more, though usually they're somewhat less. Seldom what they think they are, for most of the time. What would you expect? Most worthy citizens do not know where to locate their own heart, speak no language other than that of their own back alley or benighted home wilderness. They chatter fluently though implausibly of the future but know nothing of the past, save that 'mother's arse' were Jupiter's first spoken words. I overheard yesterday some well-educated fellow declare that Jupiter is really a woman who lives in a Strasbourg sotting-house. Another mentioned proof that China is a dead oaf's nightmare turned solid. Our wiseacres can see to the ends of the earth but not to the ends of

79

their noses. But people are also what sensible fellows like me care to make them, just as you officer fellows make your emperors. What are the odds on Aurelian? Triumph or funeral march? One, two, three – bang! All that Stoic gab about being true to oneself is very limited, a poor recommendation for one's potential. We should be true to the self we have not reached. The only excuse for supporting an emperor is that we feel we should but without knowing it. Emperors articulate longings, especially Roman ones. Mind, I've never met any real Romans save Father, Mother and, by strange chance, yourself. I rather like the sound of Goths, whom you're always overwhelming in so praiseworthy a manner. They sound fresh and, so to speak, excitingly naked.'

As so often, his voice sounded as if he were really thinking of something else, perhaps something too serious to be disclosed. However, despite his fluid praise of the joys of dying, in battle young Julian would inspire no confidence, too busy mapping a safe line of retreat.

'Brother Julian....' Annoyed, Constantius felt himself already sounding pompous, tricked by the other's mock-affectionate gaze. 'You have no love for Goths, for anyone, and not much for yourself. You have only curiosity.'

'That at least suggests respect for life and a will to survive. Even survive life. Though life itself – and who can deny it, save interested parties? – has as much meaning, I don't say purpose, as a pool of wine. The purpose of both is a good swig, or the hope of it. It doesn't burden itself with destiny. Whether we're master or slave, republican or emperor, impious or godly, anarchic or Wall-building, our essence is unaffected, its propensities are inherited, in our case from that clumsy ass Mars. Inherited, indeed, I'm assured on very suspect authority, from ourselves as shapes in previous lives. Very exhausting. I must have been a Trojan. Female, of course.' His sigh was indeed as elegant as a woman's. 'Troy, Troy ... may her moon give health to her butterfly day. That honey glow dissolves our minor lunacies.'

Constantius lost the next words as he remembered Clodia with some brilliant rapture fancying herself a butterfly.

Julian had sniggered, 'Form in space ... design, colour, quiver of sound ... they do something to oppose life's indignities. As it is written, man fears Time, but Time fears the Pyramids, though it should be added that these are excessively tedious. Almost as bad as the Officials, which in a way is what they are. A dire crew! Chrestus was right after all. Whatever slithers is not wealth. Hollowing out each day's profile to suit themselves. At a conference where I met the Procurator, his own horse had to correct his grammar.'

The narrow, composed features now seemed unwontedly concerned, the voice quickened, belying the facetious words, the slim hands still enclosing the vase but as if in afterthought. 'Armpit Aurelian gets the plebeian vote, sometimes a liability. He might, with all that energy, deserve rather more.' He dropped his thoughtful mien, remembering the Procurator's horse. 'The stink would blow any other beast out of its skin, like an advocate's clerk I met in Corduba who coughed himself inside-out when I refused his offer of a sixty per cent loan. He told me that he was doing me a favour because he enjoyed my stories. I'd told him of Flap-ears Horace agog at a former mistress plastering herself with damp chalk and crocodile dung, to replenish her beauty stocks, though by then they were as dry as a Vestal's cunt. One day we'll have to warn our little doll Clodia, if we can prise her from Isis. Thank heaven I was never a child.'

Trapped in banter, Constantius again felt physical strength and imperial commendations lying over him like fashions long derided. Confused anger threatened him, as if all colours had sprung viciously from wall and floor. So often Julian seemed testing others' self-control, jeering at the legions, at Father, at Virgil as bookish but not well read.

Soon, though, he himself would be back with the armies, venturing further than yawning suburbs and well-insured trade circuits. He too had stories. A sudden turn of battle, when the body quails but the spirit leaps in fearful deliverance, an underground voice, muffled but unearthly, in a temple of Dionysus high in Thessalonian snow woods, a criminal buried up to his neck in Assyrian sands awaiting lions and madness, cursing the noon sun, a young recruit's eyes appealing against the Emperor's inexorable sentence. These were more solid than Julian's persiflage, his desire for applause.

Yet he lingered, as always detained by inner compulson, some nervous attraction for this captious being who, wholly by some fluke of impulse or unknown, sardonic attention, was his brother, and who might yet need protection.

The vestibule, hung with afternoon heat, had indeed lost all colour. Enclosed in this intimacy, neither moved to open the shutters. The windows were flat shadows, the bust faceless. Julian had lost outline in all but voice, which was still very clear, as if dictating to a crescent of scribes.

'I was bargaining, not unsuccessfully, for a strip of woodland in Tibur, and a lady, not of the finest class and with the soft, more or less wholesome texture of a sea-mouse, murmured between bouts that in Thrace, where many live in caves, they shrill like bats when a child is born, wailing about the evils awaiting it. But a corpse they dispose of with piles of merriment, applauding his flight from bedevilled existence. They consider idleness the height of virtue and must admire our work-sky Romans. Still, they don't have to endure Triumphs!'

He remained as if goading, at last laying aside the vase, though his dainty hands remained restive.

'Father, against his most obstinate convictions, still hopes that the Wall-builder's great day will revive something of Rome's grandeur. Perhaps it will. What colour are His Majesty's eyes? We'd better dye ours the same. Token of fidelity! I imagine them very level, very rigid, perhaps closed tight. An Emperor indeed! The day will be rowdy, but at least forum agitators and know-alls will be silenced. Have you noticed that *never before* is invariably followed by complacent nonsense? *Never again* is more useful. Still, there's something to be said for sheer silliness, and indeed silliness itself is always saying it. It keeps one close to one's fellow men.' His fine nostrils could be imagined crinkling over a drain. 'It prevents values getting too solid, like this latest amenity, the Wall, which I suppose, though

82

by no means am inclined to guarantee, isn't made entirely of beeswax and chippings. Like authority itself. But will Aurelian remember poor old King Jugurtha, dragged along in Marius's barnyard Triumph? Rome, he muttered, a city for sale?'

Julian seldom referred to history, but knew more of it than he admitted. In shadows trickling through warm air in a house absolutely, unnaturally quiet, both knew of dark Jugurtha in golden chains, bracelets, richly embroidered robes, proudly facing the howling, vengeful mobs, then, lowered to death in the dank Tullian pit, murmuring: 'O God, how cold thy bath is!'

IX

A long-abandoned shrine to the Genius of Walls had been identified by a seer and reconsecrated with ox-blood. Some still feared the Wall; others rejoiced, sensing that they would now live for ever. The next day, however, a youth in green tunic, lame, leaning on a staff tipped with a golden sun, solemnly cursed the Wall, was swiftly arrested, then rescued by his followers, many of them crippled, the ringleader, one-armed but massive, snatching a crowbar from a builder's hut.

The curse was not yet effective, though a ghost was soon witnessed, swelling up from the stones in the manner of dead Achilles. However, the City was in more than usual uproar and, save in the outer reaches, the Wall was forgotten in the turmoil of the Emperor's arrival. Again the City was on display, hub of the world. From Umbrian hills, Alban hamlets, wattle fishing huts from the muddy reaches of the Anio, Sabine uplands, Istrian lime quarries, Emilian marble workings, provincials debouched through the gates, burdened with skins of cheap wine. Ethiopians had arrived, mingling with Nubians, Syrians, Egyptians, refugee Persians, not always distinguishable from tanners of the Via Appia who never quite shed the liquid filth of their vats.

Taverns and hostels, in true Roman fashion, trebled their prices, turning hundreds away, leaving them prey to the Young Patriots, Sons of Bacchus and the like, though the warm, dry nights enabled many more, avoiding the vaporous, low-lying river sites, to sleep on pavements or amongst the cypresses and olives around the Campus Martius. The first murders and rapes had been reported. Soldiers were easy to curse. Never popular, they bullied, seduced, brought plague and vile blood from unpronounceable places. Touts, money-changers, pimps visibly fattened. Small busts and medallions, of Emperor and Empress, in terracotta, wax, wood, cake, were everywhere on sale, guaranteed to cure blains, assist childbirth, move the gods. Some of these, connoisseurs considered, were modelled on earlier, perhaps imaginary, rulers. Walls sported crude daubs of the sun emerging from the womb of Aurelian's mother.

The authorities had ordered the removal of grass and nettle from the main thoroughfares; potholes were filled in; latrine trenches, particularly those alongside wells and troughs, were sanded; and some manholes above sewers were at last repaired. Steaming slabs of horse-dung were slung over the nearest wall, into the nearest porch, or into passing carriages. Known malcontents had been rounded up, the worst, trussed neat as hay bales, tossed into the Tiber. Dogs too were ambushed, killed, sold to butchers and temples. Swollen from the tramp of multitudes, the air submerged the pine scents. Twice daily, trumpets from the Capitol blared for the Emperor, for the birthday of Hercules, Guardian of Heaven's Gate, and for the Unconquered Sun, healer of men. *Io Triumphe!*

Long before dawn of the Day, the triumphal route was jammed, under blue obedient sky and clear sun. Temples and statues were garlanded, balconies hung with wreaths, leafy boughs, bunting. The seven hills, glistening with marble, trees, grass, still encircled by early mist, seemed to be floating above the City. Then more trumpets, clashing cymbals, skirl of Celtic pipes and an ascending shout proclaimed the auspicious start, overwhelming the groans of unfortunates still toiling on the Wall. Bright outriders and heralds were soon visible, their pine torches sickly in the celestial radiance. They rode, cheered throughout, to the Capitol where priests stood, white robed, with golden torques, at the temple of Jupiter, today topped with a vast, shimmering sun-disc, lion gold, an eye flashing over Rome.

Barefooted, in soiled jerkin, beard awry, hands bare, ridged, impassive features concealed by rustic cap, Julian stood near the Gate of Triumph, amongst rank, steamy drinking clubs, made up mostly of masons' assistants, already bleary, mouthing trashy jokes and catch-phrases. Secreted amongst them would be some Gentlemen of Supplies, formerly imperial grain overseers, now the secret police, so that he assiduously raised an arm to notables and appeared to join in acclamations. He was content, despite the stench of incontinent flesh, recently sizzled onion, sour milk, rancid sausage, the jabbing elbows, occasional slaps on the back, slopping wineskins. The smells would have poisoned Hades and hoisted Pluto's eyebrow. Beyond these orgiastic hordes, a house near the Cattle Market had reserved him a new boy, Cappadocian, fluent in Greek, with deliciously carved buttocks, delicately tapered foreskin, shy, graceful smile. He must forget his last visit, when he had been dry and limp as a noonday leaf.

Processions were trudging from the Campus Martius, grandiose exhalations of Rome. *Rome*, a small word inflated by too much past, crushed by immemorial Triumphs. Short, emphatic, the name matched the heavy, monotonous tread, the ruthless sword, the gasp at the Games where horror applauded extinction. *Roma Aeterna*. Aurelian's almighty Wall queried that boast: it was a grief of the soul, blocking the silvery, equivocal lure of distance, the uncontrolled joy of dancers; deadening the whirl of lovers. How different from the high days of Nero! One could, imprisoned in this dense, vulgar mob, rather admire Nero, competing in the Olympics as a charioteer, failing indeed to finish but grandly accepting the prize, the judges explaining to universal applause that, had he done so, he would certainly have won. Caligula, Gallienus, dancing into the light, ridiculing the tyrannical Roman legend. They might have discerned the cavern, abysses, faces and constellations within his coloured stones which, more than any blaring Triumph, pulled mind to its limit. Those stones which so bewildered simple Constantius suggested some truth in Seneca's sententious observation that eternity is the opposites inherent in all. A line of Propertius, a hint of Mithras's Paradise or Chrestus's Kingdom could extinguish this Triumph unrolling before him, a boastful frieze, half alive, voluptuous in lust for self-surrender to the howls of a people no longer human. How bored Gallienus would have been by these swinging blades, flaunting plumes and flags, the raucous din! A design by those who forget that immediate experience creates trashy art. Gallienus had bothered to win victories before hankering after matters more suggestive. Imagine his faithless successor, Aurelian, in purple aura confronted by a naked gymnosophist pleasantly inquiring, 'Sister, who art thou?' A Triumph only briefly smudges the irony: that, obscurely, people hanker after the lost and defeated – Saturn, Nero, Chrestus, perhaps one day Aurelian. Gallienus had lived in a radiant bubble, convinced that every breath was a spring into utmost freedom, glorious or infamous, or both. On his coins, an unblemished youth drove a four-horse chariot, galloping towards nowhere, superscribed *Peace Everywhere*, while Goths pillaged Greece, Pontus, Asia, and the Empire toppled under the stare of dead Carthage, the ghostly rictus of moribund Corinth. A ride exultant, desperate, criminal, doomed, leaving behind execration and a demonic giggle perhaps only now reaching the outskirts of the universe. How much further would Aurelian ride? Scarcely a question to be demanded of these boiled, sweating faces bawling themselves demented even before the procession had gained momentum. Was he capable of one of those gestures, useless, unforgettable, like that employed by Emperor and God Domitian who, faced by rebellion from the savage Nasamones, merely remarked: 'I forbid the Nasamones to exist.'

From the throne, the City beneath must appear a labyrinth of combustible rubbish awaiting not the efforts, plucky but doomed, of a Claudius and Aurelian, but a man with a firebrand. History is the search for someone to blame, humanity a hunting pack. This stalwart drover, Aurelian, for whose appearance they all waited, surrounded by his giant Praetorians long awash with imperial blood, must know it. The victim, when the pack turns nasty, underlies religion, art, politics: in much pain is much retribution.

Julian, covered by the revelry, murmured 'Poor fellow'. An emperor was a three-legged stallion, compounded of himself, the army, the past. In the eyes of comedian Chrestus, triumphs, institutions and laws were masquerades, dully unreal, an emperor himself a slave, ghost player in a loser's farce. Julian closed his eyes, playing with images as he did with his cherished stones: a rhetorician declaiming words too big for him, a lunatic mistaking his dung for an alp, a skinny-eyed urchin selling cocks' eggs, bulls' milk, buckets of sunlight, on the Feast of Fools. Chrestus, with his sardonic insights and passionate curses, must have felt some of the raging thrills of Catiline the destroyer. Orpheus, Socrates, Mithras, Chrestus – the wages of virtue are meagre.

Eyes open, Julian smiled, nodded, gesticulated with the rest, accepted a gulp of wine, atrocious, a strip of bread, mouldy, winked at the men's blotched faces, the women's delirium. None would remember Pompey, Pompey the Great, in his first Triumph, conqueror of eighteen provinces and seven kings, demanding a chariot drawn by elephants, then, desisting, told that the gates were too narrow. Gallienus would have destroyed an entire Section, not for a Wall but for a hundred elephants.

Ruffians were now catcalling for Zenobia.

'They say . . . have you heard? . . . She's to parade naked. A good sight, eh! Our Emperor knows what he's about.'

'Happen I'll want more than a sight.'

'I want neither. An oyster-eyed wench from behind the temple of Venus . . . more my honeycomb.'

The humiliated queen was perhaps Cleopatra reincarnate, Hellas and Asia, hateful to Rome. Again Julian sensed the City, ageing gangster and coquette, with jests, horseplay, belly laughs, belches, muffling primeval grievances, disappoint- ments, and grim fears of nothing very much. Flawed humanity. Slaves sought freedom, to enslave others. Romulus, Father of Rome, the fratricide, sacrificed during an eclipse, blood immortalizing but contaminating his people.

He would wait to see this Zenobia-Cleopatra. The streets remembered the Egyptian as offspring of satyr and snake, evil as that ruined effigy of a lion, always avoided for containing the dread spirit of Hannibal. It should be incorporated in the Wall.

Massed gladiators, some masked, all half-naked, tramped

past, brandishing swords and tridents, boastfully spitting, threatening, posturing, followed by scythed Parthian chariots surely retrieved from campaigns long past, and turbaned Bactrians and Arabs pulling wagons stacked with inferior battle trophies: cooking utensils, broken shields, tents.

The Triumph. Down Via Lata, past the Baths of Agrippa, Circus Flaminius, Augustan Arch, Altar of Hercules, Cattle Market, past the Aventine, Flavian Amphitheatre, Vestals' House, temples of Augustus, Castor and Pollux, through Circus Maximus, round the Palatine, through triumphal arches festooned with flower and leaf, through plaudits of thousands, the processions wound and coalesced, re-formed, trudging down the sacred way to the Capitol, the world saluting Aurelian Augustus, Pontifex Maximus, Tribune in Chief, Lord of the World, divine ray of the Unconquered Sun, god elect.

Aloft on a Spanish mare rode Constantius, seasoned from Egypt and Palmyra, in the wake of the most favoured general, Marcus Aurelius Probus, Probus the Handsome, another Illyrian, gardener's son, leading stocky mountaineers, beloved by the troops for sometimes intervening against the Emperor's severity, his tactful grin dislodging suspicion. Plumed, in full armour, he waved as if in gratitude to the wild acclamations, flowers falling over him from window, balustrade and roof more effusively than for any of his famed associates: Maximian, Annibilianus, Maximius, Saturninus, Aron B, Aurelian's devoted pupils, trained for victory, masters of outflanking, of strategic withdrawal, the charge and follow-up. Only Carus, the Teutonic Praetorian Prefect, actually no soldier but a lawyer, met silence, then a few hoots, his straw-headed, swaggering retinue likewise. Grimly metallic, they were the most feared arm of the State though, people whispered, not the most heroic, their loyalties revolving between mood and pay-day.

The hush around them was fearful, as if a headless man had sung.

Still far off was sounding the hysteria reserved for the Emperor himself.

Constantius, intent on Probus's plume, scarlet, dipping, remembered the Emperor's anger stopping the heart when, having granted Palmyra easy terms, he heard of its revolt. He ordered indiscriminate massacre, desisting only when Probus reminded him that a ruler requires people over whom to rule.

When a vanquished Egyptian goddess dispatched a cloud of locusts against him, he had destroyed them by firing the peasants' harvest, undeterred by the knowledge that starvation would ensue.

The Arch of Septimius Severus loomed ahead, the figures of the African emperor and his sons with winged horses flamboyant against the steamy blue sky, challenging the artificial sun on the Capitol, itself clashing with the real sun, glaring and powerful, undeterred by the dust exploding beneath.

The befuddled cries evoked in Constantius the lowering images of Rome: axe and sword, plume and horse, shield and banner, also tiptoeing spies and staircase assassins. Also Syrian desert and mirage, stink of camels, and, on a hastily built mound, brief sunset blazing behind him, the Emperor, aureoled and solitary, surveying his troops.

He patted his horse's neck; like elixir, his blood raced, loosened by the surging populace, the seething golds, the hilarity. An officer, however, is no actor deceived by vulgar applause. Like a pet tiger or favoured legion, it can without warning turn terrible. Only here, within his own battalion, was safety, cohesion, a pledge not to Rome but to the single, ever-victorious leader who had carved the godlike from himself.

The huge concourse near the Arch were still rejoicing at Old Sword-in-Hand's rout of the Sarmatians.

'A hundred thousand heads sliced off,
And one chap sliced the lot.'

Huge paintings trundled by, depicting the Emperor, imperturbable while Goths, Teutons and Asians fled, towers fell, cities tumbled. Then more infantry upholding laurel branches, growling scurrilous rhymes, preceding a line of chariots: one a gift from Sapor, the Great King, another the gold and white ceremonial car on which the Palmyran Queen, self-styled Lady of Egypt, Protector of Antioch and Syria, Goddess of the Two Rivers, had sworn to enter Rome, a promise indeed now fulfilled. Then, drawn by stags with silvered horns, later to be sacrificed to Jupiter, the black chariot of the Gothic king, followed by the jewelled carriage of Odenanthus, Zenobia's husband, turncoat senator and mock Antony, his name now reviled with sewer imprecations.

A decorated terrace beneath the bannered Palatine was nominally reserved for senators and patricians, though, Clodius Ammianus repeated testily, these were outnumbered by Equestrians, mostly the expensive aliens so flattered by the absent Julian with his indolent manners, fancy yet remarkably acquisitive, at home anywhere save in his own home, always ready for business which no gentleman should touch.

Seated between her parents, Clodia wondered whether Mother, stationed so firmly amongst the polished heads, slack mouths and heavy paunches, either heard or saw the huge tumult before her. Expressionless, barely natural, she was wrapped stiffly round herself.

Planted on a gilded chair, the Senator, too grand to acknowledge the social climbers, a very great man indeed, ready to lift his nose at Aurelian himself, remained irritated by Julian's polite refusal to join the family. The former Consul had declined the invitation to partake in the Triumph; to trudge under this broiling sun through dirty, intoxicated mobs, in the congress of senators and decurions, was unappetising, undignified, foolish, best left to those still unaware of the absurdity of institutions once revered throughout the world.

Clodia asked something but he did not hear. His face, jowled, sullen, around fatty eyes, watched with professional acumen. None, he told himself, knew more than he of the exercise of administration. He needed no military secretary to inform him of the wooden helmets and javelins painted to resemble bronze, likewise the bright, swinging targets, a reminder of the failure of a certain mineral consortium he had backed, against Julian's advice. Frowning, he noted that not all horses, even of senior officers, were of the better breeds. These mailed cuirasses and Sarmatian scaled horse-armour, were interesting, probably only of leather and a sign of Rome having to learn from the despicable Goths. Ah, Thracian light helms topped with fox-heads, rimless Syrian shields, small Assyrian craneskin shields – only yesterday Constantius had praised his memory, unsoftened by time and indulgence – oxhide Jutish shields, glimmering breastplates, another Gothic influence, dainty scimitars from God knows what pretty courtlings, the wide Egyptian axes, more spears unashamedly wooden, charred at the top, cornel bows, Balearic slings, narrow Saracenic silken bannerets streaming above the marching legions. Thickset in tawny hides, a Dalmatian cohort, sturdy fighters like all Illyrians. But see this precious pair. On archaic chariots rescued from family vaults, and borne on ivory chairs, were the two Consuls, toga'd in the old way, escorted by lictors clutching the fasces – the Consuls, once arbiters of the State, now scratching their heads over minor repairs and a blocked drain. He could repeat, word perfect, his own inaugural consular speech: *The idea of Rome ennobles the World . . . the barbarian fastness, ignorant discordant forest lives. . . .* ' Clodia was now old enough to learn it; he must instruct that capon Diomede.

Enclosed in the heat, in full senatorial robes, fatigued by the thudding momentum of this day of days, he began doing his duty to wife and daughter, cataloguing the array of peoples bestraddling the City. Marcomanni from Boi lands, Moravian Quadi, untrustworthy Alemanni federates: troopers in Celtic and Belgic trousers, Gothic mercenary cavalry, Parthian archers, Vandal swordsmen, a perilous roll-call. Flat Pannonian faces, nimble Britons, African Berbers sashed in charlock yellow, trinket strewn, all needing payment. He went silent; one would not go shares with any of them. On such followers of bankrupt gods depended all Italy. Aurelian's Wall, if the Treasury failed again, might yet be needed against these very regiments. But who would defend the Wall? Tribute, no doubt, to imperial foresight or brute fear, the Wall might yet further erode the will to survive. Instead of the Parthenon and the choral chant to Aeneas, instead of Hercules and Augustus, one must raise an arm to salute a jobbing Mason! Most elderly men, nay, mature citizens, had seen many Triumphs, largely worthless, now spectral, honouring belaurelled mummers, barbarian scarecrows in yellow wigs, with packs of the idle and unemployed overpaid to impersonate battle captives while their trumpery commander breathlessly preened himself on a hired steed, prancing to extinction through thin crowds, puzzled or indifferent. Even in the Triumph of Claudius Gothicus, upstart but a full man, true patriot, the honours had almost been stolen by a popular ballet dancer, of manhood very suspect. Very soon he must rise for a barbarian ranker lording it amongst the truly gigantic dead: Appius Claudius, Fabius Maximus, Scipio Africanus, Sulla, that brutal plebeian Marius, Pompey, Julius, Vespasian, Trajan.

Did not Herodotus cite someone remarking that when in the hour of triumph Fortune presents herself at the victor's side, he is in the most deadly danger?

This Triumph was spectacular enough, undeniably thrilling the rabble, exorcising the imps of the defeated, but much of it was disorderly, haphazard, as though the chamberlains, presumably foreigners, were ignorant of correct procedures.

He roused himself to grumble something about Zenobia, slut from camel's-hair citadel, whose lusts had redoubled the taxes, but Domitia and the daughter did not stir, and Clodia's hand in his own, despite the heat, was cold.

Probus had sat his seat well, a good fellow though, Constantius had said with the cocksureness of youth, inclined to court underlings, almost always fatal. He must be boiling within that metal casing, under the dense orange feathers already soiled by the grit, the flies, by leaves and petals and the droppings of some impertinent bird. Swirls of dust and flowers now dimmed the show, now subsided, for it to reappear in brilliance: a dream which could topple into nightmare.

Whistles, jeers, stones, cabbages, offal, dry clods erupted at sight of Tetricus, the traitor, chained, striding alone, still

93

haughty – 'Caesar of Gaul!' 'Co-Emperor' –. in scarlet cloak, yellow tunic, Gallic breeches, purple sandals, braced against the merciless battery. However, he was already forgotten, for now at last was Zenobia herself, preceded by a white caparisoned camel, another target for curses and stones. Head high, purple cloak trailing behind her, face darkened by a golden helmet, she too was trussed, in golden chains so heavy that they stretched like rays to the hands of powerful guards around her, one chain the prerogative of a clown in female dress with donkey's head, peacock tail, capering behind her with lewd antics and screeches lost in the ferocious clamour, parodying her theatrical gestures of despair or insolence, sometimes incited from all levels, crouching, aiming as if to kick her, then with practised skill tripping on her cloak, re-emerging after a somersault as if from a purple egg. Zenobia's chains forced her periodically to halt, choking, kneeling, dodge stone or egg, then resuming, the pearls encrusting her cloak, making her an apparition from the moon, but no lunar eclipse would lessen the pounding demands for her death.

Shocked, Clodia felt her eyes moisten, her throat trying to tug itself away. Perhaps – she clutched at hope – Isis might still these terrible yells for blood, the Emperor in his mightiness incline towards pity. She knew from Constantius that after his own Triumph General Pompey had freed his Asian prisoners. She lowered her head from Father. In this clink, clank, jostle and barge, the dust and roars were horrible. She had seen Constantius on his horse, but he was soon gone, and she was pitying the sacred oxen led by a splendid white one with triangular crown, which the Emperor would slay for Father Jupiter. Monkeys had agitated her, capering and gibbering in a wheeled silver cage, tribute from the defeated and as noisily mocked. Once they had been human but had been cursed for insulting gods in a garden.

From behind Father a pinkish face bobbed up, streaked yellow with perspiration. 'That lady's I O U will be paid in the underworld!' Unexpectedly she remembered an unexplained remark of Julian's. 'She's climbing to the moon.' It now sounded threatening, while all around crowed at the last of Zenobia.

Clodia glanced furtively at Mother, robed in thin grey linen. But Mother was closed like a door, absolutely still, soundless, her eyes not listless, not pensive, but as if marbled. Father was smiling unpleasantly, assisting Rome's revenge. Cold, entombed and crushed by sorrow, she slumped into herself, seeing little more of the pageant: the wheeled hillocks of spoils – wide, curtained Palmyran beds, couches embroidered scarlet and ivory, effigies of tusked monsters, gods, heroes; decorated floats representing conquered cities, the crowns dispatched to the Senate and People of Rome by nervous courts, provincial generals, wily neutrals. Mottled in the afternoon blaze, gold, heaped on crimson cushions, was carried on their heads by handless black mutes in an uncanny gliding movement as if sleep-walking, sheathed in yellowy gauze, their slippers grass green. The gold was supposedly tribute from the Great King, though scoffers chattered that much of it was but gilded acorns. A block of Moroccan onyx rolled past, which some claimed to have seen at the Triumph of Claudius Gothicus, now barely remembered.

Scarcely noticed, as though unobstrusively retiring from such splendours, the sky showed a slight haze, though the heat roamed undeterred, illuminating a tableau of Delphic centaurs prancing as if stung, Etruscan griffins, a tasselled lion with eagle's cruel head and wings, mingling with speckled giraffes slanted skywards, panthers, elks, the striped and dappled, horned and maned, the angular and prowling, concoctions flung together by a careless creator. Urchins particularly welcomed a huge wooden crab, each section painted with a naked nymph with haloed vulva, meandering with erratic jocularity, occasionally thrusting forward a claw clutching a begging-bowl. Rivalling it were a rhino's head daubed with a green, dripping penis, uproariously hailed as General Probus, and an artificial crocodile, nine yards long, lurching and rearing, snapping and hissing. All were exotic gifts for the world's holiday.

Briefly satiated, the populace was again stilled for the religious contingents, yellow and lily white, bearded, tonsured, shaved to white, the castrated, the pimpled, the albino. Priests, mitred and belted, draped and beribboned, exhalations of heated skies and magnetic underworlds. Foremost was a tall image, half smiling, cryptic, of Isis-Astarte, her tonsured priests in long white linen bending slightly forward, followed by monks, novices, children, all intoning praise, submission, hope. On caps hung small replicas of the white, satiny bull of Mithras, pink scallop shells of Cyprian Venus, lyre of Orpheus Redeemer, goat feet of the Wild Man of Thrace, though the three masks of Cybele and Attis her emasculated lover were prohibited. One of her eunuchs had earlier been mauled for accepting a large salary for telling lies. Sometimes, on public occasions, Cybele, by some sleight, became Rome's native war goddess Bellona, with shining helmet and red arms, but, with Aurelian at hand, who needed Bellona? Secretly, mothers still threatened children with a blood-crazed vengeful goddess who hunted forests with lions and in dark lust persuaded the young and beautiful to offer their joy-bags to the priest's knife. Applause revived for bare-breasted, leopard-skinned Amazons, javelin bearing, and of great stature, suspected of being Gothic viragos who fought alongside their men. Above the songs and shouts a distant thud was now unmistakable. The gigantic heart of Mother Rome! The approach of Aurelian Soter, Protector of Paths, Restorer of Boundaries, Son of the Highest, Father of the Wall. Already children were shrilling their fathers' loyal ditty about the mightiest one-eyed cod ever known. The hubbub drooped again, at tatterdemalion banners of workmen's associations and artisans' guilds, then revived for buffoons, leap-frogging, walking on hands or lemon-painted stilts to the moan of pipes, rattle of tambourines, crackle of little drums, periodically darting into the crowds, flicking the richer sort with obscenely decorated wands, spitting insults in out-of-season Lupercal. Taunts swept towards a Kushan pretender, ill-clad, barely attended with shabby crown, probably uninvited, still styling himself King of Kings, Son of Heaven, though his empire was long dissolved and scribes, letting his tale go astray, had methodically erased his name from history.

Morning was long past, the afternoon already wearing out,

periodically dimmed by the dust through which the fierce sun on the Capitol blinked and stared, and, in echo, from another thick loop of dust, from a wheeled pine trunk glared yet another disc, broad as a cyclops's face, golden as Croesus's fingers, the Unconquered Sun, purifier, begetter of rebirth, visible, undoubted Being. It preceded more effigies and paintings outspread on vast canvases of conquered cities and rivers, colonies and fortresses. Excitement brayed from wet lips, sweat-flecked cheeks, reeking breath, red, smeared eyes for the Standards lost by grovelling Valerian, magic restored to the Empire, so that again wineskins were ransacked, and bodies, soggy and tottering, kept themselves afloat by awaiting the climax, the apotheosis, the deep crimson Rose of the World. As outriders, war engines lumbered by: heavy catapults, giant rams that would split virgin, prudish Minerva, tall siege-towers, mechanical shovels. Flagging nerves again quickened, breath was held, the crowds heaved drunkenly as if under tempest, stamps and long monotonous chants and circus cries quelling an underswell of impatience, the peevish fret of children tired from delights over-prolonged. Within eddies and convulsions of sound persisted the cry 'He comes! Caesar comes!', so that the mob scarcely deigned to chuck imprecations at further manacled captives, the lesser sort, doomed to the mines and galleys, amongst them some bespattered Roman traitors, drooping, bleeding, only a few defiant, even laughing, a few spaces from death.

Always popular, old friends, were the imperial elephants – count them, twelve, fifteen, twenty – gaudily draped in reds and yellows, tusks and trunks ornamented. Led by black turbaned keepers, they swayed ponderously as, delighting everyone, they caught cake, bread and fruit in their trunks and seemed to grin. Trumpets rang out, the weapons rattled, dust surged and whirled, and faces again stiffened or trembled at more Praetorians. Overpaid louts, voices muttered again, tyrant porkers. Terrifying but hypnotic. Thick, stalking legs encased in gleaming sheaths, glinting torsos, helms crowned as if by eerie flowers washed by infernal blood. Their swords

97

flashed a path for the Supreme Despot, now very near, preceded by a huge, dragon-shaped banner, its heavy silks flapping like gigantic wings; then more scarlet-cloaked lictors clutching double-axes packed in rods, the fasces of the ancient Republic. The sky itself was opening for the Saviour, Lamb of Desire, incarnate in the present Emperor, old Sword-in-Hand, sent to steady a lurching empire. His dread laugh shook the earth, his penalties scuttled resistance.

Aurelian dominated all, standing, ivory sceptre in hand, on the triumphal car drawn by four white steeds. Abnormally tall, in high-mounted golden boots, he was square of face, square of shoulders and hands, his cheeks stained red under the victor's circlet of leaves. Under the loftiest arch he would nevertheless bend his head, as though he were indeed a giant. Beneath his purple cloak glimmered a double tunic, the shorter layer strewn with golden sun, moon, stars, the other massy with gold on purple, a silver torque at his neck, an amulet at his breast for protection against malice. Stiff as a board, afire with colours, he stared ahead as if utterly alone, blind, deaf, one small slave displaying a palm garland, another, on a silver stool, suspending above him a golden crown, while beneath him, on side-ledges, crouched more slaves with bells and whips, warnings against pride. While the soldiers yelled *Io Triumphe!* together with lascivious rhymes, the crown bearer at Aurelian's back, an African, his coarse robe hung with small leather penises, would be murmuring through thick lips the ritual caution: *Caesar beware. Remember thou art but mortal. Glory endures less than a day.*

From massed onlookers, howls were now frantic, now in drilled, hoarse, stamping rhythm as from a circus claque. All arms were extended, straining towards the new sun god, noonday hero, imperviously set for the Capitol and its beckoning deity, the columns and priests, the dark frown of the Tarpeian Rock. The merry insults tilting at authority, warding off the evil eye of the universe, the clang, the raucous immemorial paean, made a rainbow stage of delirium, seventh heaven, ineffable circle of stars, a tumultuous effort to chain greatness to the earth, while, in imitation of the golden largesse of the sun, the soul of the world, glittering coins were thrown by contemptuous officials surrounding the imperial cortège, coins stamped with *Eternal Peace* and a city of palms.

Immediately behind the Emperor but scarcely noticed rode his intimate cavalry leader, Mucapor, the two vanishing in flurry and grit at the turn near the Capitol. The imperial departure left a deepening shadow for, unobtrusively, clouds had encroached on the bright day prematurely, and as if veiling the air with flecks of soot already threatening to become clammy mist, within which gnats swarmed and birds struggled. All was so parched that a woman gasped that the Tiber must have followed the Emperor and downed tools for the day. Overheard, this precipitated a quick panic; frayed from the stretched, explosive day people fought to pull themselves free, to escape to the mutinous river and disconsolate god. Dirt and fumes smudged the pale sun. Crowds were thinning, those remaining wrinkling their faces to peer at dingy saturnalians posturing and miming on common wagons. Unlicensed, impudently intruding, pushing themselves into history, arousing desultory obscenities, three pantomine acrobats jigged with three skeletons, a winged urchin, his penis gilded, lewdly waved an ivy-wreathed Bacchic thyrsus tipped with reddened pine-cone and, ringed with screaming maenads, puffy like the drowned, some white-cheeked mountebank doctors shrilled crude rhymes, promising to cure virginity. Mincing ballet favourites posed as satyrs, drunken Silenus fondled squirming shepherd boys, Priapus lolled on straw, swaying his huge, extended phallus to flutes played by girls in loose mock-panther skins. Preceded by their flags, White, Blue, Purple, Gold, Green, Red, provoking short but savage scuffles, heroes of chariot factions drove past, trailing memories of lost wagers, sensational finishes, forfeited prizes, rowdy accusations of bribery, corrupt racing, unexplained transfers and maimings, and heavily publicized love with patrician ladies and gentlemen. Others were wildly reviled, suspected of being imperial or senatorial spies.

Intended as the solemn finale immediately following the Emperor, a stately reminder of republican grandeur, despite gibes that sufficient clowns had been seen, there now paced an irregular file of Senators in antique chlamyses, rimmed with narrow purple, their whiteness besmirched, their wreaths bedraggled. A breeze periodically revealed their ostentatiously decorated under-linen, an image, Julian could have noted, of their political impotence. Led by the venerable 'Granny' Metius Falconius Tacitus, they attempted a high, deliberate mien but were now limping, blown with lees of the japers and charioteers, and already the populace was losing interest, sinking to fatigue, irritation, insobriety, stumbling away to back streets, giving way to gangs which with cutthroat vitality, sprang from beflowered arches and porches demanding charity at dagger-point. From towards the river sounded wild, infuriated bayings of dogs, while boys climbed fountains, imitated gladiatorial thrusts, the gilded Cupid, the Priapan dance, yapping 'Sword-in-Hand', while down streets thick with rubbish a dust-storm, scolding, stinging, swooped over the stiff, grandiose Senators and almost obliterated them.

Unnatural dusk enveloped the City, white chills crept from the Tiber; the sky, steeped in greys and blacks, was not gleaming but stodgy. Statues appeared to wobble, columns to melt, the solidity of dome and roof waver as mists oozed from all orifices of Rome, and whispers of an eclipse abounded, also of a mastiff, slavering, fanged, of supernatural size, trained to protect State property, now sniffing alley and court, famished and angry. From an unseen height, above the Capitol or from deep in the curdled sky, trumpets blared, hard and coppery.

On the Capitol, now distorted, now hidden, Aurelian the Unconquerable would be wielding a bloody axe on behalf of Jupiter Optimus Maximus while priests chanted praise of the deeds of the Father enacted by the People of Rome. A white bull was offered to Clitumnus – who was he? – and, to the image, golden or brazen, of Claudius Gothicus, the chariot of the Gothic King.

Io Triumphe!

X

Summer lost momentum. The City had been picked up, shaken like a dog or child, slammed against its own Wall and now, with passions spilled and lost, it brooded in a weary vacuum. Stars were ill-behaved, Saturn balanced in an unfavourable house, the sun, shooting remorseless heat, glared like a poppy. Many crowds had departed, but those remaining were grumbling that the Triumph had failed its promises. Particularly resented was the report, at first stealthy but now boldly asserted in tavern and stadium, that the Zenobia, seen chained and jewelled throughout the phantasmagoric day, walking with undiminished effrontery, had been no queen, no Cleopatra, but a black-eyed actress, hired tart from the Subura. Of the real Zenobia, accounts conflicted. She had stabbed herself in imperious dudgeon under escort to Rome, in sulks had starved herself, had been poisoned by a Damascan eunuch. Quite wrong, friend. The truth? Bear it! The infamous traitor, perennial harlot, has trapped even our adamantine Emperor with her skills and perfumes and is luxuriantly installed in a disgraceful love-nest, in no less than Hadrian's great Villa at Tibur.

Romans, like temple fanatics, believe all stories simultaneously; contradictions make them feel at home in the world. Unease pierces one face, another fills with cunning though unexplained satisfaction. Usually concerned only with loins and bellies, citizens shy from discussion, letting further unease fester unspoken. Can those recaptured Standards likewise be false, part of the Emperor's grander contempt for his people? Some, lost in blurred, confusing aftermath, the aborted afternoon descending like a malevolent stepmother, are denying that the Triumph had actually occurred: it was but a shimmer of oriental magic, a contrived interplay of dust and the powers of the Unconquered Sun. For the price of a swig, veterans rough up a story, from 'the days of yore' or the year before last – who knows, who cares? – that, for processions, battles, sieges, the Macedonians would flaunt a life-sized effigy of world-holding Alexander, Jupiter's beloved son, strapped to a horse, before which enemies found themselves helpless, prostrating, casting away weapons, imploring mercy, like those who regularly confess to crimes they have not committed and even beseech execution, to be received naked, the men violently tumescent.

All know of Timo the Zany, hiring the Theatre of Marcellus, promising wondrous nakedness, inexhaustible blood, girls flogged to the bone, then, to an immense audience, presenting an empty arena, in front of which all sat transfixed for two hours, swelling with expectation, before, at a solitary ripple from a harp, wildly applauding, grateful for nothing at all, departing convinced of a miraculous performance. Perhaps, in an effort to overcome the flaccid or uneasy atmosphere, an unknown beggar led a troupe of droning, skeletal outcasts up the holy steps of the Capitol, which majesty had so recently ascended, while a public crier bawled 'For sale!' This satisfied none, and the beggars were thrashed, then speedily forgotten, overtaken by an official announcement that the abominable Tetricus too had received a pardon, and indeed an administrative post. Could affable Probus have interceded? Mighty general, he yet hated bloodshed, a dire condition the people agreed, forgiving him.

Questions sprouted more vehemently. Was the Emperor still in Rome? Had he ever come? Yes. You remember, friends, that some time back he had ruthlessly cleared a site on the Quirinal, dispossessing paupers, squatters, millionaires for his shrine to the Sun, designed to outlast history? Now, in solemn postscript, at midnight, almost in secret, he had celebrated its completion, dedicating it with awful rites, then stacking it with the spoils of the Triumph. Oriental sun-votives, carpets with hues deep as wells, sacks of coin, a colossal statue of the sun god Belus, copied from one near Palmyra.

102

Meanwhile the Wall still rose, still spread, coiling round Rome, crushing squalid environs, the powerful drays arriving with ever more stone, brick, cement. A woman had been strangled for attempting to betwitch a star into weakening the foundations, and many had seen a child falling into a fit after touching the Wall under a full moon.

In sinister haste, much was already in service. Several towers, high, watchful, though still empty, now supervised the populace. Pleas, bribes, prayers had failed to save hallowed temples, monuments, patrician homes and storehouses from the builders, and fragments of their marble, brick and ornamental embellishments had been hurriedly incorporated in the imperial project, so that a feathered god, moulded acanthus leaves and a grinning lion unexpectedly jutted from the gleaming surfaces; tiled patterns of flower, bird and dancer interrupted sections otherwise smooth and whitewashed, as though dream beings, distortions of time, still demanded their place, refusing to be exorcised. They reinforced those convictions that the Wall was not for defence but as a restraint, a prison. Anxiety increased when a celebrated physician, departing to Alexandria, remarked that over-concentration of population within walls caused internal bodily growth, usually fatal, particularly to the young, the middle-aged and the old.

Constantius remained in barracks outside Rome, a coming man, attending those privileged to attend the Emperor, if only at some distance. The Senator, unsettled by the Triumph, and by inevitable reports of Plague, and perhaps aggrieved by concerns more personal, consulting no one, had abruptly ordered a return to the Villa. In this heat, he complained, sleep itself made him tired. 'Nasty stuff!'

Arriving, most unusually he had demanded wine. Hitherto he had drunk only at night, and sparingly, but that hot afternoon, surrounded by slaves, tenants, the steward, assiduously fanned by a green and golden peacock feather, he flushed down copious draughts, glancing about him suspiciously, complaining

103

that certain people no longer knew their place, and laying down his goblet, expected it to be refilled instantly.

Domitia, kept standing, though wearied from the journey, would add extra degrees of water, any change of her expression being noted by few, certainly not by the Senator. Even at complaints of Julian her strong, fleshy, formalized countenance betrayed nothing.

'That son of mine repeats some nonsense typical of his exploits, that in former times people never slept. Imagine it! No dreams! He maintains that gradually they began flinching at their shortcomings and had to retreat at nightfall, scared. Afraid to keep their eyes open. Julian gives me no cause for pride by keeping himself so wide awake. He rejects his own order. . . .'

He gulped again, gazed at his retinue as if wondering whether to withdraw permission to sleep. To grant certificates of righteousness. Clodia, who had no desire to sleep, listened unobserved, brown eyes impatient, even rebellious, in a mood which made her seem sturdier than she really was, while Father painfully twisted words out of himself.

'Those journeys of his! Capua, Tarentum! Scourings! Unfit for respected families. He sails on despicable tides, curries favour in quarters at best questionable. In the Treasury, in the secret committees, scribblers multiply, their pay-roll will suffocate any honest man. Their corrupt ways would fertilize the Arabian desert.'

Clodia recognized the last phrase, sometimes used by Julian himself. She smiled inwardly, and thought of Arabia, where two-headed people must make it noisy, then minutely shrugged, in Julian's manner. She was happy to be back, the Triumph had been like gazing into the eyes of a dying pigeon, though Isis had saved Queen Zenobia. Yet, even here, there were matters to ponder. Several slaves were missing, the steward looked discontented, home appeared larger, emptier, as though sadness was at hand. She had already made a discovery. To mention it would get only a rebuke, almost befitting a traveller to Capua or Tarentum.

In a corner stood forgotten a tall, cracked vase in green colours left over from a twilit world, cold to touch, probably made by Former People, on which people walked in drooping robes, very pale and sad, a swollen bird hanging above them and, nearby, a grinning boy, quite naked. She would dare herself to touch him with her left hand. Today, back from the horrible Triumph, the strange powers of Standards, a thought of black mutes pleading with invisible hands, she had crept to the remote room and knelt to kiss the tassel between the boy's legs. Seeing it so close, startled her: she had always considered it the usual small jotting, but now it had lengthened, was sharp and pointed as a dagger which, in kitchen jokes and rude wall-drawings, it was. She now realized he was bleeding in the thigh, and enjoying it. This meant more than she could name. Her brothers would understand: Constantius would not tell her; Julian, treating children as if slightly puzzled that they were cleverer than himself, would be glad to. She would ask neither, would grow into knowledge like a flower reaching the light. Perhaps the Oscan was what Julian called a lighthouse boy, evidently not likely to be favoured by the last of the honest men.

She had learned more. In Rome she had overheard Constantius called the young master, and at once realized that Father was old, far older than Mother, uncertain of step, his skin patched, his eyes weary. His power, Mother's power, was not, as she had thought, constant and unequal, like sun and moon, but always changing. Now, as Father drank and grumbled, Mother, saying nothing, sternly watering the wine, was the stronger, perhaps had always been. Her blood chilled like the vase as she wondered who had ordered that killing of her sister.

Much was concealed, like that shrouded room where Julian had been so thoroughly absorbed with other naked doings, best kept from others. People hid from their own shadows, fled from secrets, hippety hop, like a thrush. Sometimes a slave might flap his arms like wings; Mother sang only when believing herself alone; Constantius, steadfast hero, feared his own kindness. He had once called her to help an expiring beggar, but afterwards looked down from his great height, awkwardly suggesting she say nothing to the others, then kissed her. She too had her shadows. Julian never kissed her. Unwilling to dirty his hands, he would have ignored the beggar, but she was closer to him than to others.

Finally she had escaped Father's complaints, which had become droning and indistinct. She had merged into the late afternoon as if intending to be helpful elsewhere, then skipped a few steps in delight. Safe from Rome, again Marianna, she was soon alone under a murmuring ring of oaks, the sky as if freshly drawn up from the blue sea and twinkling between the leaves. Passing along the small wood she had rejoiced in the friendliness: the bright pool, the six smiling bushes, a song from a farm, a long sound, black becoming silver sung to a harp curled like a cow's horn. Bran's vineyard showed spots of scarlet through the deep-green bush, plums were in purple bloom, crickets nattered in undergrowth. Almonds were green, cherries and melons ripening, finding new colours. Entering the wood, she avoided a certain part where trees were dry and crooked, the air cold even at midsummer, hung with a presence that did not breathe.

Before the sky faded she must reach the temple and thank the goddess for saving Zenobia, but she lingered on sunlit turf above the empty, sparkling bay. The mysterious island was invisible, concealed by haze or perhaps having drifted away. Or had it never actually existed?

A butterfly twirled towards nettles, and at once she remembered a new dream, twice repeated, in which two snakes fought, red against white, balancing, eyeing, striking, the red biting first, rearing hideously above wilting coils. A threat?

She jumped up, shaking the dream away. Birds whistled and darted in the immense blue, unaware of Bran's traps and roasting-pots in the valley. Optima Fortuna was hidden, sunlight dappled the mounds, was scented by warm grass, thistles showed purple heads, and wraiths flitted on the far side of the air. A day for wanderers seeking the cave of the gods, evening barely imaginable.

106

Climbing further, past the deserted quarry, she recalled Bran's rather tedious poem about earth and flesh coming from sea, blood from dew, eyes from sunshine, bones from rock, while thought came from the speed of clouds, veins and hair from grass, spirit from wind and gods from Mapon, Apollo the Sun. All knew that an inner year was hidden within the outer but felt only by the poor and forgotten – cast-off slaves, prisoners, Oscans. On one day in the furtive year the world would end, so that prayers, sacrifices, magic, tears helped life to survive. Also, what Father called steadfastness, though Julian joked that this was one method of always getting your own way. She must practise steadfastness, when discovering what it really was. Also, like Isis, reach for the light. As for death, Bran called it life beneath a different moon, though Constantius preferred to consider it a blacker darkness. Old people must lie awake moaning for dawn. Yet Mother perhaps refused to allow death a single thought.

Pausing again, above the elate sea, surveying the hills encircling her, Clodia gazed cautiously to where four white tracks reached towards each other, embraced, then separated. Paths were uncanny, with purposes sometimes magical. Within sight of the village roofs, one path had led her to a strange field, long abandoned, high with thistle and nettle, the stillness ghostly, in which she had stood lost and scared, while seeing quite near doves encircling the red tiles of home. She had not yet rediscovered that field. Perhaps explanations should not be sought; they would come when they wished to. One day she would understand Julian's love of pebbles, which he held and examined as though he saw things very differently. He was of course grown up, and rich, richer than anyone round here. Indeed, was Father himself rich? Questions hemmed you in, they also opened doors.

She laughed happy with the immense curve of the afternoon sky, fiery at the sea's end, warm blue around her. Wild thyme grew by a stream, splashing and purling as it dropped to the pine grove and canna reeds. Fern and moss remained undisturbed, save by animals and small gods. She had only once seen a god, brilliantly yellow under the moon, neither naked nor clothed, not tall, eyes deep and luminous. Unsmiling, utterly still, he had stared at her, fading only slowly, perhaps becoming an owl.

Walking the track just under the summits she could see far away the long-burnt hillfort. Roofless cells, a fallen tower, where Oscans had reclined in Saturn's time, king of ancient gods behind the gods. To think of them was like ripping a bandage from an unhealed cut. She hastened, now reaching the fold where, already visible, the small white temple sidled into view, domes gleaming against golden fields squared on the slanting hill. The sea too had swung back nearer, now solid, now loose, white surf nibbling the sand. Sun and moon hung above the water, broad coins on a blue cloth.

Isis was both the moon and goddess, identical but different, another puzzle not yet explained. Some dead people inhabited the moon though it looked smooth and deserted. Moon, moon, calm whatever her shape. Were such changes painful? The red snake lurked. As for the sun, however unconquered, he could be angry.

In Rome, Isis was yet again different, unrecognizable in the Triumph, a fashionable lady at ease in clashing processions, with harsh flutes and chatterbox tambourines, painted priest-esses, tawdry garlands, gods with animal heads, touched with Egyptian sickness. Father considered Isis un-Roman, but did not bother to forbid a girl to enter her temple. He agreed with a visitor, expert with horses, who boasted that he kept his girls in an old garden shed.

She would not be praying for *Roma Aeterna* but giving thanks for Queen Zenobia, a small treachery which only Isis would know.

No white robe glimmered in the sacred enclosure where myrtle and cypress beyond the arches promised happy tomorrows. Invisible in their pool, dedicated to the moon, cranes splashed and gobbled, and everywhere bees were about their business.

The way led through two courtyards crowded with blue and

108

yellow petals. In the peace under the cool white temple she thought:

> Dainty Julia free of care
> Loved to dance and gambol there.

Who was Julia? Ever unknown in her dance on the lips of the happy, livelier than the woodenheads in Virgil, though Diomede kept saying that of all tongues the most delicious was Virgil's. Actually it belonged to any lark, baked in dill with cream sauce.

Very likely, in this enchanted seclusion, Former People still gathered, unthreatened, exchanging whispers, the goddess allowing them invisibility from cruel Romans.

On a wall behind beehives, Orpheus in blue mantle was freeing lost spirits, watched by Queen Proserpine the sad. Wheels lay around him, some with small, smiling faces.

In joyous guise of Marianna she stepped into the high, incensed hall, empty but never deserted. At the far end, stationed above all other images glistening in alcoves, Isis waited, Lady whose service was perfect freedom. By a trick of light from narrow windows she appeared to be standing on air, a band of silver illuminating her dark head, one long hand, lemon-hued, open before her, to give, to receive, the other holding a golden chalice to her breast. She was smiling and gentle, in violet robe adorned with crescent moon and twelve stars. From grey, lustrous shadows a flake of white smoke drifted, vanished, from a censer in a side-chapel swung by unseen hands. Far beneath the celestial goddess, on a mauve altar heaped with corn and lilies, flames quivered. Kneeling before it, Clodia Marianna saw a petal, scarlet and fresh, hanging in a glossy spider's web. It must have meaning. The spirit of a dead child surviving within danger? Isis's promise against savagery and death?

A bee was buzzing in a corner. Footsteps sounded, very faint, then ceased. Within the lights and shades she gave thanks, then fancied the divine lips quiver. Rising, she hoped that the other

109

statues were glad to see her. Isis the Virgin, blue, with red blossom in real hair; Isis of the Sea; veiled Isis of the Nile fondling baby Horus; Isis of Flowers, has clasped hands magnolia white and pink; horned Isis of Tears mourning Osirus the Sacred One, her brother killed by wicked Set, whom she would restore to life. She was on an ivory throne, crowned with lily horn, daisy horn, moon and sun, before a screen on which, before dreadful death, Osirus, young and beautiful, offered a bowl of his own blood to the devotee he loved.

Clodia considered sighing for him, but was stilled by remembering that a sigh lost you a drop of blood. Julian said that he had removed a dishonest banker by telling him very tragic tales, the man sighing himself to death.

She was standing by a silver star cut into the exact centre of the floor, cleaving to the Lady who had known pain and grief, and, tender to all, had succoured the weeping queen of Palmyra, whose radiance might yet melt the Great Wall of Rome. A brightness behind the day, which Diomede would spoil by giving it a long name.

'Isis Queen of Heaven, Virgin Mother of Horus, receive me.'

XI

By night the Villa Ammianus received a secret warning from Constantius of unrest in Rome, advising his father to avoid the capital and particularly the Senate House, wording which lacked tact, for the Senator, never one to hide from danger, at once resolved to leave for Rome, dissuaded only by a timely, indeed tactful, renewal of gout.

Surely, Emperor Aurelian wrote later, the gods have decreed that my life should be nothing but perpetual strife. All knew the proverb, *How short, how ill-fated, is the love awarded by the Roman crowd.*

During exceptional, inflexible heat, Rome remained unsteady, vexed by a wine shortage, jolted by rumours that Aurelian was preparing a Great Measure, a currency reform to cure fifty years of inflation. Meanwhile, more sections, more towers of the Wall were completed, achieved with the frightening speed that had erected the temple of the Sun. Hundreds of convicts had already perished from exhaustion, others had been lashed for lack of patriotic fervour, Aurelian ever ready to savage the slack, disobedient and mocking. Wagers were being laid on which tower would be first manned, which gate first opened, or, others said meaningly, locked. An entirely new species of bird, though seen by none, was said to be nesting under a rampart.

Annalists were writing of three hundred thousand soldiers, slaves and criminals, conscripted from throughout the Empire, now at work. Malignants murmured slyly about inauspicious omens – rotted entrails of a cat, a headless chicken clucking inappropriate sentiments, an indiscreet flight of birds to the left. Left of what? Nobody was sure.

A new barracks was already occupied by uncouth Franks and Burgundians, late enemies, and citizens kept their distance, complaining that Rome was a cage. Chatter infiltrated all quarters about the jobless ordered to find work within a month or volunteer for the army: dissidents would be refused doles and eventually suffer death. Ghost tales were plentiful: two barbers and a praetor's clerk had independently seen a handless Oscan in mouldy burial wraps hovering amongst half-demolished tombs near the south-eastern Wall. At once, veteran soldiers spoke of distant Scythians sacrificing captives to Mars, cutting off their weapon hands to inhibit their ghosts. Perhaps – voices were agitated, a few wistful – Scythians were not really so distant.

The Wall darkened the afternoon, night itself thickened. But the Emperor, Foul-mouthed Orry, was pledged against surrender to squalling usurpers gorging on the hopeless, the debt-ridden, the crazed. Last summer an imperial rescript instructed the Privy Council, Friends of Caesar, to publish and enforce at whatever cost the Great Measure. This was a sudden issue of new coins, and the virtual dissolution of the old. It was a silent disease, afflicting many of the rich hitherto unaware of the Emperor's intent, or those deliberately debarred from it, both groups terrified by finding long accumulated cash hoards shrinking to scrap metal, grabbed at only by armourers, and the poor who knew no better. Others, particularly informed bankers and assiduous courtiers, knew that they had but to wait a few weeks before markets would resume coherence and chances indeed be greatly improved.

To forestall trouble Aurelian marched with a powerful force to Trajan's Forum, and under a slab of hot storm-cloud, before bewildered strollers, burned a pile of registers, account books, bills of exchange, castigating them as cheapjack rubbish, the middens of swindlers, misers and speculators. The idlers cheered obediently, fancying that debts and mortgages were thereby cancelled, that the Great Measure had made them immeasurably rich, only later being assured by those more industrious that they were now rather less than poor. Hard workers, the smug impeccables continued, would prosper, the Empire renew its foundations, be as unshakeable as the Wall itself.

A few days were necessarily required for *readjustments*, during which some ill-informed Equestrians, in panic, secretly conferred with Senators of like status, surrounded by the junk of incomplete property deals, unlicensed contracts, unrealized insurance profits from ships still as sea. Agitators leaped up howling that all was jeopardized and Rome overnight became a city of corners, each crowded with illicit gatherings, whispering confraternities, scared guildsmen and penniless, would-be millionaires. After two days of rhetoric, scuffles with soldiery, surreptitious hand-grips, ambiguous messages and promises, together with *attested reports* of a giant supernatural stag, leprous white, roaming the slums, rebellion swept through Rome. Who led it? No one, Constantius wrote again, was certain. Perhaps no one led it. Most plebeians would not have risked a footfall even had all those revered in the Parthenon been assaulted by Scythians. No vaunted name had assumed open command, and officially the *disturbances* were blamed on minor bakers, Asian middlemen and artisans of the Imperial Mint, who had for some days been on strike for higher wages. These last, it was alleged on meagre evidence, were taking orders from Felicimus, a freedman, ex-Mint overseer and disgraced financier who, with associates hitherto prominent in market affairs, had prospered on devalued coinage and inflated prices, supplemented by a complex system of false weights, counterfeit and alloyed metals. Such felonies had formerly endangered Claudius Gothicus by leaving him unable to pay the Praetorians, a dilemma terrifying to all rulers.

The fighting was at first to the Mint area, but soon more prosperous streets were thronged with armed strikers, released prisoners, brawny Ostian dockers, pothouse skivvies, overweight and forgotten champions from Blues, Greens, and other sporting factions, joined by draymen, gladiators, fugitive slaves, scarecrow poets eager to pillage homes, steal weapons, yell for Emperor Felicimus, reviling the swindler Aurelian and

113

his deceiving Triumph. Skirmishes overflowed into riot, arson, petty massacre, the soldiers largely remaining, on orders not yet fully comprehensible, within barracks. The temple of the Great Mother, on the Vatican, was besieged for the private fortunes lodged in strong-rooms beneath. An acrobat lowered the red flag on the Janiculum. More insurgents rushed the Flaminian Way, urging all Rome against authority. The Senate was surrounded, some applauding the sacred Fathers, others threatening them, in sublime confusion. The Mulvian Bridge was overwhelmed; a tower, men jabbered, had been destroyed on the Wall. Still the canny Emperor made no discernible move, his whereabouts were unknown. Within four days the City was submerged less in civil war than in unresisted revolution, manipulated by the unknown conspirators. Constantius explained later that the crisis had been too prolonged to be wholly ascribed to menial agitators and strike leaders. Some of the Great Measure had been prematurely leaked: on claims of defending society the Senate and the Equestrian Order had been joined by certain Praetorian officers in the Viminal Barracks, ageing men with scant prospects and sprayed with the blood of Gallienus. These methodically enlisted down-and-out rabbles, hired the ambitious Felicimus and trained claques to howl for honest money, plebeian rights, better bread, the sunlight of Old Times now soiled by the Emperor's new cult, together with a restoration for popular freedoms by the destruction of the infamous Wall.

Some provincial troops up for the Triumph had wavered, some officers had been murdered, others surged to risk all and don the purple, fighting in blooded square and park, and the fields of the Campagna. Two Sections were ravaged: attacks on the Wall, in places thinly manned, were repelled only after demented onslaughts, many artisans and masons rushing blindly against the hated soldiers, creatures of debt-collectors and the insatiable Officialdom. Hundreds perished. Then, making honest citizens shudder, property owners lament and, as a last thought, call, not on the Unconquered Sun but on old Jupiter Optimus Maximus, people understood that the

114

Emperor, Praetorian Prefect, Privy Council and the finest detachment of Guards were besieged on the Capitoline by thousands screaming for demolition and utter conflagration, though Aurelian, unmoved, grimly resolved, had by reckless horsemen already ordered the recall of Pannonian troops and Dacian auxiliaries.

Constantius cracked no oaths. He received orders and with men unquestionably loyal, moved as if by a voice intimate yet outside him, and as if in the wake of his guardian spirit, hurried to join a larger force besieging the besiegers.

'The mob was between us and the Emperor – many thousands, regulars somehow mixed up with scared rubbish who were ready to be conscripted by the nearest voice. I had my group, and attracted others who had lost their officers, or who had killed them, then panicked, or had misunderstood commands or were merely bewildered. Scores were dead or dying, putrid in this heat, dense with flies. The water supply is still fouled by blood. We managed an attack, outnumbered but properly armed. The mob began falling back, then rallied. For one instant I thought my lot had deserted, leaving me alone facing some ruffian with a spear, a stolen one. He yelped at me to surrender my own arms. I struck at him. He lost his nerve, fumbled. I struck again, slashing his wrist. He dropped his spear, howling.

'I heard a cheer from those fellows of mine who had only got separated, thrust away from me by the swaying crowd. They forced themselves through, surrounding me, and in a block we fought a path forward, killing many. The danger proved less than it appeared. A disordered mob cannot resist disciplined troops, however few. Then another cheer and the enemy trembled, many throwing weapons away and seeking flight.

'The Emperor himself was riding down the hill, leading mailed cavalry finally to settle the matter. He charged, scores fell, armed and unarmed together. After the charge, the rest of us tidied up. Many survivors, on Emperor's orders, were hustled away to execution. It was like the footsteps round Cacus's cave, in Virgil, all leading the same way, none returning. I could not pity them. Why should I? The Emperor was good enough to have me commended. I lost a little blood. Nothing serious.'

Loyal battalions raced up Trajan's military road from Brundisium, halting at Beneventum, then converged on Rome, smashing the last crazed resistance on the Caelian Hill. More captives were ejected from bulging prisons, sobbing, protesting, grunting defiance, receiving the stab or noose from volunteer executioners when the professionals became too weary. The Emperor refused to pardon one illustrious suspect, his own nephew. In the Mint the strikers were rounded up and killed, replaced with surprising celerity from Alexandria. Cowed, the City acknowledged that Aurelian had the mandate of gods. The Great Measure, the Wall, would endure. Some notables, tarnished, though without having risked any action, retired deep into their palaces. Certain suicides followed, quiet arrests, some permanent disappearances. Many Equestrians, engulfed in devalued savings, professed ruin and dismissed clients, slaves and elderly dependants. An advocate lectured bemused listeners, explaining that there had been too many coins, insufficient production, too much credit and gambling, too much reliance on slaves, too many contracts signed on inadequate collateral. Villas had been purchased, a cork forest borrowed, a collection of Cretan vases acquired from the caprice of boredom, fashion, novelty, without *gravitas*. Financial experts invested in a mine they had not surveyed, belatedly found it worthless, then held a festival to flaunt their huge losses. Rome, the advocate continued severely, had underestimated the uncertainties of tribute and plunder. Eight hundred public baths were heated from plantations never restocked by get-rich-quick owners whom the Senate dared not offend. The Wall, cursed as a dark succubus draining blood from Rome, was actually replenishing it, the Emperor fulfilling his promise of New Times.

For days following the rebellion, however, a hangdog atmosphere pervaded the City as costs were counted, damage repaired, news exchanged. The mind hung inert and shrunken,

116

or quivered like a trapped bird. None knew how many corpses had been dragged from street, cellar and attic. Patches of smoke lingered, enlarging the broken arch and scorched stump. From ashen haze a house would suddenly shoot flame, an obelisk abruptly collapse. Camping by the Tiber, a drab complained of a blood-drenched apparition standing in midstream. Doles were temporarily withdrawn, so that some professional unemployed agreed to volunteer for marsh draining or the army, swiftly regretting it when centurions listed the penalties for desertion and indiscipline. Others were forced to labour on the Wall, replacing casualties. Consus, god of secrets, was still at work, for the Emperor had again vanished, still designing the future.

At the Villa, during the turmoil in Rome, the Senator, foremost in public service, had granted a refuge to several neighbours mistrustful of their slaves and tenants. He had considered arming more of his own slaves, then unexpectedly desisted, on grounds of legality. The precaution would certainly have been noted by government agents, and Constantius's letters convinced him that the Officialdom would emerge intact.

'The Emperor', Clodius Ammianus addressed Domitia, Julian and Clodia as if in Senate, 'must settle accounts. He must be supported, despite his deplorable handling of the degenerate outlaw Tetricus, now lording it again over men of station. My son indicates that the accounts are indeed being settled, in a way indisputably Roman.'

He appeared less pleased than might have been expected. The Great Measure had first shocked him, and he explained, more than once, that its purpose was to eliminate all traces of the old society. Whatever his feelings for the Mint strikers, he did not disclose them.

Julian had arrived from Rome at the start of the troubles, then disappeared without explanation, but was soon back, stepping in without fuss, as if on a business trip of small significance. When Constantius's letters were read aloud by the Senator to his guests, senior retainers and family, in a tone that suggested that they were written by himself, Julian, very

117

politely, would request permission to examine them, scanning them minutely as if to detect a code reserved for the knowing. Seated as always well removed from strong light, he was always quick with comment, reassuring nervous visitors.

'Settling those accounts, Aurelian will charge degrees of interest higher than is customary even in Rome. Befitting his fresh-faced coins, of course. Rome's become a camp under martial law. Lawcourts are in abeyance – no great loss. Those fellows guzzle on words and get too fat to think straight. Instead, they wheeze crooked. Proscriptions are being written out for those who can't read. No evidence required. Just small nods and say-so amongst that busy constellation of freedmen and officers whom authority delights to honour. We hear that Majesty enjoys, as the Jews have it, wailing and gnashing of teeth. Periodic upsets assist old scores to be paid off amongst the illustrious. Rather healthy. I except torture, seldom my style.'

Julian had never been known to laugh, though perhaps he was tempted to do so now at the timidity obvious amongst the refugee neighbours. Yet he uncaged only a mirthless smile. Very clean, freshly perfumed, he leaned against the bare wall, in new blue habit, belted black and scarlet. Clodia gazed at him as she might at magic apples, while Domitia retained her customary composure.

The Senator, himself a lawyer though not markedly fat, was displeased. 'My son, you claim to know more than might be expected from one who so disdains what so concerns more ordinary men, and indeed women. Not least your own brother, who risks more than shallow words.'

'I've a nose for detail.' Julian touched that implement, then glanced at the guests as if for laughter. This did not come, so he smiled forbearingly. 'What we must consider is not this ludicrous helter-skelter in the City, but the real accounts. The matter of currency changes and controls.'

The silence was uncomfortable, faces contemplated particular bits of air, the Senator halted whatever he had to impart. When conversation awkwardly resumed, he started again assured and informative, to talk of a young sculptor who had lately disappeared.

'He made a bust of one of the late Consul's forbears. Mercury, though his manners methinks suggested Vulcan. Grimy hands. But he forgot the hands and left the mouth too large. A serious fault, perhaps having some effect on Mercury himself, on Olympus or wherever. The Consul, angry, as I care to express it, as a whitlow, very properly refused to pay. Our great sculptor turned insolent, took him to court, but the judges, more sensible than the last speaker has just allowed, adjourned the case until a complaint would arrive from, so to speak, Olympus. A moral, I must say without hesitation, if not for all time, at least for the times.'

His listeners hastened to agree, one mopping his brow, Julian himself nodding, as if contemplating chances of a leasehold unit on Olympus. 'The gods can be relied on, though their ironical tendencies should be remembered. Or the natural play of things. Who remarked that the divine is no more than nature? Wasn't it that old bore Pliny?'

He looked across at Clodia, for a well-reasoned and sophisticated correction, which he did not receive. Instead, she could see that though Mother was saying nothing, she was unquestionably in power. Father's spirit was elsewhere. Would the Emperor's commendation actually help Constantius's *climb to power*? She had acquired a new phrase: *Bodes ill.*

Julian, needing though not receiving wine, was reflecting that his father's unending recitation of nonsense at least had the merit of consistency, even principle. High praise.

Next day the guests departed, with prolonged gratitude for the Senator's gracious protection, praising his prophetic gifts, though, as he always foretold mishaps, these were never greatly surprising. Nevertheless, they held some prescience. In late August, Clodius Ammianus, Senator, Honorary and Honourable Quaestor, Beloved and Confidant of the Emperor, Pontifex Maximus, adopted of Jupiter, Clarion of the Unconquered Sun, Father of his Country, received a visitor, a swarthy, hook-nosed courier. With respectful ceremony, elegant sentences,

119

but the mien of a vulpine tax-farmer, he presented a letter,
sealed and ribboned, announcing the forthcoming visit, for an
amiable conference, from a dignitary of the Treasury.

XII

In Rome, on imperial rescript, markets had reopened with official guarantees. Prices first soared, then fell as goods returned under military protection, guarantees soon being made unnecessary by new, clear-cut coins on which *Peace* was replaced by *Ever-Victorious*, Aurelian's stubborn features unmistakable, fiercely distinct from Valerian, Gallienus, Tetricus – losers all. Again, public trestles were loaded with ointments against baldness and conception, elixirs for rheum, lunacy, death; figs and grapes, pomegranates, their redness very tired, stale, dusty vegetables; parchment rolls stolen from public libraries, while everywhere some wine-bar Ajax or whorehouse Ulysses bragged of saving the Emperor from traitors or, in boyhood, helping him pierce a boar in Danubian wilds.

On the Wall, Nubian slaves, notorious plague-carriers, were assigned leading jobs, bullying several hundred guildsmen suspected of treason. In the towers, soldiers were wagering that their Wall was longer, thicker than Jupiter's busy cock, let alone the seven-mile defences of Palmyra which collapsed at a nod from Aurelian. Its hollow tunnels were reputed to be stacked with emergency weapons, with outlying punishment cells and execution blocks.

On the Capitoline, the temple of Concord was reopened and the red flag on the Janiculum again proclaimed the City and the world at peace. Summer was cooling, its hectic, fractious pace slackening, heading towards luscious autumn with, as it were, dramatic unconcern. Rebellion, however, had one last flick in its tail, an unexpected afterthought which etherealized the passions, the ferocity, throwing up a dream figure, anonymous, unsuccessful, a symptom of failure to cast down the Wall and

121

overthrow the State, a tragic gesture with, as Julian said later, undertones of comedy.

A youth, slim, girlish, bare-headed, bare-legged, slightly lame, in silvery mantle over green Gallic coat, tiny bells on his feet, holding a light staff topped with a sun-disc, limped into the Forum Romanorum and amongst its shoppers and loungers, gracefully agile, climbed a tall plinth empty since Gallienus's statue had been pitched into the river, and, without effort, silenced the ever-curious crowd. At once, distinct as a bell, easily heard throughout the wide Forum, he was not haranguing but addressing them, the massed faces further held, even awed by the small, glittering sun-disc, denoting what? The Emperor? The Emperor's devotion? Approach of famine or plague? Divine protection from Eastern vengeance? Or the vengeance itself, goddess boy poised to deliver judgement? Emphatically, but light as a dancer, he pointed down an avenue of smashed colonnades and fountains, towards the invisible Wall.

'All is forever dissolving and reforming. Walls are deceiving shadows. Your Wall may stand proud but has no real being. In China some believe they can see a wall a thousand times longer and immeasurably higher than this one here. But that too is nothing, mere delusion, the mist of troubled minds, mistaken allegiances, fears of nothing and nothingness. People of Rome, recall the teachings of Marcus Aurelius Antoninus, Stoic and Emperor. That Time is a river of small events and a strong current. When anything hurries into sight, it is at once swept away. And, hearken well, he said this. That a malefactor is often he who has neglected something, not always he who has committed some deed.'

The listeners, packing the entire market, standing on benches, stalls, clinging to high statues, welcomed every word, touched by new and wilful love. Yet each word, so clearly spoken, carried meanings far from the young preacher's intention. For many, Stoics were aloof high-nosers who recovered common sympathies only by falling into ditches. Few knew of Marcus Aurelius, so that all stirred uneasily, hopefully,

122

joyously, vengefully, understanding that Emperor Aurelian, criminal or foolish Wall Lord, had been drowned in a river. What now? They felt darkly abandoned, helplessly adrift, clutching at the solitary, beautiful figure above as they would a miracle-mongering spirit from the hills.

His words spread a many-hued coverlet over them, a protection from commonplaces, the tedium of long, empty, sunlit afternoons. They groped at obscure names and tantalizing messages, appeased, rapt, calmed by sensations of a secret.

'This is the wisdom of Titus Lucretius, disciple of Epicurus. "Thus the sum of things is ever renewed, and those under heaven exist by depending each on the other." Some nations expand, others dwindle. Great Babylon sinks to a mud pie. Rome, a mud pie, becomes – Rome.'

His intonation was ambiguous, his face expressionless, and indeed many averred afterwards that he had worn a flesh-tinted mask.

'Generations are foot-racers, passing on the flame of existence. Lucretius tells us that by striving to spin out our lives we do not by one jot diminish the duration of death. But to lose ordinary life can be to acquire extraordinary life. All must flow. That is the command of atom, element, mother of gods and men. Matter is ever transforming. Animal becomes man, man becomes god, gods and man retain the primal beast. Life eternal. Death and redemption, decay and regeneration. All changes, sang Ovid, the banished one, but nothing perishes. The cause is hidden, the result is plain. To resist the flow of existence is to sin. To build a Wall is to defy the flow, defy life, inviting retribution. Rome never escapes the curse of Romulus, guilty of a brother's blood. Corn grows where guilty Troy once stood. Thereafter, rulers have ever died to ensure forgiveness, redemption. Wars and Triumphs, defeats and victories, partake of the same law, the ebb and flow which sustains the universe like breath. From the torment of Prometheus came the salvation of mankind. From the instant of light in darkness the day is reborn. But the Wall, the Wall, is a temptation to deny life, to cleave to the vanity of believing that man can contradict

123

the universe, build the eternal. It will crumble, like all else, and whoever has faith in it will fall beneath it.'

Unease trembled into fear, even terror, the fluttering soul of crowds. Could this be a call to renew rebellion, a summons to death's dark realms, or a signal to executioners amongst them? Was the City doomed to shrink away in fire and wrath? Or about to become a mud pie? This very Forum had tolled with the lament of Tiberius Gracchus, martyred for common folk, that foxes had holes, birds had nests, but that he had nowhere to lay his head. Apparently such fate awaited all, death beckoned, lush with promises which were never ascertained, while cat-napping senators, tricksome lawyers and savage emperors inherited the earth. A few, in this heavy Roman assembly, must remember dreadful words, worthy of scowling Orpheus the hypnotist, that many are called but few are chosen.

After the youth had gone, evading arrest, slipping past spear and manacle, bemusing government agents, vanishing, people were to insist, into the blue air without leaving his plinth, some remembered his citation of Ovid, the banished one. Clever ones explained that Ovid had been exiled to the enchanted North after some scandal. Publius Ovidius Naso, magic writer, now surely back amongst them, in place of hapless Felicimus, stepping over the negligible Wall, reproachful and threatening, messenger from whatever endangers empires, with bitter warnings to those who enact Great Measures, fancy themselves great ones, do evil merely for the safety of the State.

That evening, before the Officialdom reinforced controls, and the military patrolled the streets and Praetorian officers publicly reaffirmed their oath of loyalty, the Clubs, collecting through subterranean agencies, held brief, undisputed mastery of Rome, parading to honour not Lucretius, Prometheus, Gracchus, not even Ovid, but the caryatids who, they muttered, had once again slipped off their stone façades that had prisoned them for so long and were calmly grabbing the City. They assembled a moonlit counter-Triumph, marching, in submission not to Emperor or Wall but to something unnamed, perhaps nameless, through avenues still streaked with blood,

124

beneath marbled, phosphorescent heights, bearing fiery torches, pallid bannerets, blown-up pigs' bladders on sticks crudely daubed with the faces of Probus, Senator Tacitus, Mucapor, Carus, Aurelian himself, even, with lopsided, scoffing mouth and sloppy rays, the Unconquered Sun. In irregular formations enlarged by the captious flares and subtle moon, they were soon chanting '*Io Ovid! Io Ovid!*' in an Empire of moonshine where tumbling shadows, glistening and swollen, evoked further cities, further hills, simultaneously an ever-encroaching wilderness submerging the Wall as Ovid had foretold, had been foretelling for centuries, the Blessed One now returned, while an emperor drowned under a deceiving sun. Yet the official historians were already writing that the young preacher, stricken by madness, had perished in a feeble attempt to overthrow the Wall. Very rightly. They ignored the cries of the Sons of Bacchus, the Companions of Mercury, Lord of Crossroads and Scallywags, that the youth, surrounded by murderers, had dropped his tunic and sailed naked into the sky towards India where, despite snakes and witchcraft, death was unknown. Some, recalling that Land of Denos or Denosophia-Bat, so drastically flooded, wondered whether Ovid had returned there, biding his time until the universe collapsed in fire.

XIII

Throughout the Villa Ammianus all was astir, the steward in fretful charge of matters ahead, Diomede skipping hastily to his own quarters like a rabbit before a storm. Yesterday the Treasury official had arrived from Rome, to be closeted with his host so long that the household had retired before he was done, only Domitia remaining, upright and lone, gazing from the porch into the warm darkness.

The great being was a typical freedman, of indeterminate stock, small of limb and visage, bald, hard featured, skinny about the eyes, a rasping voice with power surprising from so meagre a frame. His reception must have surprised him. Usually his descents on the gentry encountered ostentatious displays of austerity, elaborately considered complaints of poverty, through which he was assured that Treasury demands, though by definition just, well-devised and committed to the public good, were alas blunted by pronounced inability to pay. But here he met no such obsequious rebuff. The Senator, in mighty toga and resplendent belt of office, had received him with all the signs of affluence, at the head of slaves and freedmen, clients and tenants, promising a supper on the morrow at which all the better-class neighbours and officials of Optima Fortuna would honour him. If these latter had flawed delight at the prospect of meeting an official of disposition so inquisitive, they concealed it, effusively professing gratification, regretting only the enforced absence of the Senator's sons. Concerns of duty, concerns of, well, business!

The morning sun was high but the guest had not yet emerged from his bedroom, though he had probably left his bed. Clodia thought him an owl, sounding misfortune, *boding ill*.

126

She was now in the bare peristyle alone with Father, an unusual and uncomfortable situation. He sat on the curved marble seat with the lion's head arm-rests, while she stood before him, head bowed, the stillness between them so severe that, despite the bustle and commands within, she could hear the far-off rustle of waves.

She waited while, robed, grand, he sat as if carved, very grey, and cracked, bearded as King Saturn. Uneasy, she wondered whether she was to be sold to the owl, the man from Rome, whom Bran would certainly call a black spirit from an evil hill. The air had been stiff with warnings. Father had hated the Triumph, had quarrelled with Julian, even complained of Constantius seeking favours from the Emperor.

The eyes, in the parched face before her with its hanging flesh and broken but stern mouth, were as if nailed. She felt that he wanted to talk but had not yet found words harsh enough. Yet he might only be wishing to lecture her about Regulus, man of honour, Cato the Just, Scipio the Conqueror, Caesar . . . but at Caesar he always stumbled, ceased, lost power, so that Caesar was left pulled apart by difficult expressions struggling on Father's face.

She stood straighter, feeling restored. Descended from Mars, Father nevertheless had weakened, blinking in the sunlight. A bee having alighted on his cheek, golden blob on the wintry skin, she expected impatience or anger, but, brushing it off, he seemed glad of the distraction.

Older gods, Mars himself, had apparently languished, and she might now learn that ancestral blood had become too thin to carry her forward. Julian would tell her more.

Could Father still be angry about the Wall? Here, by the wide sea, it was so small, and in dreams walls were soft as spiders' webs, floating between day and night.

Obviously, horribly, Father was attempting to speak. In his special robe, kept for days of grandeur, he was mysteriously stricken, struggling, and she too, suddenly wishing to help (then, how shocking it was, to comfort), but was helpless, unable to move. They were poised, facing each other like bloodless forum effigies, dissolving when the steward announced that the visitor was at hand, and, relieved, the Senator rose laboriously, as if glad to forget her.

Later, Villa and gardens were aswarm with guests painted, beringed, sedate, with austere faces and wary glances. On the edges hovered Clodia, observing, guessing, from behind a bush, from pavilion and hedge, tree and window. Throughout, she watched Father, prophet and statesman, gilded leaves on his brow, senatorial purple stripe across his smooth, plain linen, at intervals, and as if for the first time, greeting Mother, who remained quietly managing in yellow stole and blue wrap, moving little but missing nothing. The visitors deliberately remained in groups, like mobile forts. Continually their host led them forward to the Official, made sententious introductions, inclined formally when they passed on, none showing eagerness to linger with a coarse, dull face professionally trained to report on them.

He would be listing everything: the laden, espaliered pear trees, the cherry boughs lining the stuccoed atrium cooled by watered ferns, the stone Genius of the Family. Fire buckets were filled against roisterers, scarcely imaginable amongst these ageing landowners and magistrates. In the gardens, already lit by tinted lamps, were tables served by deferential though unsmiling slaves. Not once did Clodia impersonate Marianna and find herself able to eat, though spread on thin, rounded bread were mullet and spiced carp, goose liver and capon slices; salads heaped on silver platters; sucking pig aromatic from myrtle stuffing and cherry sauce roasting on braziers, apples, asparagus, truffles already prepared; olives were piled green and black amongst flat cheese, wedges of pale white honey, overripe quinces beginning to split, rubicund nectarines.

Her throat refused even favourite cakes. Save for frogs, the fish-ponds had been culled utterly and, though the sloping light remained warm, she shivered.

Frowning, spitting, engorging, the faces were also play-acting, feigning disinterest in this lavishness, the expense, the guest of honour, their own status. Lips parted for a casual whisper, an apathetic exchange of compliments, over-prolonged though empty, until, catching a glance from the Official, they closed like a lid. Few had welcomed their invitation, few dared to be first to leave. Who could be trusted? None. The noxious fellow might wish to inspect their estates, review their accounts, torture their bailiff. The Senator might be in a conspiracy to betray them. Within a few hours a report of this gathering would have reached some inquisitorial quarters in Rome.

The muffled voices floated between shrub and urn, alighted from behind tree or garden god, languished in disquiet. A very old man, his peach-stone head slanted over a crutch knobbed with an ornate Bacchus, hair moulded like confectionery, tottered to a wall darkened by cypresses. He needed shelter, perhaps safety. Clodia watched him, not with pity but curiosity. Julian maintained that years were inventions of priests, but this withered being was afflicted, if not by years, then undeniably by time. Doubtless the very old would soon be made to disappear, which would matter less than the fate of those like her sister.

She frowned importantly, stood very still, watching and listening. At last, reaching the shadows, the old man realized, with obvious perturbation, that he was not alone. A dry voice quivered like a snake.

'My dear friend . . . we were talking of you . . .'

'Talking of me . . . but who? Where? What was said?' His alarm was almost frantic but met only soothing hands, soft, pattering words.

'Nothing. Nothing at all. Only your disapproval of that woman Zenobia. That might prove incautious, but never mind. Fear nothing, you have friends. She still plies her skills, remember, with a certain personage. High perched if scarcely high born. She's living like Juno out at Tibur, every desire fulfilled. Scurrilous, I think you said. Agreed. She's not worth an opal. Less.'

'Dear sir . . . I beg you . . .'

'Say no more, old friend. Say nothing at all. We can only bear witness. But, by the way, was it you who remarked that our beloved Empress will soon be, how did you put it, placed on half-pay? "The Unconquered Sun girding himself for the Star of the East." How exquisitely you phrased it!'

The old man was almost falling in ruins before the live, ruthless shadow, but Clodia, losing interest now that Zenobia was assuredly safe, moved away, her own shadow further increasing the wretched creature's alarm.

Slaves were offering their favourite visitors best Falernian, choicest Alban, in the Senator's finest goblets, thin spun, twisted, engraved with tiny grape clusters. Tired praises greeted a dish of perch dappled with garum, surrounded by fresh sargus. Many observed that His Excellency from Rome, eating and drinking less than he pretended, was encouraging talk, admissions, even confessions from an ex-magistrate, very rich, no favourite of Clodius Ammianus, known as Four-Eyes for always looking round a speaker, seeking those more important, at this instant difficult to find. No doubt of it now, he was submitting to gross inquiries masked as polite compliments while, nearby, the Senator gazed morosely at a sullen, big-nosed lady scratching her back with an ivory stick.

Clodia had moved to a sunlit arbour where lolling figs bulged on trellises, scent drifted from roses, doves faded as the lamps strengthened their blues, greens, golds. Above, guests still massed on the terrace, Corinthian styled, Diomede liked to explain, as if unaware of flower and fruit, trees, fountains, hives. Never spoken was *beauty*, which Julian sometimes uttered, never very seriously, sometimes disparaging, probably forbidden in Father's great days, un-Roman as Isis.

'I hear ... yes ... some more of the capon, delicious.... Yes, I hear the legions are turning East again. One last charge, eh, and we'll see who's Lord of Asia.'

'He could rescue Valerian, though he might not wish to. Why add to smells already exorbitant? Legally, it could be supposed that the wretched man is still Emperor.'

'Let us not discuss that. Legality is a concept dismembered by circumstances. But I can welcome Aurelian finding something to do out there and leaving us to our own concerns, having dumped that distressing Wall on us. And is not the head of Crassus still taking up space in Parthia? He could retrieve that.'

'Ah, yes. It is said to be stuffed with his own gold. There is a story about Parthians using it in that play about Bacchus. Heartless, mysterious god, when the happy shouts die down. Otherwise . . . I could make use of the gold!'

'Friend Euripides might have chuckled at that. But the theatre today . . . depravity copulating with cruelty. I myself prefer a modicum of wit.'

This he did not show, contenting himself with a grating hiccup, then, with the dignity of a rhetor refuting an argument, spat awkwardly into an urn.

So Constantius would again be in danger. The talk sharply reflected the magnificent party in which a sort of Mercury darted maliciously behind the formal manners and amiability. From this spy-point at a gateway she was aware of rough, swarthy people, mostly men, a few with girls on their arms, speaking only amongst themselves. Could they be invaders from Villa Celsius where the family had departed by night to avoid, Father said, its obligations? These strangers had Bacchic obligations only to the supper, summoning slaves and rebuking the steward, chuckling rudely at old Ulysses exhausted on a bench.

Without orders the offended steward could do nothing, and Father was too dignified to give any.

More decorous voices passed.

'They say he's to proscribe that Jew Chrestus . . .'

'Very impertinent. Chrestus, I mean. Heaven forfend that I referred to . . .'

'Quite so! Well put! Excellent!'

Replacing the squatters was another face, familiar yet travestied by the setting: the opulent robes, lights like coloured spray, carefully shaped dialogue. Bran. In clean grey smock and leggings, an expression of superior chill on his old features, he was shuffling across grass to the terrace steps, either claiming a place amongst the guests or with news to communicate. Clodia began moving towards him, then halted, somehow warned that she should advance no further. High above, Father was flushed, as if choking; Mother, still smiling at small

131

speeches, bows, fragile greetings, was already joining him in support, His Excellency regarding them all. *Beauty* collapsed, faces bitten and strained under the lamps now souring, hands at a loss, knuckles whitening.

Before hurrying indoors, nearing tears, Clodia saw another unknown guest, tall, very thin, withered yet with eyes bright and young in depleted skin, eating and saying nothing, standing alone and disregarded by a statue of the Senator, his robe dull, as if stained. 'He is Fate,' she murmured.

XIV

'Didn't Catullus catch a chill from reading the cold speeches of his host, the worthy Sextus?'

'Very likely. And some of us caught his verses like fever. To examine that girl of Sextus, a doctor would need a dowsing-rod. Her rights of passage could entertain a horse and cart, and probably did so. No slim, ox-eyed darling. But you, my dear fellow, caught Catullus like a disease, and not the most respectable one at that.'

'Assistance for the east wind. You remember our great thinkers once believing that mares get impregnated by the wind? Spanish mares, of course. That's why our good friend Marcus keeps his spouse within doors during winter.'

'Talking of Marcus, what news of Aurelian the Beloved?'

'No news is bad news. But there are things worse than bad news. Since we're prattling about the fabulous, the lost and the doomed, we might respectfully recall that patriotic windbag Cicero once telling the not very reverential world that the future Augustus, man of the future, should be complimented, distinguished and then extinguished.'

'Well enough. You always delight me. Lovely comments! But who has the courage to intervene in such ways?'

Julian had been silent, though his presence induced much of their talk in efforts to attract his approbation, all chattering as if unaware of the secretary writing down their delicacies and witticisms. He contemplated with some light misgiving the last speaker's bracelet, its engraved elephant decoding his descent not from that animal but from Metellus, victorious over Carthage, though he himself was a briefless advocate from Beyrouth, victorious only over women. Lately, to much laughter, led by

133

his own, he had thrown away his last property at the Games, backing the Greens too often.

'On the whole,' Julian at last spoke, 'not me. Did I ever tell you of my sojourn in Armorica, where I spent some time showing the yokels how to teach money to grow up. They didn't altogether acknowledge the existence of compound interest, unlike the not wholly lamented Seneca who disdained riches and died rich. Well, every afternoon, following a morning loosely described as business exchange, to repair exertions I'd retreat to the woods to select a few juicy strawberries, then lie under a tree for a judicious doze. All very well. Then, after some days, a deputation of clients waited on me, dirty mouths crammed not with strawberries but with compliments. My acumen, my charity, my far-sightedness, my public spirit and so on. They added rather fulsome praise of my courage. Courage! You all smile, and very rightly! I'm celebrated for all the rest, but no one has accursed me of courage. What did they mean? Ah, they said, your slumbers in the wood. My dear sir, quoth a fat man, for generations none of us has entered there. But why not? Why not? It's only too obvious! Those accursed snakes! Only you have been bold enough to tackle them. Already you are being compared to the youthful Hercules strangling the evil serpents. Of course my reputation vanished like dew, and when I think of my hand rooting the undergrowth for strawberries, my sleeping body exposed . . . . ! I've always been less than whole-hearted in admiring courage, though, for what's left of our divine Rome, it can come in handy. Mind, the fellows replenished my stocks, before I taught them those niceties of compound interest. One, a rare old dog, was hereditary priest of the temple of Saturn, an edifice more decayed than Saturn himself. He'd persuaded his better self that the constant intake of plump quails roasted in goose fat with hunks of crackled pork benefited his entrails, and he left others to trace the origins of his extra chins, redoubled paunch, bulging neck. Saturn must have felt justifiable grievance. Anyway, to return to politics, I wish His Altitude the Wall-Builder would entrust me with the Department of Mixed Feelings.'

'Julian, my dear, you always claim that muddle explains all. Mixed feelings!'

'What else?'

The party was dissolving, blown petals of gaudy flowers. The young men stood on the street prolonging farewells. Pine torches upheld by weary porters threw red gleams on the green marble. The midnight stir and sough of Rome belied the empty streets. A full moon lay over the Belvedere, hard, even fierce, frosty at the edges.

Dinner had been more than pea-flower gruel and recollections of almond blossom and the honeyed dormice once supplied for Trimalchio. They had emptied curvaceous amphoras of Tuscan and Cordovan wines, washing down the baked peacock, stuffed turbot, venison and ostrich sausage and peaches, thereby reducing their attention to the mime of Perseus, satirical and indecent, performed by slave children.

Julian departed, amused by his own inventions and the wide, credulous eyes of Demetrius, loudest tittle-tattler in Rome, and telling himself that he had dined with the biggest mouth, thickest brain and longest cock likely to be encountered this side of the Alps. Altogether a collection of bodies unusual but of less distinction than his store of pebbles which at least provoked the mind to think, co-ordinate sensations, dream! Demetrius's childish face and withered hands, Marcrobius's extravagantly bushy groin and bald head, Curio's lame left leg and hunched right shoulder, none of them exactly Caesar in Gaul, Aurelian punching holes in Asia and throwing Persians over his shoulder!

The night was warm. Forgetting his late companions he was at once engrossed with the City. Each street, dimly flickering under sconces or open to bare moonlight or dense with perilous, almost breathing darkness beneath dim, towering blocks, had its distinctive ordure. Leather, damp corn, fish-gut, charcoal, stale wine, resin, horse-dung, urine, blending like friendship in sweet-sour familiarity. At each corner, usually dilapidated under grandiose and well-weathered traceries, he touched the dagger within his lambskin coat, alert for the concealed assassin, nocturnal brawlers, the swaggering tread of the Fraternal

Cobblers or the Band of Love, ranging under the moon. His wrist purse, his jewels, risked assault.

He was pleasantly, not yet urgently tumescent, honed by liquor, salacious exchanges, the tactful hands of the slave chosen to serve him. His cock, all the dangle O, could be a lord storming and irresistible, a sulky child to be cajoled into play, a ship seeking the whirlpool's cool centre, or, with sail drooping, becalmed in nowhere. In sly, afternoon sessions, while Constantius pored over Livy and Virgil, Diomede had taught him to treat his cock like a guest, slightly older, somewhat wiser, to be granted whims, soothed, petted, regularly intoxicated.

Late evening lights on a pool: now the pool is a silky, luminous cup above which, lustrous and erratic, the dragonfly darts, the kingfisher scrawls a blue flush through a network of dying light, while I wonder what the body beside me really sees – perhaps nothing but a few messy inches of rising flesh.

He swore, wiping his sandal. Augustus, great and dreary, had boasted of transforming Rome to marble. His successors had softened it to dung. Pushing deeper into a network of obscurities he encountered almost no one, though the hum of the restless City remained constant, and unpleasant eyes must be almost within reach. Likewise the ghost of his father, a bad loser, too heavily mortgaged, not least to that verbose fraud Bran. Death seldom cancels impurities despite funeral epitaphs: more often it reveals them.

Too grand to confess poverty, unwilling to plead rank to avoid monumental liabilities, the last honourable man, Republican stalwart when republics lay forgotten in dust, dignified lack of substance in a sanctified villa where the beams were older than the building, the Senator had wished his guests farewell with pompous dignity and, by dawn, lay dead in his Curial toga, swamped in his vaunted blood, under ancestral busts mildly censorious, though Mars doubtless allowed himself a guffaw at the Prophet's so clearly seeing the future and so signally failing to exploit it. Stately port and sermons on rectitude ended only in feeble attempts to bilk the State, which harried him to bankrupt death. His accountancy had been

136

amateurish. He would conceive some project, grandiose and unnecessary, reject it on grounds of expense, then convince himself that this entitled him to declare a profit and spend all the imaginary saving on inessentials.

A sudden smell of gardens wafted through Julian, fresh amongst fetid airs, a hint of better places, better days. The dinner talk reminded him of the Senator's hero, Cicero, so consistently praising his achievements to those with thoughts elsewhere. Julian, back in rankness and perils, whistled the old song, a cat at once dodging away, its green stare lurking in a ditch.

> Rome's happy fate
> Her birth to date
> From my Consulate.

Father's death would relieve the suppressed barbarities of family life. Some now held that Rome would soon be dating herself from the Wall.

Apparently Domitia, more competent than Father had ever deigned to be, had prepared swift funeral rites. Grandees had arrived scatheless from Rome, but the ceremony refused to enlarge imagination. Constantius, head of the family to the life, stuccoed with *gravitas*, twenty years older than he actually was, would have stepped glumly amongst them all, acknowledging formal courtesies, supervising the dreary, meaningless rituals, while busybody Bran kept watch for the main chance. Clodia would have followed, eyes moist yet doubtless more concerned with a pale-green vase incised with Oscans and trees, a fine little wench whose giggle outbid Father's rusty laughs and pretensions, to supplement which the meanest slave knew that the Villa was under threat. She had apparently said, rather grandly, that Father had been laid low by Fate, though her rubbish about a treacherous guardian spirit probably derived from some joker in a mask or a sponging relative of Bran.

Mother, naturally possessive, was frustrated by all save Constantius, so often at the far ends of the Empire. Her features would once have been bright and mobile as Clodia's until marriage extinguished it for ever. Sweetened for joyless lusts, she was fixed in an unbreakable Roman mould, dated as a chariot, her dreams of singing from a dolphin's back long shed.

They were all embalmed, were their own busts, unable to move save from hands not their own. Constantius, good fellow, so stern with himself, subservient to orders mortal and divine, believed that action can dislodge destiny; simultaneously that action is fated. Yet he was incapable of any action not proceeding from immemorial rules: useful staff officer while the staff endured and the general dodged mutiny.

In boyhood, Constantius, always supporting the keeper, never the poacher, had acted out banal dreams of heroes dispersing barbarians and toppling giants, never pausing to reflect.

Moonlit Rome lies like a surfeited harridan under stars shrill yet silent. The mass of the Palatine rises like a mountain of twinkling salt, ancient abode of the god Pales, whoever he was. Look closer, and around the ornate, sleeping buildings, fragile in this pallid shimmer, this petal transparency, are frozen shadows of oak groves, laurel and beech, haunted by flimsy ghosts and meaty bandits.

He stepped into a porch to allow late drinkers to pass, singing. They were jovial but wayward, liable to insensate violence, and nosy as Bran. Alone again, he saw a decrepit crossways, slushed with dried mire and excrement, but a potential investment, he noted, then thought of some false marble still unsold on an Ostian wharf, its wax already cracking, unable to survive another summer, easily procurable from the eager old swindler who had stolen it. Some olive oil was due from Athens, some Theban papyrus was ready to be inspected.

He remained in no hurry to appease his unruly cock. Sometimes it moved him like a sleepwalker to the nearest pallet or blanket, a merchant wife's crimson couch or scented bed, though, beyond each, was further enticement, a pattern, Plato's vision, the pursuit of a glimpse of perfection long lost but urging recovery. Words danced, culled from the hidden side of colour, though colour, usually potent, was also limited to but one sense. Full pleasure craved the entire body, enveloping, plunging, pouring, all nerves as one.

A shadow in huge, phosphorescent Rome, he was strolling to a quarter near the Subura, moonlight and trickly flame transforming drab alleys and stinking mews to glistening avenues, wide thoroughfares and squares to floating, transparent wastes, within which lurked the barely imaginable: a Cretan maze where loveliness entwined with horror. He was encased in himself, was a stronghold against the seething, purposeless City which, unprincipled as a claqueur, never dared sleep. Or it was a blinded, superannuated war-lord demanding tribute for forgotten services, blundering helplessly, painfully, against the Wall, where others were ready to follow Catiline or Bacchus to rape and fire and kill. Conflicting emotions whipped up by the Triumph grew deadly faces, menacing hands. A poet could create a counter Aeneas, a wilful Gallienus, a demonic Prometheus, gathering a rabble of slaves, jokers, gentleman rankers to die charred or crucified, cursing Rome. Academics maintained that, at each Roman victory, suicide increased within Rome herself. Had the late revolt succeeded, the new master would have rushed to acclaim not an Aurelian but the false Ovid. Some fun there! An anarchic reversal, the Kingdom of Chrestus. Boys, girls, parents, officials, priests, lawyers, give none of them the upper hand. If Chrestus taught anything, he taught that. Yet how little was definite. Chrestus wrote only in dust. Time was in the grasp of scribblers hired by the executioner, their pages ravaged by damp and insect, fraud, mistranslation, false rumour and – as he passed a dimly glowing column above water like molten silver, his face crinkled, his spirit leaped – by mischief. Tonight, lying on some Paula, or Paul, he could murmur a melodious lie about Aurelian, for no reason, art for art's sake.

Emperors, poor wisps of being. Gallienus had enjoyed triumph and failure, extremes of lust and love, and, with rapt sensations of pleasure and pain, must always have been awaiting a sound most terrible. To show approval, the brutal soldiery clashed shields against their metalled knees, but when loyalty slumped, through bribery, caprice, grievance, they clashed weapons against their shields. The raucous anthem of Fate.

In a pool of reddish sconce-light, he bent to examine words chalked on a grimy wall:

> Be
> Be low down
> Be now

Scarcely a martial epigram, more a whimper from a horde barbarous as Finns. Few would bear children or wish to. Curses abounded here, on the founder, Romulus, renewed on that day, centuries ago, when in the Cattle Market the Consuls had buried alive two aliens, stamping them deep to appease the gods as Gallic armies neared the City. People were now gibbering that the Wall contained signs, round as a Babylonian coracle, triangular as the female pubis. Visible only to eyes in the sky, itself crippled by star clusters with mendacious analogies, evidence for conceptions of Fate, powerful but absurd. Little separated modern Rome from the Thessalonian witches smearing cunts with magic dyes so that men would flee howling, leaving their cocks inside them.

> No poison bats in old Thessaly
> Great Nero swiped them all.

Throughout Italy, that diseased leg, were blighted cities, residue of disgruntled gods. Rome had swallowed them, then swallowed herself.

He stepped aside again for an almost soundless file of expensive litters escorted by torch-bearers, armed and barefooted, and leaned against a door god, double-headed against sorcery. Moonlight's very purity was a reminder of its opposite, the noxious stench of wolf and boar and shambling bears from rocky Abruzzi slopes, creeping in dim masses to occupy an eerie, deserted Rome, with, like poverty, their own ways of overcoming the Wall. Was the Wall indeed garrisoned with troops, sharpening weapons in towers and secret galleries, or was it a stupendous bluff, an elaborate allegory of the weakness of power, a folly left void when the Emperor, the Saviour, trotted away for yet another assault on the improbable?

Questions maintain existence; answers tend to kill it. There was that queer farce in Diana's shabby wood at Nemi where the priest, red-eyed and sleepless, having killed his predecessor must hold the job against all comers. But why should he wish to? Who paid? Diana herself! Were such priests madmen or escaped criminals? Surely not salvation seekers. Did the business still continue, with idle sightseers? Perhaps expeditions to Nemi could be staged profitably.

The litters had gone. From several streets away a scuffle, a cry, running feet, then again the low, underground murmur of the City. Nocturnal saunters, doss-house prowling, suggested many Romes, layers of time, packed so close that each affected the others. Had he shouted, he would have been heard within several millionaire palaces, yet he was now treading cautiously through a collapsed arcade thickened with shrub and thistle, where beggars slept, or guttered out, and cutthroats hovered like grim marsh spirits. Again he touched his blade, outside a decayed Sanitation Pavilion, hearing grunts and sighs and kisses, those tiny compacts, truces within the turmoil of existence. Cloacina, patron of shit, give me a little more time. Here was the realm of the strangler, stabber, the fellowship of the hook, the Clubs, the orphan killers. Before him, almost snow-like, stood a deserted bridge curving over a rancid canal, still, as if painted, with fireflies dancing on the moon's glare. Crossing, he reached the House of Poppaea, nicknamed the Bed of Apollo and Diana. Through paying protection money to the Clubs the establishment was superior to those below in the crumbling Subura, with its sister houses in Naples, Syracuse and Pisa. These assured a constant supply of bodies, new, if not precisely fresh, and guaranteed more to glut curiosity than ensure refreshment of spirit and immunity from infection. The poet Nemesianus was reputed to have been a patron, and, in tribute Julian murmured:

> But we will hack out new paths
> Rather than traipse along the old.

Feeling for his tablet, he scratched a few further lines which trimmed life like a blade, until desire mounted and, at his tap, the small door opened. How awful the new so often was!

Respectful greetings and open palms, a rush of perfume, an oval of tired, still smiling faces. At once, the sight of previous lovers, some winking and over-familiar, others tactfully looking away. Down the thronged, arched vista, naked, by a plaster Priapus on whose jutting phallus hung discarded gowns and silks, lay his one-time favourite, Absalom, quick with hands, eyes, wits, blemished only by circumcision, tonight mitigated by a pig-bladder foreskin painted green. Barbarous rite, ugly, perhaps vestige of a loss grimmer, bloodier, demanded by some devouring Good Goddess. Already, his appetite was flagging. With whom here could he exchange such thoughts? None. Again, oh again, he was immersed in the fatigued coterie, bizarre decorations, whispered proposals, and behind affability and compliance the keen calculation. A bubble in which all was on offer.

Recovering, lust enjoyed its own life, snooking a cock now here, now there, suddenly hot, unexpectedly cold, as if at a magician's whim. Dawdling through bodies down the wide central hall, past candle-lit alcoves, exchanging soft gibes, invitations, jocularities, he felt the silver cord binding flesh to spirit had loosened, freeing him to dissolve, as it were, into the tints everywhere quivering: black of Bacchus's eye on the nearest mosaic, pink of Venus's carnation, streaky silvers in the marbled pool, ivy green and rowan red struggling through drugged air alternately roseate and violet, hung from ceilings painted with clouds and Olympian peaks which periodically divided for a deity, naked as glass, to descend in a dove-drawn car.

142

Everywhere in this playhouse was the Dionysiac toad, carved, painted, stamped, whose warts, if swallowed neat, induced descents to the underworld where, prone and immobilized, you relived previous lives, wallowed amongst flat, yellow faces, animal gods, moonflakes that reassembled into leaves, snakes, tortoises, Isis's fingers. There, Aurelian washed platters, the Wall toppled over, crushing Rome. After a swab of aconite, you flew without moving, eyes closed, through air which swiftly thinned; roses blazed, the sky, washed with unguents of unearthly blue, opened as if at a discharge of arrows. From smaller rooms, faint through chatter, strings were plucked, songs quavered, lapsed, abruptly stilled. All walls sported mirrors, and paintings in which satyrs with rutting penises rhymed with the mortals writhing and straining on couches beneath. In a brilliant wall mosaic, Lusitanian girls, lemon-skinned with crimson pubic fuzz, copulated with purple Titans awash with grins and taunts, agonizing them on dripping tools sharp as javelins. One girl, impaled, drooping, screamed while masked dwarfs slashed her buttocks. Could this be a travesty of Chrestus's Kingdom of the enlightened, the nonconformist, the free, of love suppers and orgiastic ascensions?

A bare-breasted girl smiled teasingly at him, fumbling in her saffron loin-band. He gave his practised nod, but was at once accosted by stumpy young Curtius wreathed in silk, a fringe of artificial yellow curls on his bald head. Curtius grinned, opened his mouth, but could only burble. Very rich from his mines, he had once come here to be thrashed silly and had never recovered. Julian had earlier requested 'the high priestess' for an option on Flavia, but had been preempted and had to pleasure himself with the ironies of rebuff, resigned to prospects of Tullio, effeminate, deceitful, with urchin malice and gloating mouth.

In the mirrors, fixed at many levels, all was fleeting, exorbitant. Gazing into them, faces saw themselves flushed with seaweed dye, breasts hung with pearls, scallop shells, medallions of gods, emperors, beasts, famous courtesans, loins downy as if from powdered gold. Only connoisseurs would

143

distinguish payer from paid. An exception was the most flattered jurist in Rome, lolling with his fat piled up in terraces and utterly submerging the source of whatever thrills yet remained.

Tullio too was invisible. Discontented, simultaneously relieved, selecting a decorated shellfish, a goblet of Surentine, too flimsy for serious drinking, he shouldered through to a smaller apartment where Julius Caesar was supposed to have used adultery to extract secrets of rivals. A small group was watching a pantomime in an arched, red-lacquered recess, the evergreen Triumph of Neptune, reminder of the Villa, the salt-crusted, blue-maned god, enacted by mincing 'Pylades', the name filched from a more reputable predecessor. Neptune was already ramming himself into the rear of a silly, bleating youth, girls with smartened-up nipples clicked castanets and, on another little stage, Clytemnestra beat her lord, a slave, until blood glistened and the onlookers awarded her with lacklustre applause. Circe too was, as it were, at hand, opening herself to a bull, her voice, caressing, half singing, calling him Ulysses's pilot. It was a theatre of listless, well-polished squirms and jabs, feigned ecstasies, while, on a tapestry above, the Persian godling plunged his sword into the Bull of the World, the scalding blood gushing through a grill to drench the initiate, promising new stars, inconceivable visions, another soul.

Watching with barely suppressed needs was Flaccio 'Footrot', Galilean financier whom Julian had last seen refusing to pay his forfeits after a board game with a brace of tarts. Julian gazed firmly at him, to make him sure that his presence was observed. The Galilean's embarrassment might be useful in the bargaining promised over the Sullan Arch repairs. Around him were prominent Treasury gentlemen, the breed who had finished the Senator.

Already the place had staled, was rank as dead daffodils, lust thinning into temptation to spit and as though these languid forms were struck into a very slow, eldritch dance and, at a touch, would collapse into dust. The equivocal blessings of freedom. Ready to depart, he met a priest of Minerva who had

144

lost his beliefs. A fellow to be teased, always earnest, worried, pleading for certainties, failing to realize that zest for life is maintained by the reverse, by reverses.

Stout, shaven, the other embraced him profusely, nodded at an empty couch draped with soiled gold coverlets partly detached from the rest by garish screens decorated with suggestive scenes of a walled garden, locked, with tight roses and tall, tapering bushes. Seated, they resumed a debate which had neither beginning nor end, only an indefinite middle.

'They say, Julian, that you're still concerned with Chrestus. But I'm unsure about who he really was. Sage? Mystic? Conjurer? Can a Jew really be a god? Tell me what you know.'

'Nothing very much. I doubt if he himself was always sure. He claimed to be on divine business. A mission to enlarge understanding. Seldom productive save in cash terms, which didn't interest him. He got entangled both with Rome and the Jerusalem authorities. Torture wasn't allowed but he was crucified under a yellow star, and either died or was allowed to escape. His friends seemed to have decided for the former but claim to have seen him alive after his death. An act not without precedent in divine circles. Nothing's quite clear. Some say that he retired to India, where there's no tale of any trouble. I haven't heard whether, on his escape, his dog died of joy.'

The priest sighed, dissatisfied. People said that Julian was sober only when drunk, serious only at play. Rescuing a youth from drowning, he had profoundly apologized, explaining that he had mistaken the swimmer for a gambler who owed him money, then inquiring whether he wished to be thrown back. Despite his talk of high-minded poets and sages, he liked to claim that *worldly* was of all words the most lively.

'I'll tell you what you really don't wish to know, how I first began questioning the untruths surrounding us on all sides.' Julian frowned as if at an uninviting prospect before signalling with one eyebrow for wine. 'I went out with my tutor, Diomede, secretly, to witness the village spring rites. Harmless enough for an ugly boy. Playing bowls with painted eggs, swallowing little cakes and, more to the point, some rather questionable dances which, for his own reasons, on the whole unwholesome, Diomede wanted me to see, if not partake in. A corrupter of youth, that one, who could have taught Socrates a bit. He fattened on curious lusts. My brother was too high-minded for him, wanting no more than grammar, rhetoric, numbers and so on. Insufficiently human. Diomede shook his head, sent his lusts elsewhere, unravelling for me the showier portions of Propertius, Catullus, Ovid and indeed of himself.

'Anyway, at this spring festival, the god Faunus always appeared. Wolfskins, hairy legs, a brace of horns, that kind of thing, all very rustic, pipes, a blessing or two, some vigorous pulling under the gown, on which, as an applied art, Diomede was a full, an engorged professor, may Priapus drink from his dirty eye! But this time, before I'd learned the tricks of the trade, there were two gods, identically clad, quarrelling like centaurs about rights to the pitch. Their language set a local barn alight. I was green enough to be upset, but acquired a scepticism that now passes as natural. No use, henceforward, to rely on gods, family, hoary wisdom, respectable zealots and reputations. I had to polish my wits, realize that to outflank a rival does not disgust any god worth knowing, that sound law can be sound injustice, public opinion is usually public folly, that gods emerge from our own riven selves.'

The stout man gazed moodily at gamblers squatting at small tables, drinkers confiding in low, cautious tones. Splashes and laughter flicked up from gratings above subterranean pools and steam baths warmed by illegal timber transactions with certain officials who were regular clients.

'How assured you are, Julian! I have the trappings, my priesthood, respect from matrons, a certain position, and revenues of course. But I'm lost in darkness, my head's a prison. As if I'm only pretending to be myself.'

'You could pretend to be rather better. The art of life, perhaps the point of life, is in transforming setbacks to assets. From the fall of Troy one can extract a lampoon. My family never understood that life is simple. Take no thought for the

146

morrow. So. . . . ' Julian refilled both goblets, looked from under lifted eyebrows at gauzy, twitching tableaux around them, sighed disparagement. 'Do use your brain, your Minerva. It can be done, it really can. You've read Democritus? Well then, here's your faith. Perfectly easy, not an ounce of pain, or very little. Only a bit of an effort. A stupid man only barks, but you can learn to speak, clear as the letters on Trajan's fancy column. Mellifluous words, they come easy to your profession. Find a creed, though, otherwise words only buzz. Atoms establish being – there's a start for you. Refreshing. Cleaner than elo-quence and conjurer's fingers rummaging through a domesti-cated universe. Marcus Aurelius, you remember, gave us a choice between atoms and godhead. They may be identical. Go ye forth and find out.'

His narrow cheeks creased, he pressed the other's shoulder and, nauseated by sweaty, panting flesh on wholesale offer, was already outside in a cool, salty breeze from the Alban Hills. The tired moon had lapsed, leaving an ashen afterglow in which the City slowly resumed her morning shape. Freed from heat, languor and curdled desire, his blood revived as he strolled beneath an aqueduct, legacy of Rome in her prime. Ahead were high, shabby tenements astir with waking life and, fragmented by distance, a tower rose from the whitewashed Wall, glimmer-ing deep in the pale light. Ah, the Wall! A cruel trick played by Aurelian on his people, on himself. Elaborate defences confess lack of defence. The more strident the symbol, the weaker the situation. The powerful ruler expresses a society cowardly, cowering, cowlike. Meanwhile he was content, feeling his shapely hair ruffled by the wind. Life was to be lived, livelihood assured, lively as crickets.

A fountain, still intact, halted him, and, drinking, soothing skin and hair, he lingered over the tritons and mermaids spouting almost alongside a stinking midden, on which an infant girl rotted. Throughout the City were hundreds of fountains, mostly broken, dribbling into stagnant filth, haunted by graveyard shapes. But a fountain, ignored by an Aurelian, treasured by a Gallienus, was a rival Capitol, hub of a world,

147

glittering, cascading, foaming, tinkling, waving spray like fans iridescent with stars and jewels, like a sibyl dropping arcane messages from the secret and imaginary. Secrets remained, but ears had withered, infected by the tragedy of Rome, a pile of boulders and cavities for the toad, the fern, the untamed boar.

XV

Granted leave for the funeral, Constantius, entering the Villa, immediately noted a crudely cut ash stick. Bran's. Puzzled, uneasy, he mentioned this to Domitia.

'He has been helpful. To us. No doubt he does not forget himself.'

Her voice and eyes, usually dry, now had a new expression: resentful, even harsh. Matters, however, were better than he had feared. She had always possessed a little property and, well versed in law, had resolutely preserved it from the Senator's schemes. It had been managed by a bailiff, only now revealed as a cousin of Bran. These two, nominal slaves, though likely to be forced into freedom by the State, and thus liable for increased taxation, managed the sale. After payments to the Treasury, then to creditors, a sufficiency was left for Clodia and herself. The Roman mansion was also to be sold.

Contemplating his mother, he reconsidered her duty to family cohesion, her part in the mystery of women. In funeral blacks she had cut her long hair, like a priestess detached from normality. Never admitting it, she probably shared his relief at the Senator's death, itself no sacrifice worthy of the Rome of his beliefs. Without respect a man sinks beneath his Name, and beneath her calm, ridged features, Domitia must long have withheld respect from one whose affairs were culpably awry and whose personal integrity was suspect. By so dying, Clodius Ammianus, holder of great office, guarantor of probity, had revoked his own principles: fidelity to ancestors, Rome, contracts. He had broken a pledge.

Funeral rites had been punctiliously observed: black cock and raven had been sacrificed, though no black ox could be procured. An official deputation represented the City, accompanied by a few old friends. Aggrieved, the clients, parasites and dependants had not come, and from surrounding villas many mourners had been merely hired. The ravaged corpse had not been formally laid out, no funeral mask of the veined, weighty face exhibited. All wished the ceremony to be finished quickly, the unnatural death forgotten. A nameless guest, very thin, silent throughout and the last to depart, had been identified as the Senator's guardian spirit, abandoning the Name.

Great through our misfortunes, the actor Diphilus had declaimed to Pompey, but, in his humiliation and defeat, Father would never be great, and of his public undertakings nothing survived. His contempt for the Wall might be a fitting epitaph.

The Senator had always asserted that he had been just to all. Few such remarks are true and, moreover, he had cared for none but himself.

As if knowing her son's thoughts, Domitia broke a long, troubled silence. 'He cherished what he called Rome. Nothing more.' The words distilled from a lifetime of bitterness. To Julian she might have said more, but Julian had not come, neither of them mentioning his absence.

'But how is Clodia?'

'She has broken a vase. A green vase.'

Further grievance underlying simple words, though the girl had loved that vase, deciding that it contained either starlight or a god's missing eye, and he agreed that in a certain thin light it did brim with peculiar shimmers.

Uncomfortable with Domitia he sought his sister, finding her alone at a high window, gazing at what could be seen only by herself. Turning, she brightened, her eyes glad. She was growing up, he noticed, discomforted by Domitia's unconcern. Rather clumsily he embraced her, and they sat together overlooking a yard empty and dull.

Summer was passing, an occasional leaf fell on the paving, and the sun, streaking clouds above the hills, though fiery, was cool.

150

She slowly looked up, needing him in unforced grief for the Senator, though he was convinced that she too would have preferred Julian to have consoled her.

He could not tell her that, at the outbreak of the revolt, Julian had sidled out of Rome. Unnecessarily, for he was one of those always inexplicably immune, like well-oiled gladiators stark naked yet as if armoured. Like handsome actors, irresistible singers, graceful courtiers and crippled buffoons, or, more strangely, those without looks, talents, patrons, who yet advance, effortlessly overcoming by an inflection of tone, singular half-smile, insidious small talk and unspoken flattery.

Clodia too was thinking of Julian. In his light way, he had said that nothing lasts, that people were ice awaiting the sun.

'Constantius, I felt I might have been alone, that you too would stay away. That night . . . I dreamed of great Hercules, after terrible death in fire, reaching heaven but. . . .' Her voice was small, shy, belying the eyes still shining beneath the trim fringe. In a few years' time they might lack gentleness. 'Have you ever seen the dead?'

No answer was obvious. Dead bodies he had often seen; he had killed people. The slashed and gouged, the skewered, the dried, ripped throat and oozing stump, the stare when all light had gone, the mess of brains on a fallen shield. But these she did not mean.

'Like most of us, Clodia, I never really know. Sometimes the dead are thought to be standing amongst us, obstructing, helping, or merely weak and wretched. I know little of dreams, though the dead fill them. They may be messengers, or bits of other people's thoughts that have somehow got lost, or spirits trapped because none cared to attend them in death. Outside Palmyra is a city kept for the dead alone. It has tombs like small temples, houses, squares, parks. Many cells are underground or hollowed out of great rocks. Paintings too, scorched by the sun.' He laughed, trying to liven the peaked, solemn face. 'There's a painting at Scyros of the great Achilles. But, imagine it, dressed as a girl!'

As he said it, he fancied Julian responding gravely that

151

Achilles was dressed most fittingly. How else? Clodia, staring at the barren yard, did not smile again. Both would be thinking of the Senator demanding admittance to the city of the dead, very peremptorily, expecting to be escorted to the best quarters by patricians of the first rank.

The girl remained silent. She had wanted to confide her dream to Julian, though he would only have thought her silly. Kind Constantius always tried to explain, but his words sounded unfinished.

Two days after Father's death, Isis had appeared, crowned not with a star but blood-red blossom, and she had woken in pain new, scarcely bearable, the blossom harder, more biting than the coloured spray swarming behind closed eyelids. She found herself unable to tell Constantius about the vase. Holding it, she had trembled as if at a cruel stare, and it had jerked away like a fish and at once lay smashed. That too must be a message from someone who knew her better than she knew herself. Isis? Could the goddess be jealous of the vase? Or, amongst the ghosts, did Father need it? Or it may have returned to the Former People inscribed on it. Or ... but imagination fluttered, folded inexpert wings and was still, leaving her only with that thought of the baby, her sister, deliberately killed, and left to wander unburied and unlamented.

Without warning, brother and sister realized they were watched. Robed, bearded, somewhat masterful, Bran, who had been standing motionless behind them, now approached, finally disposing of the possibility of closer intimacy. Seneca, Constantius reflected in helpless anger, had called slaves unpretentious friends, but he might not have said this of Bran.

The next day, having laid salt, eggs and lentils on the Senator's grave, reciting the customary prayers, while knowing that dishonouring of contracts reduces the dignity of death, Constantius was back in barracks, a temporary camp established for the extra forces needed to crush the revolt. This day was consecrated to Augustus's defeat of Cleopatra. All shops were shuttered, street banquets and sacrifices to Mars the Avenger enjoined, together with heady libations to the Emperor and the Unconquered Sun. Swiftly, excitement soared, for Aurelian then published his intentions. Not for him Hadrian's gardens and fountains, nor summer bowers graced with the charms of Zenobia. He had decided to move against Persia, planning to reach Ctesiphon, the old Assyrian city on the Tigris, before autumn. Officers agreed his motives were political. Violence in Rome, so swiftly succeeding the Triumph, induced him to postpone further reform before he had again terrified opposition by yet another victory. To overcome the Great King, perhaps rescue Valerian, would crown what Pliny had hailed the unfathomable majesty of the Roman Peace. Old Tacitus, one of the few senators respected in the City, confirmed this, and his approval erased all doubts.

From an orderly, Constantius knew that omens were favourable, better than those for the Triumph, which the Emperor had impatiently disregarded; better even than those for the Wall, which he mocked in language regarded in certain quarters as unseemly.

Furthermore, as all knew and none uttered, if left too long unoccupied, the legions became fretful, apt to quarrel with civilians, particularly those in Rome, excitable yet bored, now complaining that the Emperor's gift, the Wall, exuded poisons imported from Asia, which would render women sturdier than men, and already girl babies were being inspected for outsize limbs, exorcisers and chemists doing a brisk trade.

Meanwhile all frontiers were quiet, barbarians at a standstill, tending their wounds, and the Wall, now fully manned, overshadowed Rome. On the last day of August a priest of the Fetiales, an obscure, virtually forgotten brotherhood which in antiquity had supervised magical ceremonies when wars began – rituals to fracture enemies' images, subvert their gods, tempt their goddesses and wives, emasculate their warriors – was unearthed, or seemingly so, to proclaim destruction for the Great King, and hard-headed Aurelian Augustus, Aurelian Soter, on foot, led a procession through cheering streets to the Campus Martius. Surrounded by upraised Praetorian swords he exhibited a spear dipped in blood from a sacrifice to Bellona.

153

Abashed by such grandeur, plague abated and, by grace of the Roman Emperor, the Unconquered Sun penetrated everywhere for the healing of all.

Constantius was happy to escape Rome with its stench of disease and crowds, its Hippodrome crazed between Blues and Greens, its cruel, repulsive stadiums. A Claudius, an Aurelian, manifested that all was not hopeless, the Empire had a future, wielded by forthright hands. He craved fresh wind and high air, a gallop towards broad rivers, a light twinkling on a darkened mountain. His body was trustworthy, its leanness, its blessed fatigue after a march, rejoicing in the wine, the cleansing from dust and flies, its confidence lying in danger and receptivity of long sleep in which girls offered themselves weakly before fading into pale clouds. In battle it might first stammer incoherently, incontinently, even waver, but always recovered, spurred by rivals until, attacking as if in song, defending with agonized exhilaration, it shed all fears in frantic need to survive. Once, in a skirmish by the Euphrates, forgetting all others, pulled by incredible suction, it had rushed him forward alone, routing a Palmyran cohort.

This new campaign, with its hazards and casualties, could bring him closer to the Emperor. Aurelian knew his name, had approved, perhaps instigated his promotions. On formal parade those flammable eyes, unblinking, straight, the chipped face battered by demands not only of endless challenge but of known character, had always recognized but not yet addressed him.

In mess he was reckoned courageous, reliable, but better in receiving orders than initiating them. Whispers seeped through of 'excellent Constantius, our permanent second'. Such scorn could be dispelled, but by action. Battle alone would ensure him a Name far beyond the Senator's.

Brother officers sneered that he kept to the straight path, though, if they themselves had strayed, none had outmatched him in Egypt and Palmyra, and, in the rebellion, some had quailed, several pleading sickness. Aurelian must know this, or be made to know it.

154

His own flock, 'the Gulls', depended on him, likewise he on them. Manilius, chief tribune, with coppery Umbrian face wrinkled as if against glare, had sure judgement in managing polyglot rankers and surly conscripts. He had won rapid promotion from Claudius Gothicus, who knew of the lost estate, the grim wink of Fortuna, and recognized a loyalist who, though forced into the army by State tyranny, regarded his badge of office as an entity almost numinous.

The legion was at full strength, some five thousand, with newly serviced pontoons, battering-rams, store wagons, and vital complements of Greek engineers, doctors from Pergamum, from Bordeaux, scouts, runners, Jewish and Persian interpreters, a cavalry force, volunteer Palmyran archers. Daily the commissariat received freshly salted pork, newly baked loaves. Pay too was punctual, not in salt, bread tokens, promissory tallies, but in honest coins stamped with Aurelian's head.

All could mock the Great King, enthroned in feeble Persia like an effete moon, with his summer-houses and pleasure pavilions, scheming satraps and fraudulent soothsayers, his eunuchs and catamites like soft peaches, his concubines and golden bowls of grapes in snow.

> The Great King's in his castle,
> Get down you dirty rascal.

In song, rank, status and time collapsed. With sudden tenderness a scarred, brutal mouth had crooned *O Rose of the World*, and another's eyes, filthy, butcher-like, went soggy with longing, like some Oscan primitive hearing a poem to love and death.

Urban classes had long ceased to volunteer for the legions, and the Gulls were typical, mostly rural, impoverished conscripts or fugitives. British, Gallic and Galatian Celts, youngsters from Sicily, Syria, Spain, unseasoned tribalists from Teutonic and Dalmatian frontier plantations and African colonies, they were ignorant of Rome, of the Wall, but still

155

aglow from solemn oaths of loyalty to the god Juventus, patron of recruits. They were raw, but fine material to be sifted and tested. The great Antonine emperors had been provincials; likewise Claudius Gothicus and Aurelian. There were deep thrills in instructing and leading, even risking, these slowly conforming limbs and faces. One could envy Hercules training young and dazzling Hylas. At Palmyra, such lads had followed him, many to their deaths, one, struck down beside him, gazing up, incredulous, bewildered, sighing his last into a froth of blood. He had failed to save 'Commy', a fat Ephesian known as 'Compliments to the Cook', collapsing with a dart in his throat.

Their voices jarred, where eyes and disposition did not. Incomprehensible tongues jabbering barbarian secrets. His orderly, Ammas, trim, loyal, even affectionate, was illiterate, ignorant of Roman speech and gods, given to sudden tears which bewildered him as much as the others, residue of some outrage perhaps deliberately forgotten. Like many youths, like Manilius, Ammas worshipped Mithras the Persian, inappropriate for the forthcoming war. At his neck he wore a tablet depicting the god in blue, youthful radiance aloft in a sun chariot and promising to save his own when the world burned. Once, when asked the number of tent-pegs needed, he thought long and seriously, then answered 'Blue'.

From such stock Constantius acquired engrossing facts. Very serious, novices struggled to explain ancient lore. Certain simples plucked seven heartbeats before dawn routed all sickness demons save plague. At Sowing Time, Celtic marriages could be forsworn by either spouse after a year and a day, new gifts being accepted or rejected under divine eyes. Manilius, wizened as an apple, tough as oak, spoke of vines as life everlasting. Commy had seen six *proud ones* stalking the night sky, 'Titus', a name adopted by a grinning, uncouth Briton, condemned hanging as unjust; by trapping the spirit it prevented flight to the Other World on behalf of the rich who objected to their air being sullied by a felon's soul, they themselves insisting on being beheaded, leaving the rankers to be hanged, clubbed, burned alive, thrashed to death. Burgundians told camp-fire tales of a one-eyed war-lord with chapped face under a broad hat leading a spectral hunt with fire-rimmed hounds.

> Muot, with the big hat,
> Has more guests than the wood has twigs.

All this recalled childhood, and Bran, not Diomede, with talk of an enchanted cauldron refusing to boil for cowards. It would not be needed by Rome during the months ahead.

Constantius had his own knowledge. An officer of the illustrious family of Cinna had been feared throughout the legion, not for his severity, for he was just, but for his tarnished aura, a reputation for ill-luck, indeed the evil eye which more than once, under a particular moon, had emptied the mess. He was found stabbed, his eyes covered by a rag, and senior officers, concealing the matter from the Emperor, so quick to punish, knew better than to force an Inquiry, secreting it even from the Gentlemen of Supplies, seldom recognized but always at hand, keeping notes, dispatching reports.

Yesterday had seen an execution of two young Pannonian brothers for disobedience, though evidence suggested an order misunderstood. *Emperor's command.* Generous to high-born captives, Aurelian was pitiless to mutineer, deserter, striker: even a small suspicion of dissent exasperated him. But Constantius was happy, out of range of Julian's mockery. Already new recruits, however alien, were manipulating weapons with feeling for balance, precision, will, while genuine Romans loafed at home, demanding hand-outs, casting hawks, chasing hares on the Sabine Hills, and, like Julian, shrugging at victory, defence, law. Never wholly obliterated by turmoil and usurpation was an ideal legion pledged to a City of orderly living, wise fatherhood, brotherhood of the handshake, keeping at bay the Scythian forest and Hunnish steppe, the Scanian furies, the perfumes of Asia. To kill in a righteous cause was condemned only by those with safe billets.

Father had accurately, if tediously, reiterated that Roman

157

greatness had been founded as much on the spade as on the sword. Brute conquest had been followed by dykes, aqueducts, roads, temples, senates, theatres. Planting, draining and protecting constituted true empire. Aurelian and Probus knew this, seeing the army as a tool to repair, punish, mould. Probus indeed, having scattered a barbarian army, had bemused his men by foretelling a world so at peace that no army would be needed, the men wildly applauding, though afterwards wondering why.

These modern hirelings, though affectionate as dogs, carried no spades, despising simple tools, but might yet be taught.

Twice weekly, Constantius attended an officers' council, inferior only to the Imperial Staff and the Privy Council. Assiduously he had construed Aurelian's celebrated map, which reduced overall strategy to a few stark simplicities. The Rhineland, richest area of Gaul, concentrated roads and waterways essential for defence. The Danube frontier, so often vulnerable. Dacia, now deliberately blacked out. Rome, red-ringed by the Wall, but now less vital than Ravenna and Milan. Antioch, necessary bastion, Spain, source of minerals and ports, with the name 'Tetricus' grimly crossed out. Trier, loyal but needing refortification: Lugdunum, Gades, Alexandria, listed with tax returns and responses to the Great Measure.

Throughout camp, morale was brisk. Weapons were still arriving: helms, cuirasses, shields round and oval, heavy infantry javelins, old-style swords pointed and cutting, *ballistae*, those gigantic catapults to pound enemies with blocks of masonry from dismantled temples and confiscated dwellings, or discharging clouds of darts, *Wild Asses* on wooden trestles, whose windlasses, releasing the beam, would hurl a boulder into any defence, battering-rams with which Septimius Severus – as any officer should know but not all did – had crushed Babylon and reconquered Britain. Dying, that charmless conqueror had groaned to his son and successor, Caracalla, witless as Gallienus: *Pay the soldiers. Show contempt for all others.*

Whole fields were filling with horse-blankets from Cilician

158

goats, wine, vile but ample, from South Britain, transport mules laden with mead.

Aurelian had never lost a battle, had never endangered lives by such a gamble as throwing a Standard into the enemy centre and daring his men to retrieve it by a demented, victorious charge. He was the master smith, forging the new but riveting it to the best of the old, recasting elements. The real marriage of Vulcan and Venus, strength and survival. Despite their speedy enactment, his projects were methodically deliberated: recovery of the south bank of the Danube deemed so needful by great Augustus, conquest of Palmyra, restoration of Egypt, Spain, Gaul, Britain, quelling of restless Alexandria. Sun temples, Wall, Great Measure. Tutored by Claudius and himself, the High Command was more emphatically borrowing from the Gothic riders. The Empire must be guaranteed by cavalry, formerly small, somewhat despised, gathered from allies and federates. Surprisingly, Julian's ignoble Gallienus had anticipated this, using swift, independent horsemen to forestall danger. Aurelian had extended this practice in Syria.

The eve of campaign: the Eagles again flying east to bleached lands and deep-green oases, remote hill shrines, the domain of Bel Shamin, Lord of Heaven, desiccated birthplace of the Unconquered Sun and what precious-tongued Julian called the blond wind of the desert.

Julian! Again the sensations of irritation and inferiority, contempt and a sort of love. Julian, always disappearing, unexpectedly returning, never standing in full sunlight. He himself could be a tree, deep rooted, giving shade, unmistakable: Julian, a flower of many colours, spreading fragrance and some pleasure but planted shallow, drooping at fierce suns, quite soon forgotten.

Preparations quickened. A legion had already embarked at Brundisium, set for the Straits before the late autumn gales, scattering the pirates and island scavengers. The Gulls, with two further legions, led by Aurelian and Probus, would march down the coast of Hadrian's Sea, slowly, elaborately, to overawe the provinces, cross water, incorporate some waiting

159

Pannonians. Imperial glory would be paraded through Macedonia and Thrace, towards small, well-sited Byzantium. At nearby Heraclea Pontica the legions would divide for winter, and in early spring pass through the Straits to march unopposed through Bithynia, Cappadocia, southern Armenia, Mesopotamia, an itinerary as much political as strategic. Deploying along the Euphrates, Aurelian would confer with vassal rulers and clients, collect supplies, before moving towards royal Ctesiphon, gateway to Persia.

Constantius was further absorbed. Julian had mocked his military dedication, his lack of intimacies, and indeed throughout he had sought but never reached particular friendship. Here in camp, however, attracted to him alone, of equal rank, was a newcomer, Gaius Valerius, an Illyrian peasant, not always intelligible, as if biting words before releasing them, nimble, despite heavy trunk and slightly bandy legs, a youth of short though nondescript hair, capable hands already calloused, greyish blue eyes staring out from above thick nostrils as though laboriously striving towards answers to questions clearly important though not readily understood. Frequently silent, when he did speak he showed curt certainty, sometimes a strange arrogance which could ruffle one proud of book learning and patrician ways.

Trained for present and future, Gaius Valerius was ignorant of the past, dismissing most references to it. For him, Augustus himself was but one of Aurelian's titles, Nero only a Greek godling, Domitian a disease – suppositions, of course, not wholly inept. He seemed always to be thinking seriously about more than he revealed.

On their first encounter, the newcomer had at once greeted Constantius with a warmth he denied to other officers, unexpected from his pursed, unyouthful features.

On a calm, russet afternoon the two stood together, saying little, but at ease, glad, the camp encircling them. Armour glittered outside a tent, ready for polishing, a horse was being exercised by a Nubian, all grins and teeth and, across in the main field, soldiers noisily wrestled, played catch, quoits, touch, jostled amiably for nothing very obvious. Crossing a dusty patch towards Probus's quarters, stepping grandly yet slightly awkwardly like a waterfowl on dry ground, in ceremonial buskins and striped cloak, was 'Eros' Mnestheus, Chief Imperial Secretary, professional civilian, with fat, doughy cheeks, gummy smile, chins loose as if unfolding. Respectful clerks followed, clutching rolls and quills, one bearing a tall, three-legged golden inkstand on blue linen, all professing indifference to the loud, vulgar soldiery.

'An uncomfortable fellow. He needs watching.' Gaius Valerius was doing just that, intently. 'They call him the Hencoop. Much clucking, plenty of scurry, with only muck to show for it. Don't know how the Emperor stands it.'

Sentries saluted unwillingly. Probus's door opened from within, Eros vanished. 'The air lightens.' Gaius Valerius's grunt might have passed for a laugh, his hand tightened on Constantius's shoulder, then they resumed earlier talk, careless of the knowledge that two officers talking together would be noted, from a tent-flap, window, from behind a fence or tree, by those one-time grain contractors, the Gentlemen of Supplies.

They had been attending Probus's staff lecture on tactics. Very upright, jocular, formidable within his grace of hair and bone, the general had cited Hannibal's genius at Cannae, exploiting Roman flank weakness, not risking headlong assault but inexorably surrounding defenders doomed almost from the start. 'A lesson, gentlemen, signally acknowledged by our own commander, with results known to you all.'

Later, Constantius laboriously explained that Probus was a Stoic, practitioner of *ascesis*, body and mind exercised to control excessive ambition and wayward thoughts. But his friend yawned. 'Too much thought already, blowing about unneeded. Probus don't need it, he sees straight. That's all. I don't know about Stoics. They sound like Galileans. Aurelian doesn't like 'em. He'll be rooting 'em out, maybe quite soon. Dangerous breeds. Not in this world, not out of it either. Because they're not mere rabble, they're hard to squash. You and I together could clear it away without wasting much muscle. No need to arm the slaves for a long time yet. But here's danger, in Galileans, I mean, listen to me now. They understand slaves, they've plenty, they've learned to give 'em easy promises, without being too sharp about paying 'em. They understand cash, useful to governments, but governments must keep their eyes open. Galilean women pretend to understand everything. But loyalty they chuck away like dirty finery. So the Emperor'll round 'em up. For that, for disloyalty, or ...' – his face, young, but lacking youth in its hard, inflexible lines, smiled mirthlessly – '... he'll save himself risk and do 'em in just for thinking of disloyalty. He can depend on me. I say, better bad government than no government.'

Constantius glanced hastily around, wary of informers. He too had heard speculations that, with the military – Probus, Saturninus, Mucapor, and perhaps Senator Tacitus – the Emperor was planning to act not only against sectaries but against the quasi-independent Officialdom, where despite ever-swelling hands, business lay clogged, the sinews of empire atrophied. Then he smiled affectionately at Gaius Valerius, whose unaccustomed surge of words seemed to have exhausted him more than an afternoon's march. This rough mountaineer from an unknown village was more Roman than most of the legion. He would appreciate Father's tale of Gauls rushing the Colline Gate, storming the Senate House, then halting, trans-fixed by the Senators, seated in glistening togas, calmly silent, indomitable. The tale should have ended there, but finally an invader stole forward and dared pull a dignified beard. Out-raged, the old man cracked him on the head with his ivory staff and, freed from the spell, the Gauls slaughtered the lot.

He was about to speak but cheers interrupted, resounding from the outer encampment. *Io Aurelian!* The Emperor was back from hunting, already in view, riding with Praetorian escort, the horses in flowing, continuous undulation, Aurelian's favourite boar hound trotting beneath him, looking about with an air of aggrieved authority. His master's face, under jutting casque, was dim, his outline shut in a metal corslet. *Io Aurelian!* Sincerely applauding, gathering cheerfully, the soldiers never-

162

theless kept a respectful distance. Formerly, Aurelian would have jumped down and walked amongst them, friendly though taciturn; with crowds he had always been at ease, despite natural peasant aloofness or suspicion. But he was no Hadrian, ready to risk his dignity by chucking a javelin with the first challenger and greeting even the humblest by name. Since the Revolt, Aurelian had been fully Augustus, forbiddingly paternal and reserved, though hailed not as Father but as Ever-Victorious.

Already he was gone, leaving the men docile and satisfied. None had dared address him singly, but, cheering in a mass, they were safe, anticipative, rejoicing that he was again to open the East for stupendous plunder, rapine and, oh yes, heroics. Had the Emperor *Fortuna*? Who could deny it?

No plaudits had welcomed Carus, Praetorian Prefect, broad nosed, pitted, black bearded, riding ahead of the tight-mouthed Guards, on whom no ruler should turn his back. Constantius had seen Italian villagers insulted, kicked and robbed by these huge-headed, insolent Teutons, who conscripted them for forced labour, jeering at their protests, their rights as Roman citizens.

Constantius and Gaius Valerius, young men with a future.

XVI

The year darkened. Letters from Optima Fortuna reached Constantius by military couriers. They were not from Domitia, always grudging his absences, his freedom, the freedom, Julian taunted, of obedience. Not from Bran, pleased to feather his own nest unquestioned. They were from Clodia, less simple than he expected; usually, behind sentences modelled on Diomede's slightly archaic prescription, perplexed or troubled. She probably confided more freely in Julian, who would grimace pleasantly and forget to reply.

Constantius always replied, encouraging her into life. He had duties towards her and methodically compiled his replies like lessons. Though young, he already felt himself an experienced veteran. He had undergone battle and siege, drought, ambuscade, a plague of snakes. Around Palmyra he had seen deserts produced by ancient peoples building fine dykes but allowing the salt to form hard craters, blighting the land. Some nomads had refused to fight, afraid not of death but of contamination from Romans, men of the plough, the plough being source of all wickedness, for violating the earth goddess. He had watched a man going to execution, stooping, anxious to retrieve an artificial tooth. She must recognize life, discover ways of death, ever ahead, like the light blinking on the night-filled mountain. She loved rambling alone and he described strangely sited boulders, wild lavenders, firs sticky with resin, sometimes cut with runic signs: a distorted sun, a severed head, a crowned bird. She must absorb smells of damp leather, horseflesh, trampled grass, the powers of starlit frost, glimpses of distant heather and forest swept by salt winds during an easy crossing of Hadrian's Sea towards lands without known limits. Emperor

Marcus Aurelius had, imagine it, dispatched traders to China.

Much could not be mentioned, for reasons other than her sensitivity. Officers' letters could be opened by other hands. The most fervid loyalist yet knew of immemorial aspects of government seldom spoken, everywhere known: the dagger at the neck under question, the hidden cellar and darkened pit, the knots, lead weights and pincers, the rat and cobra. The hand-cutting and torn mouths. Clodia had wept for Zenobia. In a few years she would weep for better causes, entering risks over-hanging all that breathed, slave and emperor. The deadly recesses where lurked such flabby tyrants as Eros the Hencoop who lived by anonymous scripts, covert accusations, rewarding the horrible, whispering to the inescapable Officialdom, with access to the Highest, promoting decisions never proclaimed but which might convulse the world. Eros's hand on the Trea-sury was said to control two-thirds of the revenue. He had an entourage of two score literate faithfuls extravagantly paid to nod assent and silence dissidents.

When the war was finished he would use long leave to instruct her further. The outburst of the preacher 'Ovid', reaching him through much garble and floridity, had nevertheless induced him to resume his own studies. In a temple library he read that through effort, tribulation, knowledge, the mind could reach *ataraxia*, internal balance. Lucretius, the Epicurean, had written: *O wretched mortal intelligence! O blind emotion! In what darkness of life, in what dangers, you spend this brief span!* Words not dispiriting but challenging. Clean, pure, they confronted the future; simple and direct as an abacus, easier to cherish and use than 'Ovid's' interchanging patterns and Julian's ribald intri-cacies in which misunderstandings become gods who fade to misunderstandings. The empire of the clown: leaderless, law-less, cruel. The Galilean threat. For Julian, life was play, subtle approaches to personal gain. A soldier felt deeper, remembered the plight of others.

Suddenly, almost overwhelmingly, he needed to embrace, then confide in, not Julian but Gaius Valerius. Unlock secret thoughts. Meanwhile, winter had set in, mild enough. Snow fell, but intermittently, gently. The troops remained cheerful, sustained by the efficient commissariat and by the presence of the Emperor amongst them, though veterans complained of his invisibility within doors heavily ranged with Praetorians. Manilius spoke of the men seeing ghosts on the mountains above the coastal road, and swapping tall stories of vampires. Constantius, while manipulating them into soldiers, watched and listened. For such lads, towns were sunless slaughter-houses, the Wall unimaginable. Sometimes he suspected that their native diet forced them to live almost wholly within dreams, so that orders were misunderstood, death was a phantom, demons and queer, indescribable colours haunted them, and they believed that emperors and generals were able to fly. One boy spent his leave not in a village wine shop but in digging an immense hole, which he then methodically filled in. With what spirits and curses had he peopled it? A thunderstorm that night must have been his answer. Two others, unwillingly conscripted, had lately, tearfully, presented him with a skinful of water, imploring him to wash in it, then drink it, explaining that they had gathered it from where 'two rivers kiss'.

Their fireside songs drifted to his tent where he discussed tomorrow's work with Manilius.

> Sometimes I can't thrill you.
> Sometimes I want to kill you.
> Leave me wet but suck me dry.

Manilius, avoiding familiarity, was forthcoming. 'They still find weaponry difficult. They're more used to plough and hoe.' His educated tones at odds with his attire.

At Constantius's reference to the Emperor's seclusion, Gaius Valerius gave his short emphatic nod. 'Happen he's wise in that. He used to spread himself too far, too often. Emperors can no longer pretend to be one of their own men. He's learned not from Rome but from the Great King. The secret of rule is to remain up there behind the mask with all eyes straining to see you, and finding only the mask. What they call the Diadem. If the Great King don't even exist, no matter. People think he does, the Diadem glitters for all. He must be hidden, yet sleep with his ear to the ground. Inescapable, but invisible, a god. Aurelian's behaviour, very good. He too sometimes puts himself under a new Diadem, Eastern-like. The Triumph was his goodbye to the herd. These are new times. Emperors must be guarded from their own Guards. Those Praetorians must be tamed, even terminated. And no more donatives, cash bribes. Give a fellow one sesterce and he'll demand two, turn angry if only offered three. That's the record.'

He spoke as if he had long pondered these matters and was prepared to maintain his beliefs stubbornly, even ruthlessly, when opportunity approached. Self-evident, they were also essential. Likewise, when he spat, which he would do on occasions usually inappropriate, he did so as if taking a momentous decision, spitting fiercely, apparently at an invisible target. Of the Diadem he had spoken correctly; no previous Roman emperor had adopted such formal splendour.

'Government's not quite science, and not what an educated fellow like you'd call art. But has one nostril in both. Balance, hard unmistakable forms, colour of men's hearts, their strength of will . . . all to be set against the daily work. The one set against the whole. See! More difficult than music, painting and the rest. More plain spirited than anything in the gymnasium, arena, racecourse. The theatre may be closer to what I'm saying, gods and diadems, but I've never seen any theatre.'

In the cold light thrust through the tent-flap he glowed. His face, grooved, usually rather immobile, had an ardour which briefly replaced his expression of absorbed, somewhat defiant purpose.

Next morning the two were standing over a brazier, superintending auxiliary troops defiling into a narrow pass. During the night Constantius had realized, in dismay, that here too, insensibly, he had been 'second', deferring, behaving to Gaius Valerius like a subordinate. As with Julian, he could feel his advantages a handicap with this peasant who, at a casual mention of Cicero or Cato, would look bored or uncomprehending. He once interrupted a fine quotation with what from anyone else in their mess would have been rudeness. 'I don't want things perfect, I want things better.'

His grasp of life, obvious ambition, fascinated Constantius. He had desire, still muffled, to surrender utterly, offer the embrace he had occasionally yearned to give Julian, and once to the neat, dark-eyed orderly, Ammas.

Gaius Valerius nevertheless had acquired more knowledge than he sometimes pretended.

'The Persians had a spring festival, saluting the equality of all men. They say nothing about women.'

'Like the age of Saturn.'

'Can't talk about that. But for that day the Great King had to accept strange company, the likes of shepherds, vine-trimmers, fishers, the dolts and nobodies like my brothers. In return for a good feed they told him their grievances and wants. He allowed the dirtiest on to his own couch, shared goblet and platter, showered them with honeyed words. From your toil, said he, we gain our well-being. From our care you keep your jobs. Since we need each other, let's dwell together as one. As a family.'

They smiled, knowing each other's thoughts. Aurelian, though himself lowly born, would hear this story with some grimness. Possessing an empress, he as yet had no family and had shown no desire to incorporate any dolts and nobodies and notoriously preferred injustice to disorder. 'Like Plato' Constantius wanted to say, but at the thought of the look he would receive, he desisted.

When Gaius Valerius spoke again, his voice sounded like the regular chop of a woodman's axe. Sharp, strenuous, calculated. Like Ammas and many barbarians he used words either as weapons or very cautiously, as if they were liable to break.

A soldier replenished the brazier, saluted, ran off, but Gaius Valerius seemed not to notice. 'Dedication! Well, our generals have that. Honesty – well, maybe. But I don't care for the civilian lot and, if I hear aright, nor does Aurelian. Something's afoot. We've both heard of something they call the One.'

Nebulous but clinging, the word was heard everywhere, still undeciphered, faintly ominous.

Gaius Valerius shrugged. At the brazier his hands, pliant like all his body, clenched, unclenched, as if over a hilt. Throughout the talk his eyes had not ceased to follow, like those of an assessor, missing nothing, the men before them marching briskly against the chill, disappearing in regular formation into the steep, cavernous heights, bare against the muddy sky. His manner had a vehemence subdued only with effort.

'Who knows? Who cares? Me. But listen. We're talking of new times. Rome's finished. Bunged up. Trapped in a curse. Too far from what matters. Bag o' nuts for them that don't like nuts. Body o' lot. Part of the old ways. Facing what we'd call goblin night. You wouldn't know of that, Constantius friend. Sometimes you speak too fancy to be understood by some of us. Anyway, that Wall of our chief mason, which cost a hefty pile, must be a feint. The Empire's got all the walls it needs. Sea, river, mountains. But Rome's Wall won't mean much. Military like. But could mean a heap if people think of him always behind it, at a peep-hole. I've never been to Rome, probably never will. I'll keep in the thick of things and one day will hear of Rome disappearing for ever behind her Wall, leaving it as a big block, monument to Aurelian the Great. Anyway, I say it, Italy's dead, only ghosts come from a burnt-out field. But there are new lands, new cities ... Trier, the Bosphorus ... new Romes. We'll rebuild Ephesus....'

The deep eyes, almost colourless in the dreary afternoon light, even the cowhide face, were supremely assured, and Constantius once again felt himself submitting, almost awed by this Illyrian, elsewhere somewhat despised or resented. Yet Gaius Valerius was the intimate he had always craved and never found, least of all in Julian. He disliked hearing of others' dreams, hopes, fine intentions, was interested only in what they were actually proposing or doing. Gaius Valerius was no dreamer and disliked speaking. Commissioned by Claudius Gothicus after bravery in ambush, advanced further by Aurelian, having disobeyed orders during panic on the Rhine and leading the counter-charge, he had gathered more recognition, and jealousy, against Tetricus in Gaul. One sensed that, despite informers and spiteful colleagues, he would survive. Usually silent, he was never, so to speak, dumb. Words were always waiting within his thin mouth, seldom to confess ignorance or ask help, but, despite wretched schooling, ever ready to dispute, assert, demand.

Constantius thought, Together....

The last troops had returned to quarters and the two strolled forward to the tedium of mess supper. The laughter at worn-out jokes, the cool stare and surreptitious gesture, the swilling, quarrels, accusations of favouritism. Dusk was swelling the hills, transforming trees to a single overhanging shadow. Each was reluctant to meet indoors, perforce as mere professional associates. Intimacy between officers was always noted, was disparaged and feared. The Emperor required obedience, distrusted bands of brothers.

Gaius Valerius paused, just out of hearing of the sentries ranked before the low, single-storeyed wooden mess-hut.

'Yes, Constantius. Listen. We've fine leaders. Probus for one. Energetic, keeping things moving. But Aurelian should given 'em some of his load. The Empire's too big. Throwing away Dacia was good sense. I'd place a commander I trusted in each centre, with a force dedicated and expert, doesn't matter how small, ready to be rushed to wherever danger's heard. The roads are being repaired. These troops, backing up the frontier defences, need to be trained to move swift as hawks, with no regional ties. No nonsense.'

Gallienus's method, though used too languidly. But Gaius would know nothing of Gallienus, be healthier for it. Almost from darkness, he touched Constantius's arm unexpectedly. 'You've told me much. Too much, maybe. Me, I've nothing to tell. I came from nowhere, will probably get smudged out, not in battle, and for nothing, catching the eye of some Praetorian oaf or paymaster hanger-on who hasn't earned his wages and is jealous of those who have. But listen, I may feel too little, but you can feel too much. Inheritance – that's the word, isn't it?

170

Your old man's breed has died out, like the giants. We can get nothing from there. My parents were born slaves, but they fought their way up a bit. You too must grab your chances, savage-like. Life's getting shorter, you can rely on nothing at all 'cept your own right arm. Changes must come, to stop everything slipping into disaster. We can't let everything depend on the Emperor's life. He knows it. He's reorganizing.'

He seemed to smile, his features rough and bristled in the gloom, harsh as his voice, though the words were unwontedly negligent. 'The crow or the horse!'

Both laughed. The latest camp story was that when the Praetorian Prefect asked the Emperor for the night's password, Aurelian had hesitated between *Crow* and *Horse*. Then a crow had flopped from the pines and Aurelian immediately decreed *Horse*, and, against his usual custom, deigned to explain. He refused, he said, to submit to superstition.

Night was all around; a rising wind suggested more snow, whispering above. The two men were still unwilling to part, held together by a tangle of premonitions, desires, affections, outside the ring of fires, sentry calls, horse movements, the vague tent shapes, the quick-set hedges. Gaius Valerius stood like a boulder, obscure, of unmeasurable stature, a threat to men, to spirits of the dark. Constantius felt his own words seeking utterance, but confusedly, almost in panic, so that, beginning a sentence, he stammered and, attempting to resume, was interrupted by scuttling feet and a voice quite close, gasping to the nearest sentry: 'Have you heard? The Hencoop's been arrested!'

171

XVII

In the mess, none could clarify what had really occurred. Eros, Imperial Secretary, had long been the link between Emperor, Privy Council, Military Staff and the Praetorian Prefect: secretive, unpopular, respected only for Aurelian's backing. Aurelian seldom overlooked mistakes, retained ministers only on extended probation, was probably suspicious of all of them, and wanted to prune the suffocating Officialdom, drastically.

Publicly Eros was accused, by Carus, the Praetorian responsible for the Emperor's safety, of accepting bribes from the Great King, of accumulating property and gold by blackmailing notables and senior officials. Oddly, however, though under arrest he was not yet in prison: execution, surely guaranteed, was not yet ordained. He remained in his offices, under guard, but still examining certain papers on behalf of his master. All agreed that 'The One' had been the Hencoop, synonym of personal greed rather than conspiracy, the nervousness of a civilian facing a rigorous campaign and apt to overreach. Conceivably the matter had not very much significance. Probably the Gentlemen of Supplies, taking a hint from the Emperor, had initiated the move against a man who could look for no support either from the Guards or the legions. The exact process would never be known. The intricacies of power would be left to annalists generations hence. Persian bribes had becomes little more than a formula to halt the progress of those whose usefulness was over.

The army again moved forward, Eros accompanying it in a closed carriage, through towns, villages, valleys, past old sites of battle and massacre, and meeting delighted acclamations. No dissent was observable, no disease loped out of the East. The

winter had been mild, 'Emperor's weather', obsequious courtiers chorused. At the Macedonian border a halt was called for
recuperation, review of supplies, the arrival of reinforcements
from Scutari and Egnatia.

Constantius alone was disconsolate, feeling clumsy, uncertain of his standing, misshapen in sullen loneliness. Gaius
Valerius had vanished, withdrawn, no one knew where, along
the complex webs of army command, probably on a mission to
regions with which he was familiar. That he had been involved
in 'The One' was unthinkable. Meanwhile Constantius was left
isolated in the mess, with its bleary swagger about women and
boys, recollections, often spurious, of blood and revels. Here
Gaius Valerius known as 'Docles' had been distrusted as a
pushy, taciturn, ungracious yokel, not much better than a
gladiator, and too respected or feared by the troops. Such a man
would return, would always return, unannounced, very simply,
claiming his due through those clotted, jerky sentences without
air between words.

Performing his duties, exercising, strengthening his body,
conferring with Manilius, instructing his band of Gulls, Constantius thought of Gaius Valerius: very probably that mission
of his might make an Ammas feel queasy. Constantius worked
harder, forcing such youths into cohesion and purpose. Their
eyes shone, lit by prospects of hacking out lumps of rich Persia
– one boy imagined Persia was a golden palace, another that
the Great King was a blinded giant upholding the world but
vulnerable in the heel.

Had it been permitted, Constantius would have messed
cheerfully with Manilius and young Ammas, both, in their sep-
arate ways, devoted.

His letters to Clodia revealed no sadness, though to Julian he
could have betrayed some of it. Writing to Julian, however, was
like dropping a gift into snow. Poring over his accounts, his
pebbles, keeping one appointment, avoiding another, flitting
between anonymous beds, Julian, man of concerns, lacked
personal concern.

To Clodia, reaching womanhood, Domitia would hand down

173

some chilly precepts and discouraging warnings. He could not, so continued his conscientious descriptions: a general's scarlet cloak, gilded cross-leggings and belt of an Imperial Companion, the small dirty towns, the people thronging in imagined freedom to cheer the Emperor from mountain settlements, hidden temples, caves. Even for the meanest, the Standards were uplifted, Eagles of Rome flying towards the lands of the Unconquered Sun, the wind tipped by acrid sands, blowing from deserts where palaces, domes and bright cities rose on the horizon, pink, yellow, green, reflected in glittering lakes, surrounded by trees, very clear, a call to the heart, but already receding, fading to harsh sunlit sterility and the wreckage of long-lost people. You remember, Clodia, that at Palmyra I saw a golden lion nailed to an upright cross, eagles screaming above? He had not mentioned the black collar of dried flies at the throat, another mass quivering in the eyes. Soon enough she would see such things. Ammas he ignored, but she might be interested in Manilius, more so in Gaius Valerius. A marriage there? The Senator's shade would be outraged but the outcome might be good. He would work towards it, though his friend had shown no hankerings for matrimony, even love. He might indeed have wives already in Illyrian squalor, too unimportant to be spoken of. Lovelessness, of course, need be no impediment to successful marriage and Clodia might yet be a general's wife. After briefly trifling with Zenobia, never truly ascertained, Aurelian might agree. His Empress, whom few had seen, was awaiting him, to accompany the army towards Salonika where a Persian embassy was said to have arrived with servile terms on offer.

Unable to describe the Empress, he ended with the conventional admonitions, wasted on the young.

His depression increased, his squad wondered at his face, whispered about women. In the mess he could hear or ask nothing. Discussion of the Hencoop was forbidden, but others too seemed uneasy, anxious to confide what they should not. The sudden arrest of so lofty a personage unsettled the younger men. The insidious and hidden might still be at work, despite

174

the reassuring presence of Mucapor and Probus. All awaited a gesture from the Emperor, customary from a man who had known life in the ranks; the exasperations and exacting preliminaries before a campaign acquires momentum, the tensions between veteran and conscript, volunteer and certain officers claiming privileges as yet unearned.

Amongst the auxiliaries, never the flower of armies, and even some regular officers, the Emperor had acquired a new nickname. For the legions he had never been the World Saviour so popular with stay-at-homes; Old Sword-in-Hand was more usual, affectionate enough but keeping you at a distance. The tendency was now to term him the Chief Mason, jobbing at walls and temples, as if the nickname had been a frightened rejoinder from the disgraced Eros. Gaius Valerius himself had used it, surely unwittingly.

Constantius reckoned himself no fool. Here, in Asia's backyard, he could agree that the Wall might indeed lack military significance, might have been a shrewd distraction to reduce the restless, the jobless, the apathetic, perhaps also fulfilling some urge within Aurelian himself. Rulers enjoy sensations of storming time and events by the force of sheer size. Most great rulers since Augustus had been builders, adding to their name, their Genius. In Rome the army had saluted the Wall as another feat of their leader and of themselves, a new wonder towering above Italy, posterity fearing it as the work of giants. Now, however, with a sea overcome, great distances mastered, with fathomless Asia lying before them under the painted, supine gaze of the Great King, the men were forgetting the Wall, which most had never seen. Until the next victory, as 'Chief Mason', Aurelian might lose some grandeur, though to ban a nickname was what no ruler, however tyrannical, had ever achieved. Julius Caesar, Tiberius, Domitian had suffered worse. Constantius, nevertheless, was not quite appeased. Julian had thought the Wall comical. Should others do so, danger might revive, worse than any contrived by Eros. Respect for the Emperor underpinned the Empire. Within the comic was also the cruel, the vengeful.

Days passed, seemingly normal. Some manoeuvres were held, conducted by Probus under a cold bright sun and scatters of snow. The Emperor rode away with the cavalry élite for exercises elsewhere. Constantius was glad to work himself to exhaustion yet found sleep difficult. For three successive nights he awoke, startled, shivering, from an identical dream in which, returning home from but a few streets away, he nevertheless got lost, wandering through places queerly lit and wholly unfamiliar. Houses had shortened, slanting towards him, time as if gulping, hurried from noon to dusk, and in near-darkness he reached the Wall, indistinct, colossal, menacing, though effortlessly he leaped over it and found, not the wide country-side but, in the blurred light, another City, lofty hills crowded with windowless dwellings and turrets topped by empty granite crags jutting as if about to fall, occasional brilliantly green streets showing between the buildings. An apparition torment-ing, unendurable but presumably a sign, though from where? Again he missed Julian, so at home in the shadowy and con-cealed. Much of life, he would say, remains, very fortunately, unexplained, some of it inexplicable, the remainder explained unsatisfactorily. He had joked about a father god needing help. He might interpret this dream as further confirmation of the deceptiveness of walls.

Constantius had never succeeded in answering Clodia's questions about dreams. Years ago, Bran dreamed regularly of a snake which, with each dream, had crept nearer him, he himself being inextricably bound, heavy as iron, unable to move. Finally, with the snake almost upon him, Bran dared not sleep but, waiting until noon, searched the woods, found an identical snake and killed it, whereupon the dreams ceased. Julian had interpreted this as envy and resentment of his master, the Senator, but, though always grabbing the last word, he admitted that last words are seldom final.

In camp, nothing remained still and something of the expec-tation tainted with unease must have reached the Emperor on his return, he the master of circumstances and ever alert to moods. Cancelling staff festivities to welcome the Empress,

176

renewing an edict against infanticide, issuing a threat against Galilean subversives, he appeared in his office of the High Priest of Jupiter Optimus Maximus and ordered the auguries to be taken. Predictably, they were signally favourable and many grinned knowingly, though an Armenian archer was punished for, in drink, insulting not the Emperor but Jupiter himself. 'Wet dream old ram with bollocks of brass.'

Aurelian, for whatever reasons, professed dissatisfaction and announced that on behalf of Rome and the army he would consult further.

Not far off, up-country, on the further side of a wooded pass, was a temple reputedly founded by Aemilius Paulus, with a once-famous oracle, Sibyl of the Four Emperors, so named because the priestess, two centuries old, had foretold four perishing within One. This had occurred: Emperors Nero, Galba, Otho, Vitellius, all killed within a single year. At this time, however, throughout most of the Empire, oracles were in disrepute for corruption and deceit. Notorious was a temple where Alexandrine machinery transformed water to wine, warm air moved objects without hands, statues glowed red from within, while hydraulic bellows produced music, flames, thunder. Everywhere, imitation Chaldeans patronized the future, alleging kinship between stars and sleepers' guts. And, on a warm mothy night at Optima Fortuna, a masked and horned figure, capering, intoning, had led the villagers to start grunting, singing, then rushing to strip and rut brutally beside the phosphorescent sea, knowing, yet also not knowing, that the shaman was merely the cobbler from over the hills.

Aurelian, nevertheless, in aftermath of treachery or a treachery perhaps secretly manufactured by intriguers who might have included himself, decided, at the fateful turn of the year, to visit the oracle, now renamed the Temple to All the Gods, still advising the occasional pilgrim, a merchant anxious for his fleet, a pretender short of confidence.

Constantius was roused from melancholy by a summons to accompany the Emperor's staff, the order coming not from his immediate superiors but directed from the Imperial Adjutant, delivered by a certain Gavian, handsome youth, no surprise, with blue, somewhat ingratiating eyes under a litter of bright hair and set in silky skin, beardless, perhaps washed too often. He must possess, had possibly earned, court favour, though of indeterminate rank and duties save those which attracted ribaldry. A *palatine* officer. Parasitic.

Gratified by long-awaited attention from on high, Constantius received congratulations, their noisiness admitting envy, even rancour. An important eye was watching him, perhaps with some reminder from Gaius Valerius. Aside from ambition, he was curious about Aurelian's mission. His own religious feelings were more staid than Julian's quicksilver flourishes but were open to the unexpected and unexplained. In Egypt he had seen mysterious tricks ascribed, perhaps correctly, to magic and divination, but vivid as the ever-distant walls and pinnacles hanging above sweltering sands yet eternally vanishing. A man had stood unharmed in fire, another survived five weeks' burial; a stranger accosted him in a bazaar to tell him his age, his name, that he had a brother who enjoyed riches, a sister who would be almost a queen, and that he himself would rule a province. Ghosts were commonplace in the desert and a statue was known to speak, seldom to much effect.

His dream of the City, grey as pumice, beyond the Wall, and of losing his way, must have significance designed either for him or by his own blood. Diomede had once quoted Alexander's mentor, Aristotle of Stagira, a Macedonian: *It is neither easy to despise dreams sent by oracles, nor yet to believe them.* Lucretius had written: *Nature works through bodies unseen.* Life was protean. In Rome he had encountered his friend Quintus Emilian, in a carriage with a small, unknown girl. Quintus had stared at him without recognition, but the girl cried excitedly, 'Look, it's Constantius!' He had seen a dog bound towards a hut absolutely empty, then stop at the threshold, trembling, then beginning a terrified howl, refusing to enter, bright with sweat, eyes dilated in horror.

In childhood, the strange was, as it were, the ordinary: that lost time, seldom recovered, of huge secrets, endlessly broken

178

promises, pain, marvellous mornings and sullen afternoons, the momentum of *tomorrow*, the clear cloud of being, as Julian called it, which Clodia was losing. A small boy, he had walked with Julian by a river. Returning, they found themselves on the opposite bank, though they had crossed no bridge and the water was deep and fast. What had occurred? Little Julian had smiled, then said they had learned to fly. Some held that the earth contained nerves influencing blood, plants and metals, with help from the dead. More believable, after death the spirit became a circle of light visible on the midnight bridge reaching to the shades, though a hero might add his lustre to a star. Julian sometimes spoke of descents to the underworld, sometimes with obscene meaning but more often referring to Mysteries in which initiates seem to die, receive ghostly instruction and visions, are reborn into a secret brotherhood of salvation and knowledge. No very desirable knowledge!

On a windless night guaranteed propitious, some sixty officers assembled on foot, the oracle having to be consulted after dark. A Pannonian general had addressed them, speaking thickly, as if knocking words from a block. 'Inside the temple, say nothing. Nothing at all. Don't offend the priests but avoid their questions. Keep your distance. That's the order.'

No Praetorians were seen, allowing sensations of comradeship. Also, a group so chosen might have excluded Gentlemen of Supplies and scorn-a-penny malcontents.

The march, torch-lit, silent, lasted about an hour. Stationed with unknown high-ups towards the rear, Constantius had not seen the Emperor walking forward with tall Probus. Aurelian would probably not hear, and would certainly not announce, bad news. Whatever the nature of his pledge to the Unconquered Sun, the army had guffawed at his retort to a college of busybody priests: '*I* decide when Mithras was born.' Careworn from his lifetime of labours, he was entitled to divine secrets and goodwill.

Few stars were visible, mists enlarged the heights on either side. All too aware of the seasoned officers he had joined, Constantius felt very young, barely experienced, yet immeasurably older than those he exhorted, punished, taught and, in a manner, treasured.

The Temple was visible from afar, its lights gleaming on all levels with a radiance suffusing the wastes around it. A breeze, scattered as if at a signal, immediately withdrawn, dropped a flake of pine-sap, a suspicion of salt. On surrounding scrub grass, spectral in the false lights, white oxen stood as if carved. Under the pallid arch an old flamen was ready to receive the Emperor, stooping, the intruders seeing eyes tired but shrewd in flesh papyrus thin.

Aurelian, Probus and Maximus were absorbed by a blaze of light falling from lamps of finely wrought bronze. Incense pervaded all, sickly, slightly toxic. The officers were escorted to a high, domed hall, watched mutely by priests sleek in white and yellow robes with tasselled belts, lurking in and out of shadows, faces sleepy with disdain, the slow pout of Asia. Their air of idle well-being forced questions of how in terrain arid and sparsely populated the luxuriant shrine supported itself.

Joined by Gavian, friendly but unspeaking, Constantius looked around. Oracles might be unfashionable, but he could now detect in shrouded side-chapels a number of votaries in soiled garb and ragged shoes grouped before image or ornament, one elderly man staring as if hypnotized at a small, impudent face moulded on a lintel, mumbling words which a priest, ostentatiously inattentive, affected not to hear. Carefully spaced ledges and columns shone with ivory and silver fittings, tortoise- and scallop-shells were ranked on maplewood altars, behind which loomed porphyry inlaid with gold, a clinking metal water-clock, an Indian crucifix. In one blue cell, the inquisitive debarred by a silver grill, lay artificial palm leaves, inscribed with unknown lettering. One wall was splayed with a celestial map woven in green and scarlet silk, depicting the moon hung with emblems of childhood, pale, adroit Mercury the Instructor barely restraining a chortle, naked Venus, red, glaring Mars, Jupiter bearded and clasping a thunderbolt, Saturn worn, hunchbacked, suffering.

Unable to escape Gavian, both flattered and oppressed by the other's flamboyant good looks, Constantius followed him down the vaulted, aromatic building. Colour smarted on wall and casement, writhed up slender pillars, hovered in recesses. Elongated figures painted on a stone screen were sooty and vague. Patches of gloom were conspiratorial between lamps roseate but giving scanty light. At intervals a flute began, solitary, birdlike, then abruptly subsided. The two examined some icons, none very alluring. The three Cretan shepherds adored the infant Jupiter. Another child lay smiling under the sign of the Virgin. Orpheus, Good Shepherd, tamed striped tigers with his lyre. A cross suggested Chrestus the latecomer. From Mount Oeta Hercules ascended to heaven and, in a swollen river, carried the young Bacchus to safety. A man was flung from a ship, a peacock preened its golds, blues, purples, perhaps denoting death overcome. The fane's alternate light and darkness must echo eternal conflict: Cybele against Apollo, West against East, Life against Death.

In a mosaic surmounted by golden candles a naked youth, haloed, holding a cross-shaped hammer, rode the sky in a chariot, scattering storm-clouds, doves and lilies streaming behind him.

The young officers, bored, uncertain, suspicious of the lurking, barely visible priests and thickening fumes, were startled back to duty when tall doors opened as though from a kick, a scared face blinking above a saffron robe, then, pushing it aside, the Emperor strode down the crowded aisle, his retinue parting in front of him, starlings before a hawk. Impatient to be off, he acknowledged none, seemed to be ripping apart the dense, heated air in his need for the night air, not pausing for the ritual gulp of water drawn from a consecrated brook. Striding after him, Probus signed for all to follow.

The priests or their masters must have taken umbrage. Regaining the pass the imperial delegation suffered first a concourse of bats flapping from the blackness like angry guardians of the infernal, then thunder cracking the cliffs, blocks falling with titanic din, great men dodging for safety while hail and lightning tore down the night, leaving them in a frail, chilled dawn, the landscape withered and ashen.

At the camp entrance Gavian clasped Constantius's arm. 'I trust you.' The words, the blue eyes and fluent smile contained some invitation, almost a plea, then, turning quickly away, he was gone.

Though visited by no dream or apparition, Constantius's sleep was troubled. The Emperor's graceless departure, the temple wavering between shrewdness and enchantment, the storm, then Gavian's farewell, perhaps a mere courtly gesture, perhaps a spasm of lust, perhaps something more serious. A well-favoured youth can turn wolfish and his love dangerous. Shy, dainty-handed Ammas was more tempting, though forbidden.

Though not a virgin, Constantius had bedded few girls. One, a Roman cousin, dark-haired, olive-skinned, grave, he was expected to wed and would probably do so. The family Name demanded rehabilitation, which would scarcely come from Julian, certainly not from dreamy Clodia, despite that mis-applied Egyptian prophecy, and moreover he wanted a son.

Secrets do not long remain secret. Some concealed witness is always taking notes, preparing evidence corrupt, distorted, misheard or honest, on which historians hinge their master-pieces, finalizing truth for the credulous. Fate can be nudged by long ears in corridors, suspicions murmured in ante-rooms, barely fledged rumours. By the next nightfall the army knew the words uttered by All the Gods: *Nineteen careless heads melt with the Sun*. Delivered pat as grocery, the Sun could be only a compli-ment to Aurelian notwithstanding his ill-tempered response, but *nineteen* was obscure and men of that age at once felt uneasy. All implications were sinister. Wiseacres, barrack-room lawyers, amateur soothsayers and rich know-alls recalled old scrolls, runes, traditions; they argued, quarrelled and decided nothing. Nineteen was neither sacred nor inauspicious. Doubt-less the oracle had been bribed to confuse the Romans by the Great King, abject on a throne too large for him, bleating for help from a languid heaven.

More realistically, a majority finally calculated that the Emperor, beloved of the Unconquered Sun, would require but nineteen days to crush the Persians.

There followed a rumour of the private crucifixion of Eros, henceforward unmentionable, erased from history, and, to extinguish all whispers, a trumpet alarum from Imperial Headquarters preceded an Order of the Day. The Emperor was formally to review the army, and at once the blood quickened, as, from the wide fan of tents, portable cabins and wagons, couriers sped towards Milan, Ravenna, Strasbourg, Vienne, Rome.

Outside the encampment, a natural amphitheatre was formed by an immense grass crescent stretched beneath steep slopes, pine-clustered, the higher reaches jagged and bald. Crocus already gleamed yellow and white amongst rocks veined with silver and the scraggy clusters of ilex. An empty platform hung with flat purples dominated like a grim scaffold, the afternoon sky florid, roughened, small black clouds crusting the horizon untouched by the orange sun. Behind the dais in gay shawls and headpieces the Empress and her retinue were flimsy and birdlike against the metallic Praetorians encircling them.

Black lambs had been sacrified to the Sun, the imperial standard, the *Labarum*, flapped and honked in periodic gusts of wind.

Thousands paraded, in long, strict blocks trained on the purple dais, arms meticulously polished, a monotonous sheet of light, motionless, until, finely timed at the turn between excitement and fatigue, trumpets again rang out, their echoes bouncing between the slanted rocks, falling amongst high trees and now, escorted by more Praetorians, corsleted, sheathed in iron, plumed, striding, amid utter stillness, Aurelian ascended his rostrum. Some of those beneath him would have marched in the Triumph, men drawn from Caledonia and Africa, Lusitania and Syria, bound by oath, to Rome, to the *Labarum*, yet also to their particular general, himself so often storing up treasonable promises and donatives. Sententious fellows might at this thrilling instant remember what an old playwright had dared repeat to Julius Caesar in supreme power: *He must fear the many, whom so many fear*. A few might still ponder the fate of Hencoop Eros, 'The One', hated, friendless, mincing towards a dreadful end. In some minds must be that puzzling Nineteen. Most, however, would be conscious of little save pounding blood, the inescapable gaze above them, aura of power, the spoils of Persia waiting to be grabbed even by those with hands sliced off in battle. A rapt hunger for lights beyond the world.

Arms stiff at his side, disdaining theatrical gestures and rhetoric, Aurelian Augustus, crested like some antique, even supernatural Trojan, was uncompromising, stark against the blood-red sky, his voice coarse, even ugly, distinct, reaching even the furthest, neither conversational nor hectoring but stern, then indignant, addressing children unloved but part of a Name.

'Men, we have marched from one end of the Empire to another. We have never ceased. Invasion, rebellion, hardship, sickness, we have overcome all, aided by the spirit of our beloved commander, the Augustus Claudius Gothicus.'

Thousands would not have understood the laborious, unschooled Latin which hidden clerks were no doubt assiduously correcting, but centuries of authority spoke through him, no one-legged cripple anxious to lead the dance, no Chief Mason, but Alexander reborn, a flash from whose eyes would scorch the barbarian world. Only the front ranks could see that those eyes were morose, almost dull, as if still grudging time wasted at the oracle. Within his broad, massed frame, barely withheld, vulnerable to the fickleness and deceit of trusted followers, was the ferocity that had destroyed Eros, hurled armies forward, raised the Wall, decreed the Great Measure against the entrenched, the purblind, the interested parties. Behind, the vast, cold sun lay still, as if at his order.

His voice lowered. Even the most ignorant could recognize a threat.

'I have uncovered conspiracy. Treachery against myself, against you ... Empire's defenders ... no mercy....'

184

He named no traitor, the threat was both vague and deadly. He ended in a dangerous silence, the suspense in which a regime may collapse. At last a stir rippled over the gleaming, outspread concourse, first hesitant, then gaining pace, until surging upwards in acclamation, shields clanging against knee-plates: '*Io Augustus! Io Lucius Domitius Aurelian!*'

XVIII

Spring had painful birth from sleet and iced winds sweeping from the sea over Forum Trajani while men fretted at inaction, staring at horizons broken by ravenous waves. Earth, nevertheless, fulfilled her contracts more readily than mortals, and now a warm sun gleamed on eucalyptus and palm, the breeze splayed with blossom. Along wide, straight avenues and marble arcades, orange trees displayed tinted, cloudy fragrance, tall geraniums showed tight, whitish buds, tiny, clasped hands thrusting from the green.

Trajan's military outpost had absorbed two crumbling fishing villages dedicated to a forgotten goddess born of sea and mountain though, a little beyond, hyenas roamed wastes polluted when forests were ravaged for ships of Phoenicia and Carthage, Corinth and Rome. A cult of Thracian horse-priests was said to survive in still-wooded mountains, with bloody Mysteries forbidden mention, save that initiates were dispatched to kill in neighbouring lands, filling small jars with tallow melted down from victims: this made candles, the light of which rendered murderers invisible. An aboriginal tribe survived, unscrupulous fighters federated by Rome to defend the coastal road to Salonika, financed by what the Officialdom termed wages and the local ruler boasted was tribute.

Ramparts strengthened by crenellated towers and deep subbasements enclosed the town, Jupiter Victorious replaced Baal the Lord, established by a Phoenician colony in times no longer recorded, though, beneath the new imperious temple with its roofed colonnades and Olympian portico, were still sold emblems of moon goddesses and garden trees encircled with snakes, figurines of the rising and setting sun holding torches in

186

darkened grottoes or catacombs. Here, the chief priest was paid well to avert the end of the world, a bonus being added each fifth year. An arch, honouring Trajan, overshadowed all surrounding houses and, implying the passage for a giant, topped an artificial Capitol with zigzagged terraces raised above a forum always teeming with water-carriers, beggars hiccupping from hunger or feigned hunger, cookshops, stalls of figs, gourds, lemons, ruddy beets, hard-boiled eggs painted blue and yellow, Parthian torques, Cretan jars, brought from the harbour on pack-mules. Parasols all colours twirled, Alexandrian fashion, red fly-swatters fluttering in the new light.

Small fluted obelisks darkened the courts of Venus-Astarte, east and west fused within a goddess more voluptuous than befitted the mother of austere Aeneas. Nearby, enclosed by wispy tamarisk, sweetly toxic terebinth, wide-leafed, not yet displaying full blue, and tall, trellised vines, stood Isis, cut from fresh marble clutching a winnowing fan, a sacred knot between her breasts and glowing with the sunset pink of flamingos. The eye turned upwards to Jupiter on his column, to Juno Regina, Minerva, to a winged head with onyx eyes radiant against the newly washed sky. In a garden of silvery fountains, asphodel and blurred yellow bushes, the air resin-drenched, stood a stone tableau of a haloed child lying under a pine guarded by centaurs and goats. The circular House of Vesta reproduced the one in Rome. Window-ledges sprouted lavender, hyssop, sunflower, and beneath, citizens stepped gracefully through the transparent sheen of colour. A block of adamantine, dedicated to Mithras, assembled in gold the seven stages of illumination, the adoption by the god: Raven, Bride, Lion, Soldier, Persian, Sun Runner, Father. Children were always gaping at them, imagining toys forever beyond reach, though women ostentatiously averted their heads, indignant at privileges permitted only to men, who would exchange mysterious finger signs and murmur such male nonsense as 'I strive to become myself'. Galileans, despite their forbidding cross, at least gave women their due, especially wealthy ones.

In the central forum, mounted on a stone platform, was the

alabaster tomb of a Roman general, the lower reaches swamped with graffiti, *Titus's bottom reserved for Marcus. My wife's dying, I get richer by the hour*, the tomb itself moulded with apples, pomegranates and listless captives chained to each other. Before the trim Basilica boys played 'It', trod out mazes, capered in and out of sunlight, captious as minnows. Overlooking them was a library of white brick, gift of the Emperor Gallienus, and, above the heavy doors, glittered a dedication to Aeneas: *Each man seeks his pleasure; Destiny and the City appeal to him to seek further, even at the cost of pain.* By it, transported from Veii, with features diseased by age, was a statue, allegedly of Hercules, backed by a complex of baths, a stadium, and the foundations of a theatre.

Trajan had sited well. The broad, curved harbour, with moles and lighthouse, now served substantial trade. Ships, in convoy against pirates, brought Bilbilis iron, Cordovan copper, horses from Epirus, Arabian cassia, Lebanese spices, Bahrain pearls, Indian teak, ebony, sapphires, an octopus for the Emperor's table. Quays reserved for export were piled with Arretine jars and dried figs, though seldom with much else. Several effigies, youthful and naked, were so aligned to the sea that, in changing lights, they seemed to be strolling on water.

In such honeycomb air, in streets paved, planned and symmetrical, distant Mother Rome could be envisaged as a murderous confusion of speculators, rentiers, fraudulent contractors, subletting landlords with thieving agents and cutthroat bouncers, yet all scurrying beneath the wide, lidless eye of the Officialdom and by night crouching behind their Wall like scared virgins. Yet, like a bland mountain-locked lake, like Rome, in this fair haven a riot could erupt without detectable cause or purpose, and as swiftly subsiding. Meanwhile, on quays, in markets, in public squares and garden cemeteries, voices chirped and chattered:

'Armenian girls now . . . once married, have their mouths blocked by a cloth. To preserve peace in the home.'

'My wife could learn something from that. As for Armenians, I know what you don't. When their king visited our

Nero, a star moved ahead of him, lighting his way to Rome. A stuck-up brat.'

'Both of you have your minds on inessentials. Mouths, star. Absurd! No, it's not her mouth my girl keeps covered, alas, but something more inviting. My lot's a sad one.'

'I hear complaints, I smell rubbish.'

The group, laughing, parted to make way for foreign soldiers sauntering to quarters improvised in the unfinished theatre. The town for these weeks was overcrowded with the military, though Mucapor had led a force to Salonika and two legions had advanced with Probus to Heraclea Pontica to join those landed from Brundisium. The Emperor was said to have left with the Praetorian, Carus, to hold conferences at a place still undisclosed. Officers left behind exchanged news or would-be news, agreeing that Aurelian had, before the crucifixion, watched Eros flayed alive, screaming for mercy, promising to betray a batch of conspirators, confessing that he had cast the Emperor's horoscope, a criminal action.

Told that they would be stationed here for several weeks, the recruits were happy. Most, hitherto so fearing towns, rejoiced at Forum Trajani, and were easy prey to wheedling street-pedlars, plaited whores in brilliant sandals, fancy-boys awash with perfume. They stood astounded by lofty pillars and clean terraces, gods floating in air fresh as Carpathian snow or Rhine cascades. Sometimes the sky was white with heat-haze, promising radiance, soon packed with unsullied blue, rhyming with the light, provident sea tumbling on sands of extravagant yellow.

Nevertheless, the campaign could not be forgotten despite obliging flesh and cheap liquor. Arms were delivered daily. Tokens of blood. Captured Gothic mail for the cavalry, Frankish throwing-axes, Sarmatian tunics strewn with iron plates, piles of infantry jerkins of leather or thick linen, javelins mostly too light, the know-all veterans declared, some actually wooden, German style. Too many helmets had not yet arrived. Spirit, though, as Probus always insisted, outweighed trappings and here, in great Trajan's city, men told each other that they

189

too possessed a Trajan, invincible offspring of the Unconquered Sun. They did not need the auxiliaries, mostly light cavalry, Parthian deserters released from island gaols or the quarries, despised by regulars, suspected of loyalties to the Great King, apt to provoke fights in street and tavern.

For the local regulars, Constantius felt misgivings. They were nominally quartered in barracks, but many had, against regulations, married, acquiring farms, shops and market-stalls, becoming only part-time soldiers, living at home with their families, their officers shrugging aside queries about their availability in emergency. When he gained his staff appointment, Constantius determined on changes.

His depression, begun by Gaius Valerius's departure had not dispersed. The snake had moved closer, judges deliberated, their eyes forbidding. From that one friend no word came. Confident that he would soon reappear, Constantius bore no grudge but could not join in general elation.

Occasionally he considered the Emperor's visit to All the Gods, and the oracle's message, cryptic in the way of all oracles. Aurelian had probably set no great store by it, and the army had unanimously interpreted Nineteen as the love-bites on the Empress's bottom. The Sun was most surely the Emperor himself, which as yet explained nothing. Oracular prophecies usually contained some speck of truth.

Two months had passed since then, weeks of marches and debouches, through small towns with acclamations, addresses of welcome, bags of small coin for the Emperor. Throughout the Empire the Imperial Peace held. From dank forest, overcrowded plain, from fen and river-mouth no threat was uttered, no pledge revoked. The Great King himself had moved no army, his ambassadors, gathered on the frontier, murmuring soothing diplomatic phrases about their sacred Lord willing to surrender this world, for, as all knew, he possessed several more.

Constantius, a professional, strengthened his Gulls. More sword drill was needed, the arm should be lower, stabbing not forward but upward. One lad was borrowing too much, another

190

too obsessed with women. Unspoken intimacy bound him to these exuberant, fatalistic youngsters trailing across the world at the behest of those indifferent to their concerns. They would learn that fear is a wise companion, enabling you to overcome all, even itself. That no battle is predictable, not all victories are conquests, that men in struggle will endure, not so much from bravery than insensate delirium or fear of taunts from others. The inevitable never happens. Battle itself was but one means of victory, often the worst. Julian would have smiled at a conscript's story of an Armorican prophet who saved his village by persuading Scanian raiders that it was invisible save to those whom the gods had doomed.

At swimming and weaponry, on the march, round pine fires at nightfall, he knew them better than he had the slaves at home. Mountain boys had abrupt changes of mood, sullen depression succeeded by manic excitement, aggressive or affectionate. Gauls had queer unease about crossing boundaries, even a mere stile. Teutons despised Italians, jeering clumsily at their rapid gestures and careful hair-styles, yet proudly, ferociously, declared themselves Roman. Brother officers would be suspicious of his private knowledge. Of Alaric, proud of knees scarred by a wild pig; Klos, with ears which, the rest clamoured, could be used for target practice; Quint, with feet too small for army requirements, though the recruiting sergeants overlooked this shortcoming, desperate for anyone with or without feet – and, compensating, owning a nose large enough to carry an apple while he charged. And, in his own tent, shy, over-devoted, Ammas, volunteering for the most menial jobs, eager to follow, though Manilius shook his head. 'A dog-type, sir. Worshipping any master. I'm keeping an eye on him. He may come to fear it.'

Constantius was happiest away from the mess. In the army, all depended on each other, for an officer, an emperor, the least detail vital when battle began: an unjust punishment, thoughtless curse, an unaffected smile might, in turmoil, earn death or rescue. Manilius knew this well, reporting who wanted a girl, who a boy, who would settle for an indecent picture. When far from towns, Manilius encouraged them to masturbate only in groups, honouring a god, fostering cohesion. Mind itself was perhaps the outcome of groups.

From Constantius they received simple Latin, a certain strategic grasp, an inkling of Rome's story. He was a court of appeal against the stickler Manilius, he represented the godlike Emperor. Their demeanours were also a language needing interpretation, liable to gross error and in which consistency was not to be expected. Churlishness might conceal an appetite homicidal or inarticulately gentle, resentment an inordinate bewilderment, mute obedience a desire to argue. Tears could flow from delight. The language of animals. The artful, the shrewd, the timid, all were forced to renounce some bit of themselves on behalf of the group. The Roman way, though they would never be wholly Roman. The Rome of exhortation and oaths was a dying magnificence attached to the towering Wall, with a future, as Gaius Valerius liked to insist, lying elsewhere. They would remain hired, often less than slaves. Some would desert to become thieves, drunkards, brothel-birds. Many would die, a few die well. This they did know: suspicions, antagonisms and jealousies were slowly crumbling, each knowing that against Persia he must trust the fellow next to him. Knowing too of field punishments pitilessly enforced by a ruler to whom failure was treason. They shivered at a villager condemned for pilfering army stores, led to execution preceded by a bell, warning all against his bad aura, a harsh voice which sounded as though the world was cracking. Reports of the Hencoop's death awed some of them to sickness.

At Forum Trajani they were entranced by the graceful dodges and feints, the adroit, curved sticks and sudden flashes of the ball-game players, gay parasols flowering everywhere. Baying like hounds they rushed towards water, a horse-pond or the sliding waves, exclaimed delightedly at early mist through which columns, globes and statues seemed daily reborn from the thin, golden sun, then quickened by rich light striding over the sea. Hitherto, mist had been a threat of malaria, ambush, or worse, a looming shape, without mouth or eyes yet poised inexorably to fulfil a curse.

Had they been more numerous he would have been suspect to the inescapable Gentlemen of Supplies, alert for conspiracy and corruption. Doubtless in the mess they thought him in brute need for love or power, but would thereby respect him more.

At Cetenzi one lad had suddenly died, killed, several muttered, by somebody's violent dream. He had been disliked, but his corpse, chilling, clammy, demanded full rites, his companions pouring cock's blood to strengthen his spirit and soften its anger, then carrying blossoms, listening to a gruff laudation from Manilius. Afterwards, tearful, they carved his name on a tree, to endure until the world's end.

Gavian had made several visits, each time remaining longer, bringing superior wine and news that had not yet reached the mess. Officers had arrived from Trier, the Empress had embarked for Alexandria, while the Emperor, after his conference, had a slight fever, surely from the stupidity of auxiliary leaders. Probus had departed, on duties undisclosed.

Some covert purpose must underlie these movements, about which Gavian did not risk speculating. Constantius's welcome was cool. The greenish bracelets, luminous eyes, the inviting manner and high-nosed ease suggested the adroit, ambitious court toady rather than a valiant survivor of battles. The pale skin had been too long indoors, the teeth too undamaged, the hands more readily imagined caressing a Persian cushion or wooing a sunflower than wielding a sword. His tread, like his stare, was feline; those eyes were older than his elegant face. Such personages had sometimes gained, rather than won, the throne itself, only to regret it, gibbering for mercy at the end. When frontiers topple, such as Gavian auctioned their commissions. Yet, unmistakably, this unexplained acquaintance enhanced Constantius's prestige. He remained a coming man, to become more than an Eternal Second.

Did friendship need explanation? Almost certainly, yes.

Gavian appeared unaware of Constantius's lack of small talk and smart wit. He smiled, gossiped, sipped his own wine with courteous restraint, smiled again, departing always with an unspoken hint that he had some preoccupation not yet to be disclosed. Once, trapped by his long need to confide, to cry out, Constantius was tempted to question him about the Emperor, touched by that courtier charm which suggested that the other had been treasuring the delights of their last meeting though, douched by Constantius's reserve, these must have been few. But caution and Gavian's silky prattle intervened. 'You see, my Constantius . . . with mating time rife amongst the soldiery . . . beasts of burden, you may say. . . .'

Beneath, he must have some design, perhaps planted from above. His negligent tone was probably assumed. Swiftly chilled, again the meticulous officer, Constantius warned himself against revealing his misgivings of the last months. He had always avoided candour, with associates and with slaves, too often treated not as spies but as furniture. For Julian, of course, almost all were slaves, especially the rich and fashionable.

Julian's opinion of this purring Gavian was easily imaginable. He would have spoken affably, announced himself bankrupt, concealed his purses. I am sufficiently superstitious, Julian had said, to trust only myself, a very trustworthy fellow indeed.

At once Constantius breathed freer, convinced that he had escaped danger.

On some other matters, common views were forbidding, or worse. Constantius pondered them. Earthly misbehaviour could provoke convulsions within sky and earth. The vicious tantrums of Gallienus were followed by earthquake in Pisa, then by fire speeding from peak to peak of the Julian Alps. The thunderstorm after Aurelian's return from the oracle had been fiercely argued. A god's rebuke to the priests? A warning to the army? A threat to Persia? Or . . . but here voices ceased as if at a signal, and faces glanced uneasily over shoulders. Within the temple itself an officer, renowned for lack of feeling, had seen a candle-flame turn black yet continue to give light.

Constantius brooded over Aurelian. For too many weeks he had been remote and brusque, few but Mucapor, Probus and Carus being allowed regular access. Some captured Aegean pirates had been drowned without question, as were certain

194

Galilean dissidents. Order, the Emperor reiterated through his generals, preserved the Empire, civilization itself, the many deserved more than the few. Remember the horrors of those decades before Claudius Gothicus, bloodshed caused by protest, spurious claims, too many demands from those who produced too little. Also, he probably added, too many emperors.

Aurelian's passions worsened during the shortages and hardships before spring. They were witnessed by Constantius himself in an old sea fortress, briefly imperial headquarters. From an aperture he had gazed into a square empty save for a sentry. Unescorted, the Emperor had entered through a narrow arch. The young sentry instantly displeased him and he spoke to him angrily. The soldier, a Vandal, understanding nothing, shook his head helplessly, then, in terror, dropped his spear. The clatter on the stone was hideous, the sequel more so: Aurelian's infuriated buffet, then another, the soldier buckling at his feet, a rasping shout, hurrying figures, the sentry hauled away barely conscious for the flogging under which he died. The incident brought to mind a saying ascribed to Julius Caesar himself, that recollection of cruelty is a wretched crutch for old age. Such death availed the Empire nothing.

The continuing absence of Probus was now disturbing. Believing like Clodius Ammianus in the virtues of the spade, knowing that, even in peacetime an army was rebelliously inclined unless at useful work, Probus was ever-trusted by the Emperor, a restraint upon impatience and wrath.

Constantius brooded, waited some inadvertent word from Gavian that might reassure him about the Emperor. Aurelian was his leader, his guardian to whom he annually renewed loyalty. Breaking an oath, Father would say, loosened whatever bound heaven to earth, and these beliefs rose from the shades to confront him. Without Aurelian, prospects were unthinkable, a rag-picker's vision. Beyond frontiers the interminable forests bristled with tribes living in dreams of plunder, faces turned westwards, averted from eastern steppe and desert where implacable, slit-eyed riders waited, barely in check. Aurelian had for years fought disintegration, dispersals of spirit, collisions of peoples bloodshot with memories, fragmented, a goddess demanding human throats. Another time of troubles would link Rome with Carthage, once teeming and opulent, then utterly finished; trade, colonies, navies gone, a name without a dwelling, a desert. Nightmare days had succeeded Marius's defeat of the Germans at Aquae Sextiae: officers had lost control and the victors had rushed headlong to scalp women captives who, witless with terror, began stabbing each other, to demented applause from men calling themselves Roman.

Constantius, alone for too long, thought of Clodia, gravely picking up aged or dead plants uprooted by gardeners. These she planted in a small unwanted plot, hurrying out in the morning hoping for a bud, a fresh leaf, a pink blossom out of season.

From talk in the mess he understood that 'the Eros plot' was not finally stilled. More names might be denounced. Gavian, for once careless, remarked that something remained to be unravelled. No one seemed to have actually witnessed the execution. Always, among Praetorians, within Imperial Staff and Privy Council, existed discontented potential, criminal ambitions. The narcotics of power, the beckon of the Diadem poisoned at the rim.

Eros had accumulated wealth: with it he may have meshed some now striving to destroy evidence and escape doom.

The mass of the army was seemingly content, in complicity only in protest at tavern prices or the ill-managed auction of a girl. But officers were more secretive. In the mess, Constantius sensed glances exchanged behind him; voices lowered at his approach. Yet perhaps Gavian had indeed increased his stature, perhaps he was mistaken. Perhaps, perhaps. Then with warmer days his spirit lightened, until blackly checked when he overheard a single word, *Galba*, murmured amongst a group of officers who, when he entered, instantly broke up, three others, grinning over a wine-jar, already inviting him to join them. But they appeared over-cordial and faintly awkward, and he soon left them, smiling pleasantly but inwardly suspicious. Were they so innocuous? *Galba*. An elderly general who had over-thrown Nero and seized the throne. A dark name, a secret pass-word or no more than a word misheard. Certainly insufficient to report to superiors, even to Gavian.

The more nagging such worries, the sterner his need for routine duties. Gulls wondered at his unwonted impatience, his strained face, and joked lewdly about 'officers' habits'. Ammas's deft attempts to please were wasted. Manilius said nothing but accompanied him uninvited whenever possible.

On his next visit Gavian spoke with trained unconcern about Persian affairs. The Great King was affronted by a northern revolt, and had impaled a leading satrap. As they sat in evening sunlight, little fires and cooking-pots around them, he added in the same indifferent tone that 'Docles', Gaius Valerius, had been made assistant governor of distant Maesia.

So their friendship had been noted at court.

'Gavian . . . is that promotion? Or a setback?'

'You speak of dimensions about which you and I can only guess. I myself venture to believe we shall hear more of him.'

Useless to demand more; to mention 'Galba' would be risky. He too affected unconcern, and mentioned that, at the last oath-taking, a bemused Isaurian, instead of pledging himself to Aurelian and denouncing Persia, found in terror that, mis-understanding the interpreter, he had sworn unbreakable allegiance to the Great King.

Good humouredly they swapped tales of interpreters, so powerful in a polyglot army, but seldom reliable. They were suspected of pronouncing the first words that came into their heads, and in battle panic yelling 'Retreat' when the general ordered 'Charge'. Gavian, more interesting than usual, cited several treaties, bloodily short-lived, through the malice, ignor-ance or clumsiness of interpreters. In one such treaty, 'Five years friendship' which, for Romans, had literal meaning, was, for the enemy, slang for 'a false promise' and was treated accordingly.

They laughed again, and, as though under cover of their mirth Gavian asked a question which Constantius had often pondered to himself. A coincidence, but coincidences could be less accidental than they seemed. Here, quite possibly, was a trap.

'When the oath is taken, is it to your particular general, or to the Emperor?'

'Cannot both be one?'

'That of course can happen.'

His smile gave away nothing. He was a well-mannered young man, relaxed after the day's fatigues, enjoying wine in simple light while the camp hummed with good cheer, the frogs croaked and the cicadas clicked.

'Yet, Constantius . . . in a situation, let us imagine, of the last months of the late Gallienus, general, Emperor of Rome, where would your own pledge go?'

No laughter in that. Gallienus had been too recent a disaster for an officer to find anything but an honesty which hurt.

'Gavian . . . I suppose we must admit . . . without Gallienus's destruction, no Claudius or Aurelian would have worn the purple and recovered the Empire.'

'Well spoken! Killing a madman is not murder but duty. Like disposing of a lunatic bull. We both know that we swear obedience, let us say fealty, to the Emperor. But . . .' – even his immaculate unconcern wavered, he paused, involuntarily glancing about him – '. . . there is a further oath. To Rome. Senate and People. The Idea.'

Roma Aeterna, behind all life, as behind any emperor was the ideal Emperor, perfection of society, and behind that sun now in its last gleams across the sea was Helios-Apollo-Mithras, the Unconquered Sun.

Gavian yawned slightly, appeared satisfied, gossiped a little, departed. Something was afoot. Could but the Emperor now show himself, a guest amongst his followers, doubts and puzzles would disperse.

Spring, however, glided forward like a galley perfectly launched. The sun climbed, Forum Trajani rejoiced in glittering leaves, calm seas, the arrival of trade argosies. Leafy rites celebrated the resurrection of Attis, of Persephone, and many

198

marriages. Hope was born of fresh light. No statue of Fortune was reversed by an earthquake, no Mars left facing the wrong way.

Constantius felt little part of it, convinced he had signed some pact with Gavian, accepted an unwanted mortgage on his prospects, with benefits unspecified and probably empty. But, in answer, an order arrived. Again selected for higher purposes, he was to lead his battalion forward to Byzantium, where the Emperor waited.

XIX

During critical events leading personages are often not present: actors deeming themselves not yet called, leaving the stage for supers and hangers-on; lords failing the desperate pretender; a god missing his appointment. Others resemble the crows collecting round aged, proscribed Cicero a few hours before his execution.

At Byzantium, small and undistinguished though on shores useful for traffic with Asia, few notables were discerned. Probus was at Heraclea Pontica teaching Scythian and Alan auxiliaries some notion of Roman discipline; Saturninus was superintending naval transports to cross the straits; Maximius arranging supplies at Caenophrium; while the Praetorian Prefect, reporting illness, remained at Forum Trajani. Mucapor, alone of Aurelian's intimates, remained at court, now established in a small sea-girt barracks, the Emperor unseen, visiting no troops, but apparently tireless, punishing, rewarding, releasing couriers to all parts of the Empire.

Predictably Gavian had already arrived, soon making himself agreeable to the higher ranks of the Gulls, always pleasant, with the right word, the correct salutation, the exact degree of smile, natural to one always fresh from some imperial function with flattering hints and amiable half-promises, a graduate from that closed world of secret assemblies, whispers in corridors, ears alert behind pillars. Glad to welcome Constantius, he implied that he had energetically supported what must surely be his friend's deserved promotion, and Constantius could not deny him some gratitude. Here, the chances of encountering Aurelian might be considerable, his flair for obedience be acknowledged, his good record scrutinized.

Summer sun, glaring at noon, lit early mornings with soft lights rippling over ilex and thyme, swooping in patches of yellow through clouds high above brilliant water. To Clodia he described the twisted pallor of asphodel, gay tinge of apricot, sudden spurts of grass, the sea breezes streaming from distant lands.

Busy, more content, he was then horribly dismayed by a word from Gavian delivered urgently, though after some hesitation: 'Constantius, you are in danger.' He spoke rapidly but fluently, as though reading aloud. Eros the Hencoop, though dead, was indeed not extinguished. Papers had been discovered, perhaps planted, written in his own hand, perhaps in panic at threatened exposure or improvised after arrest in a frantic attempt to shift accusations elsewhere. Chiefly they listed officials, commanders, 'Friends of Caesar', palace attendants, postal and revenue underlings whom Eros recommended should be secretly examined for purging. Or – even Gavian, smooth and experienced, seemed to falter – Eros, in a last unavailing complicity, had written the names at the Emperor's dictation, Aurelian's own script being crude, even perfunctory. 'The One' might have been the many.

The summer evening turned terrible. Dry throated, Constantius heard many names which he was too shaken to acknowledge, until, at last breaking through, there sounded *Probus, Saturninus, Carus*. . . .

Probus, unbelievable, a false plot. But Gavian was still speaking, tensed, blue eyes stricken or artful. 'I am on that list, and some very great names . . . most of the generals. So, Constantius, are you. You had an associate considered, let me put it so, undesirable. We need not name him. At Maesia he may be safe, may yet be of service. Meanwhile we must look to ourselves.'

'But the Emperor?'

The reply was a whisper, low but with a player's distinctness: 'He's sick. Very sick.'

In normal tones, Gavian explained that from prolonged overwork, and perhaps as a threat against the presumptions of power, the gods had afflicted Aurelian with delirium. To safeguard his life and authority, restore his senses, he must, if necessary by force, be delivered to doctors who would insist on his retirement to Baiae or Naples, for a short holiday with the Empress, freed from the toils and hazards of campaigning. The excellent Probus was riding with all speed to join Mucapor at the Emperor's side, scornful of that list of black forgeries and ready to borrow the chief command until the gods relented.

This was plausible, explaining the Emperor's impolitic withdrawals and savage outbursts.

'You are one of the younger men, Constantius, respected by the Emperor, with a future, but like many of us, unjustly accused by a known traitor. Trusted officers are now asking you to support Probus, and join them in consultation, on behalf of the Empire. Like myself, you will have to take an oath of secrecy. That you are known as a keeper of oaths stands in your favour.'

Henceforward, days and nights were distorted. Details magnified: a line of light glittering along a sword, a trooper's hesitation at an order, the theft of arrows, all might have sinister significance. Angles of the day became strategic, time quickened, slowed, in nervy convulsions. Mind and dream swayed between doubts of opposing, or seeming to oppose, Aurelian, and belief in Probus, respected, even loved throughout the legions. How many such officers were implicated, he could not know. He saw them moving as usual, yet at times felt himself drugged, sensing them as brutal enemies, immoderate friends, conspiracy enveloping all.

Of his own men, Manilius's strong, weathered face showed no change, but the rest he fancied, perhaps erroneously, were obeying less promptly, averting their eyes. Even Ammas was sometimes listless, as if scared, sometimes over-eager in devotion, perhaps comforted by Mithras.

Already the consultation was behind him, though he remained fixed within it as in a web. Officers had sat in an oval headed by a Praetorian, none of them save Gavian known to him. An oath of secrecy had been pledged, another to the

202

Emperor. Each man had saluted him, enfolding him in the design – even to himself he could only name it with a word commonplace, neutral. The Praetorian spoke with a softness at odds with his heavy accent and hamlike face. In the coming days he, respected Constantius, whom Majesty gladly honoured, need lift no finger. Only his goodwill was needed, for Probus's stewardship, goodwill, favour – even, the Praetorian seemed to add, his assent. On recovery, Aurelian would hasten to thank him. He need only watch and wait, whatever the orders for the rest of them. All rose at his departure and, accompanying him, Gavian kissed him on the mouth.

Now, awaiting Probus, he brooded over Roman lessons, Roman fables. The Senator had liked speaking of Hercules, tempted to make himself tyrant, but choosing to labour for the public good. Hercules, rebelling against Jupiter his father, then resigning himself to the divine will. At his death the earth had shuddered.

In a lonely forest we can at once be with a god, the sum of existence. A rowdy camp, where commands were incessantly cried, weapons sharpened, wheels and field weapons oiled, horses exercised, groups set wheeling, dividing, scattering, re-forming almost beyond their limit, fostered fear rather than devotion. Again, the thought of Clodia worried him and he ceased to write.

Spring had brought ambiguous gifts, yet it was the healing time. He missed not Father's fussy gravity, not Julian's slanted, sceptical grin, but the calm assurance of Gaius Valerius.

Nothing was heard of Probus, but at last a staff officer brought orders. The Emperor, in whatever health, had repaired to Caenophrium, whither Constantius was to follow with a detachment of Gulls.

'You can select your own men. You will be required for nominal guard duties. Don't choose full-blooded singers and jokers. Majesty's in need of rest.'

Excellent. Manilius must go, of course, and all his trusties, the young barbarians he was welding into a family. And Ammas. The expedition, small but consequential, would cure the youngsters' moods. They would all stand together in precious quality, a brotherhood on watch for the suffering hero, saviour of the West.

On their last night, however, Constantius himself awoke breathless, choking as though the air had dwindled in a deceiving season, poisoned by vermin bloated in its own filth, though the morning resumed its simple blue, innocent white, the sea wind clean. Caenophrium was reached without incident, a ramshackle village straggling under gashed, tawny hills, almost all its trees ravaged. The Emperor lay in a turreted mansion built by long-ago Athenians surrounded by walls and courtyards, officered by a few Praetorians.

Manilius and the others, glad of the change of routine, settled cheerfully in comfortable quarters. Ammas, alarmed by Constantius's bad night, was reassured by his master's quiet reference to a dream. For Ammas, dreams, the night, were more natural than the day. Sickness, pain, destruction, all derived from daylight in which unknowable figures governed, punished, made incomprehensible plans. In dreams, all were equal, animals spoke, gods embraced mortals.

Constantius at once realized, in relief tempered by renewed unease, that whatever his condition, the Emperor was refusing to acknowledge anything but duty. He had outfought all enemies, would fiercely overcome his own body. Apparently he was still forcing himself through his customary paces, ignoring physicians' pleas, and presumably countermanding Probus's proposals. He maintained his methodical ways, dividing his day into offices through which he moved in turn. Paperwork he had always disliked, leaving it to Mucapor, for some days unseen. He ruled through his mouth. Here at noon he would inspect the Praetorians in the largest courtyard, ready with the impatient rebuke, the hard stare, then stand rigid while the Standards paraded, Rome's blood embalmed and shining, cowing the nations. At sundown he received the duty officer, giving the night's password while the Gate guard changed.

Always too distant to judge Aurelian's health, Constantius found the days unexacting. Gavian was not with whatever court the Emperor maintained here, and for once he missed him as a conduit of news. Manilius too had heard that the Emperor, grossly strained, was brusquely refusing to admit it.

This was confirmed by further orders. The Gulls were, at noon tomorrow, to protect the Gate against all intruders while loyal officers were to surround Aurelian and induce him, perhaps forcibly, to submit to the finest physicians of the Empire. In one report the Great King himself, with the courtesy once customary between monarchs, even when warring, had offered the services of his own most confidential medical aides.

Constantius slept better than on recent nights, tensions easing at the resolution of the intolerable.

Again the day dawned in customary lack of significance. No Bacchic irresponsibles danced free of the earth and flung themselves into celestial space, no cock crowed before midnight, no owl screeched, no voice blared from the starlit sky, no cloud was suddenly inflamed as a Fury scrawled her signature on a passing breeze. Only a few civilians were on the street by the Gate. A few fishermen lingered on their way to the shore; a blind beggar stood under a depleted oak; several women had paused with their water-pots, others with baskets of dried fish and apples. Children squatted to play with dust. A washerwoman and her slaves were waiting for the inspection to end, licensed to fill churns with camp urine for the purpose of cleaning linen.

Constantius, barely aware of them, stationed his men on the street, he and Manilius keeping the Gate, which was barred. All, though with swords drawn, placidly awaited dismissal, though Ammas's slender face seemed somewhat parched in the strong light.

A bell sounded. Constantius gazed within at two small lines of Praetorians, behind whom a door was opening for the Emperor, bareheaded, informally mantled, moving towards them quite alone, as he always preferred. Then came a blurred impression as of rain against trees, the double line of Guards was converging inwards towards Aurelian, and, as though drowning, in a swift instant Constantius saw himself helpless

205

in a squalid drama, debarred by the Gate, unable to strike out for the land. Weapons were flashing in a fierce bubble of light already reddening, metalled feet sounding, the Emperor, with mastiff tenacity, fighting back, obdurate as he had been throughout his life, refusing to bow, against all odds, until the Praetorians ringed him utterly, one, the tallest, directly at Aurelian's back, his arm rising drenched with blood, gripping a short blade.

For an instant Constantius was convinced of Aurelian's animal eyes entreating him for help that could not come. The murderers were already parting and, silently, smoothly, as if from the wet stones, head high, a camel leisurely, casually loped towards the stables, eyes bored, ignoring the prone body far beneath, the curled, mottled limbs, gaping head, already clustered by a black helmet of flies.

The camel seemed to crumble and vanished, no part of history save perhaps for some sardonic epigrammatist. For Constantius it had been the stage prop befitting a day all at once abnormal, wrenched out of true, as the mortal world stumbled.

The Gate was already unbarred. A hand gripped his arm, a rough voice spoke, a smile sat on a jowled, beardless face.

'He has lived.'

None would directly mention death. Constantius realized that he was being led to a dark arch, while behind him more Praetorians were harshly advancing down the street, a mass of glints and blanks, outnumbering the Gulls, now irresolute, gazing from them to Manilius, who was staring after his commander, so unaccountably removed.

XX

To the always courageous, ever fortunate Legions, and to the Senate and People of Rome.

The wickedness of a single individual, Eros, and the mistaken beliefs of many, have robbed us of the Emperor Aurelian. May it be your pleasure, Enrolled Fathers, respected gentlemen and citizens, to admit beloved Aurelian to the fellowship of the Immortals, then to appoint in his place whomsoever your just consideration shall deem fit to assume the imperial purple. None of those who, by guilt, error or misfortune, had complicity in depriving us of the best of rulers, will be considered fit to rule.

Just so. Old Sword-in-Hand had lost grip, poke-nose Aurelian out of the race, a mountain tortured by a wasp, collapsing into hell, done in by his own will-power so commended in virtuous quarters. One more stalwart magnifico erased, the show-off Wall not yet paid for and, despite pompous announcements, probably not yet completed. By the fountain, laughing on warm, ochred stone, children had declared that the Wall was made of butter cake.

Aurelian, overbearing general who disdained to be a statesman, had refused to acknowledge any judgements save his own, was deaf to discussion, unaware of jokes. Romans were attributing his death to the wrath of gods insulted by the Wall, which showed insufficient trust in themselves. The Empire had cocked one snook too many and, easily stepping over the Wall, a primeval goddess, deprived of her dues, had catcalled that in much pain is much retribution, without adding that pain can advance understanding. Under snow lies bread, the peasants say. Young Sextus must be reminded to pay cash for losing the wager that Aurelian would not survive the year. Imperial luck had faltered as the Wall rose. Capitol, Wall, Pyramid were gigantic efforts against death, condemned from the first brick, unable to staunch the blood of Aulus and a pool oozing from beneath Pompey's statue.

Constantius must have missed a few steps and was still under arrest. A good man, elder brother, but too earnest for his own good. Sincere, but sincerity is the swiftest path to the infernal. More bardic than intelligent, never quite comprehending that life is a rich matter not of beginnings and endings but a purposeful middle. Stolidly free of corybantic urges to spin into the unknown, pour himself into flame, Constantius yet had nerves too thin for his martial conceits, brave reputation, convictions stoical if not entirely Stoic. Had he not been taught to read, he would have learned more. He inhabited a past invented by writers of best quality, a Rome without people.

Julian was fond of his brother but would not weep if the axe fell on him. Doubtless it would not, though, in these circumstances, vestal Constantius would accept guilt and utter no protest. Should he survive into marriage, he and his lady would be casualties of nothing very much. The wife might need tusks.

Ah, well! A new pebble lay on his table washed by sunlight, while down in the street a closed litter lurched by, preceded by Africans, their gilded spears clearing a way through amiable saunterers who, in this notch of orchard summer, appeared briefly convinced that after all life is simple.

With Aurelian's death the ordinances proposed against Galileans might be revoked so that certain contacts could be safely resumed. Their denunciation of military service made them disliked, particularly in quarters by no means martial. Chrestus had shrugged away armies, not because he valued all lives indiscriminately but from scepticism about the reality of the tangible. His own technique was sometimes as disarming as brute force – unexpected retorts, angry sarcasm, sardonic passivity, cryptic sincerity. His followers were less lofty, apt to terrorize women by threats of fire, blackmailing adulterers, inducing conversions by magic devices to escape death and punishment.

Self-seeking had two meanings, profitably fused by this ambitious sect. Meanwhile he wanted no talisman or fiery disaster. Briefly, he was content with this pale, speckled pebble, its lines and crevices, cracks and profiles more suggestive than any stolid Wall, a replica of the world itself, its secret places and paths, valleys, endless patterns, smooth indifference to public events. Staring at it, into it, round it, beyond it, concentrated on its tiny compactness, simultaneously image and symbol, he was enveloped by scents of a garden, sweetness of hay, flutter of blossom, a goatherd's pipe, long dissolved or imaginary contours of a world without frontiers where the traveller descends to heights, strides the untraversable, lit by a moon afloat in a cracked mirror. Here, in a counter-Empire, Clodia might one day venture. Her delicate glance had the knack of transfiguring the mundane: fauns prancing in mosaic or tile reverted to birds, collapsed into sheer colour. She understood that a riven stone disclosed a face, then a message; foliage, like love, was a mass of suggestion; the desert blazed with lions, some of them live.

Yet she will never stray very far, this little Clodia: however great the distance, she will remain at home in herself. She will bear no children, though she may marry a regiment.

Domitia might once have dared a glimpse beyond news, markets, documents, then dutifully withdrawn into best Roman marble.

Pebble in hand he lingered in the spare, sunlit room under the apple loft and the swallows and storks scratching on thatch and under the eaves, watching the lizard motionless on the sill, green shadow amongst fig leaves bantering with a placid breeze packed with resin and birdsong above the glow of wild jasmine. A porch opposite was painted with Juno, her huge golden triangle slotted between swollen thighs and leered at by Priapus, straining towards high heaven. Reluctantly, he prepared to descend to sup with the passing riff-raff, the chance opportunities always encountered on journeys, with their sluttish stories, thieving hands, a few employed by the Officialdom.

He was at a guesting taverna at a crossroads town, making for riotous Alexandria where Aurelian's widow had been proclaimed for a mayfly reign until, following an unexpected request of the army, for the first time within anyone's memory, the Senate nerved itself to enthrone the civilian, Senator 'Granny' Tacitus, loaded with some seventy-five winters and, looking like a decrepit tortoise, and known to disapprove severely of the sacred Caesar Augustus, whom even he could scarcely remember. A reluctant Emperor, Granny, though the legions, still numbed by the extinction of the Saviour, the Invincible, assented, acclaimed the old man's visit to the camps, and easily dispersed support for the imperial widow. He, Julian, had arrived from Antioch, a favourite place, throbbing with novel philosophies and bizarre variations of familiar notions. Plague, Eastern ghoul, had returned to Rome, usefully disposing of the unwashed and insignificant, less important than a threatened gladiatorial revolt. Sensible fellows exploit plague and earthquake, together with those grandiose displays of human folly, idealism and despair, though the muscles of Empire droop and rats gnaw through the Wall. Sites, like flesh, are always on offer, insurance plums gleam within reach. Losers can usually be soothed by eloquent, vaguely flattering reference to Orphic austerity and discipline, the escape from the tired wheel of death and rebirth.

Life is pleasure, my friends, if possible pleasure with profits, a matter of securing options without temptation to conceive existence as metaphor or hoax.

In Rome, dwarfed further by the Wall, bereft of their tremendous protector, pondering the death of the deathless, people moved slowly, slightly groping, as if under water, as if summer had thickened, discoloured by an aggrieved sun. The fate of emperors had ceased to be unusual, but this was different. Meanwhile they dragged on, endlessly ranging the streets, acting the parts allotted them by whomsoever, whatsoever, the noisiest the most obedient.

Far from Rome, this trip was as pleasurable as ever. Random encounters, amusing and inconsequential, were more numerous than those piles of books at Pergamum. Small, odd anecdotes pattered down, half-promises and queries were wined

210

into contracts, landscapes exposed the provident resources of colour – he had identified ninety-one phases of green. The broken bridge at Aquilia Minor, which decades ago, rumour had it, contractors were coming to repair, survived. People gathered from failing villages for the spoils anticipated from the project: casual work, casual pilfering, lackadaisical gambling. The contractors never came but the vagrants remained, the village swelled to a town, slum suburbs without a centre, sustained by the conviction that, like old-time gods, the builders would yet descend. At Antioch a youth, sporting emerald earrings and a gummy smile, introduced himself as 'Juvenal'. A few years back he had been secretly kidnapped by the Gentlemen of Supplies. Accused of attempting to poison Claudius Gothicus, he listened politely to the prosecution, then demanded with pleasant assurance, 'Did you speak? Or did your nose waggle? Or did you lay an egg?' In baffling response, he was freed. In his cups a banker, unnaturally lean, confessed he acquired sexual joy on the cheap, having discovered it by climbing trees and masts. The cock is a various college. Gifted, subtle men abounded, who, to escape the Officialdom or onerous office, had sold themselves as slaves, bemusing their masters and particularly their mistresses with questions wittily suggestive though delivered with shallow innocence, with dumb insolence, indelicate quotations from impeccable sources, respectful mention of labour laws and compulsory bonuses of which no one had heard. Quiet praise of a noble wife as 'Ganymede' was accepted as a compliment. In all, each journey tested the versatility of the eye, which can arrest a stranger at fifty paces, hypnotize a lion, jib at an imaginary snake, declare love or forteiture, stimulate bad verse, detect a long-smothered battlefield, discern confusion within order, and bamboozle juries. A direct stare can infuriate or paralyse; the imperial privilege.

Supper provided the usual wine, rankest Massic, indifferent food, small, hard radishes and too much fennel heaped on too little carp and pork, clumsy strangers beseeching his attention, erroneously scenting an easy outlet, a foppish amateur. Every-

211

thing fully enjoyable. Eating, pushing aside the tiresome fish, raising his eyebrows, those of a long-weary connoisseur, he again thought of Clodia, feeding the carp, gravely intent, like Plato reading, calling each by name, convinced of its intelligent response, telling them well-turned lies culled by Bran.

He dominated the talk though saying little, while from moist reddened faces, voices clattered around him.

'Landlord, sharpen your wings. I'm in need. So hungry I could eat a horse.'

A reminder that he would probably be doing so might check his vivacity, though not for long.

'I'm the ugliest man, Marcus, you're ever likely to see.' He spoke with some pride and considerable veracity. 'Should we not indulge ourselves further and offer a toast – I'll put it better, a libation – to this new Emperor, not, they tell me, in his first youth. Our goodwill may waft him skywards to further happiness in luxuriant company.'

A stout Cappadocian in canary gown, hitherto sleepy from grappling with intricate accountancy, jerked himself forward. Julian had met him the previous night and distrusted him for being not quite so silly as he appeared to others and perhaps to himself. Could he be a Treasury agent? His father, another acquaintance, was said, though by the son, to be a ghost though, if this were true, his resemblance to life was uncanny.

The Cappadocian waited for silence with the prosperous air of one with something precious to deliver.

'I met Junius once . . . or was it my brother? He enjoyed putting on airs, like a magus. At Milan I was alongside him at a banquet. I can hear him yet. "I have", he informed us, "certain gifts, I refrain from calling them powers, I call them certain gifts, which enable me at once to apprehend the nature of a person's ancestry. For instance . . . here." He pointed to a lady allowed by the new customs to join us. "This charming creature is the daughter of a butcher." She gazed at him, very nervous, yet resolute. "No, no, Senator," she quavered. "My father was a court chamberlain." But he shook his head, like

Jove. "My dear," he told her. "You're quite mistaken. Your father too was wrong. He was a butcher." '

Another voice intervened.

'That's nothing, my friend, or very little. I've plodded about the Albanian mountains and, mind you, very loathsome it was. I once found villagers howling obscene jests while they buried their chief . . . I dare say our barbarian defenders did much the same for the regretted Mason. Laments, you see, would force his spirit to flee the clan, mirth would keep it amongst them. They blocked all his holes to retain it further. A drunken fellow, wearing only a necklace of teeth, caressing a mouldy cat, was forced to prophesy before showing us where the ghost was hovering. Actually in a privy. I did not care to investigate fully. The chief lay in a ditch with his weapons and hounds and clutching a bunch of his own hair, and, beside him, not exactly our Roman way, his favourite wife, her throat like a red rose gone wrong.'

He chuckled at his own wit, revealing teeth surely too heavy for the slack, narrow mouth. Silence followed for a period of gobble, led by a currant merchant, angular as a crane but more greasy. Scarcely comptroller of Olympus, he could be led by the nose – a nose pulled forward rather too emphatically – towards the purchase of a copper foundry not of the first rank. Gulping more wine, he grinned happily.

'Julian, your judgements are impeccable. Money dances to your tune. Jig-a-jog, all the time. But tell us, is it true that after death the soul lingers three days above the body?'

'Julian, though Mercury to the life, mixes with Galileans, to stiffen his moral fibre and doubtless more. Tell us, did Chrestus haul himself from the grave by his own bootstraps?'

He could tell them that Galileans pretended absolute truth, very presumptuous, though in the process they might have turned up a few minor truths. Collapse, revival; the potency of words; the disconcerting effects of the unexpected. Rome, soon to finish, yet remain permanently incomplete. That sententious old owl Cicero had once 'condescended to opine' that intellectual certainty is impossible but, for mortals, probability is sufficient. Yes, indeed. But this sweaty, jovial crew had never heard of Cicero and next week would have forgotten Chrestus. With know-all shrugs he described, not Chrestus butting into eternity, but the Pisan financier boasting that the god Pan would attend his river party. Pan indeed came, though confusing the revellers by knowing neither Greek nor Latin, only a vile Hebrew dialect. From the Pisan he shifted to the Pious Ambrosius who had begun, though not completed, an epic on the delirious sizzle when the sun sinks into the sea at dusk: *O Mighty Orb, O Golden Blob of Splendour*.

Julian enjoyed watching the listeners, who were uncertain whether the words were absurd or miraculous, experimenting between degrees of considered gravity. Misunderstanding, slaves hastened to refill the wine-jugs.

Suddenly bored, Julian rose. 'I must leave you, ascend to my arbour, sleep with gods.'

Actually he did not. The air under the low, dirty rafters was too hot and, save to a hardened anchorite, the bed lacked charm. Lying restless, he planned the morrow. During a quiet stroll along the town walls he would pour some soft words over Long Nose, hint at confidences from on high, a wink from the Officialdom, gratitude to be expected from Emperor Tacitus, and ease him into acquiescence.

Sleep remained aloof. Morpheus, prince of dreams, lend me sweet juices.

He slumped into a thin doze pursued by fragmented images, wrenched-off bits of life. Seas were said to be rising, a tiger roamed loose in Alexandria, a cloud rained snakes over Strasbourg. A tavern song clinked stupidly about his head:

> The way the dead were sleeping
> Before the dead were sleep.

From nowhere, light and rock collided. Sudden flame. *Zeus*. A stage in the illumination of mankind.

Then, as if prodded by javelins, he was out of bed, naked and alert, poised in a darkness acrid and thickening. Breathing, he felt his brain reel and, staggering, feeling his way to the door, he jerked it open. Stairs were in flames, smoke rushing to stifle him. Blinded, choking, he kicked it shut but was enveloped in dark fumes fighting for his throat and lungs, gnawing at his eyes. Staggering towards the window, propelled by instinct, he reached only a bare wall at which he clawed frantically, struggling for air, desperate for refuge, striking out without direction, sensing, as from far away, a clash of buckets, a hiss of steam, before collapsing.

For several days he lay almost sightless, periodically choking and vomiting, tended by assiduous women, submerged in sick fantasies and wandering worlds. Faces peaked and askew with broken eyes seemed to tilt from a curdled sky, a worn-out heaven. His jokes about the Galilean threat of fire and agony might have induced a spell that trapped him in flame inspired by angry shamans. Jokes, flames hid further realities waiting to be uncovered. Now, beautiful bodies were gliding past, but his own body made no stir. His limbs were helpless, but within his head pictures flashed, swift but with startling vividness. His pebbles welled into galaxies, sketches of the unborn, faces without bodies. A gigantic copulation of giants clarified into Aurelian's triumphal entry into Rome. A patch of yellow air became an apothecary's beard dangling above him like a parched forest.

Lying thus, he felt shapeless, an essence with consciousness barely within reach. Unknown influences lurked, dull fish beneath bright-green scum.

Recovering, with balsam rubbed over him by delicate hands, he mused about humanity developing a flair for self-torture, babbling about gods born in silence and fear. Truths were accessible. A Jewish sage in Alexandria, Philo, had written a thesis about an eternal Word begotten by a Father on everlasting Wisdom. On evidence the universe was a unity, its multiple contradictions posing as gods but inextricably mingled. One had little freedom of choice, though some struggle more energetically than others. Life had now reminded him that complete independence was illusory though he would continue to behave as though it were not. More ordinary folk,

bundles of inconstencies, laboured on, at the mercy of darkness
that Persians condemned as Ahriman-Shaitan, and the Jews
cursed as Satan, endlessly fighting the light, their struggle
sustaining existence by preventing stagnation. Failure pro-
motes success, a Gallienus makes possible an Aurelian, a Wall
excites discussion from minds preyed upon by armies and
officials, magicians and saviours, tutored by fraud and mischief, the deceptions of paradox, seeking protection from Time,
welcoming ghosts and demons, fairy gold, and periodic, deadly
proscriptions. Deep in humanity lurks a desire to be crucified.
The visions assailing him during illness a lesser being would
have accepted literally, instead of stripping the symbols from
ancient tales, heroic misunderstandings. From peril and
mortality, one saw life naked. No vulgar Elysium, no Platonic
garden existed. Olympus was a rudimentary stage in efforts to
prolong rapture, Hades the last despair, the extinction of spirit.
Earthly death was final, though moribund selves could be shed
in rebirth of spirit, resurgence of appetite. Chrestus's
Kingdom, total acceptance of paradox, nourished only a few;
unless the Galileans had lost or destroyed some vital evidence,
some proof that particles added up to more than themselves, the
extra momentum loosely termed divine.

By now freed from bed, Julian sat at a window watching crisp
light, the steady alterations of the day, the encroachments of
darkness, new pebbles enlarging his hold on life. He had survived, had emerged keener. Prayer creates the god it addresses,
the dance requires a song. Needs require pattern. A Trinity:
Jupiter, Juno, Minerva; Hercules, practical and responsible;
Orpheus, teacher of knowledge; perhaps Chrestus, with
purposeful love and astringent demands. Such a Trinity was
still weak, requiring human help against darkness, was only
slowly being born, needing no sacrificial blood but dedication,
so that it might coalesce into One. To fly too near the sun, stare
at a gorgon, seek a golden fleece, descend to underworlds, all
were wayside physicians, warning, healing, like the flames on
the stairs. Clodia must have dared herself down the path to the
bolted door, changed to bird, tree, rose, pool, vase, supped with

gods in her quest for light. In the riddles of childhood she watched enchanted seas, sailed to Colchis, whispered spells, in fearful secrecy lest she turn to ice and melt in the arms of whoever loved her.

But did anyone love her? Julian gazed into the infinite recesses of a green and white stone: from such a question flow new stories, sad jokes, angry rhymes, initiations into the wild fact of the world. That fluent young parrot 'Ovid' spoke sensibly, in his denunciation of the Wall as a negation, sterilizing the warm pomp and flux of existence.

Clodia would probably live, perhaps live well. She would learn that life periodically requires a shove.

Julian smiled, fondling the tiny stone. He himself might die, but generations hence. His nose would not waggle, he would never perhaps lay an egg, but on occasion he would say a few quiet words.

XXI

Midwinter. Birthday of the Unconquered Sun. The Saturnalia was still celebrated, the reversal of norms, the master waiting on his slaves, children taunting or preaching to adults, animals decorated with finery.

In Rome, some now rejoiced that the Cage had opened, though knowing that it had not, or that no Cage existed. The late Emperor's decree against Galileans had been rescinded. Others flocked to the Wall as defence against the destruction of the world, of which Rome was the hub. Plague continued.

No letter from Constantius reached Villa Ammianus, but after some weeks Domitia received news of his promotion to the staff of Emperor Tacitus. Her face expressed nothing, but Clodia clapped hands; then, abashed, desisted. Later, she asked whether Aurelian had had a proper funeral, remembering a Greek princess disobeying a king and burying her brother so that his spirit could free itself and drift to other worlds. But Domitia did not know, and certainly did not care.

Without formal permission, Bran had moved into the Villa, occupying the Senator's old quarters. No common spoon hung from his belt, but a jewelled dagger, and he dressed in purest linen, telling no stories, immersed in estate matters, and insisting on being served his meals in private. Meeting Domitia in a passage, he told her roughly that old Tacitus had died at Tarsus, his brother reigning a few days before being killed by the troops, who then, ignoring the Senate, empurpled their hero, the conqueror of Egypt, Probus.

No officer had suffered for Aurelian's death. Constantius's arrest for complicity was followed by a few days' confinement without formal trial, then, without explanation, he was released, swiftly receiving an invitation to join the Staff, in one more tremor from the mist of unwritten compacts, shadowy conferences and whispered decisions.

The army had held a solemn, sincere wake for Aurelian, clean flame devouring his ravaged body, his worms leaping and twisting. On the place of his death, juniper, sage and thyme were heaped, burned, purging the stench of blood, the lingering apparition of guilt. Men threw a prisoner to be killed by wild bulls, the victim said to be Eros, after all preserved by Aurelian, but no one was certain.

Carus, the Praetorian Prefect, Probus and Saturninus grandly reappeared for the imperial obsequies. Mucapor was loaded with rich insignia, praised, embraced, then he vanished, none daring to ask whither. Men would never be told whether Eros had left any list, whether many or few had been duped, whether in all his life Aurelian had undergone real illness. His personal attendants were seen no more.

Under old Tacitus, Aurelian's generals governed well, in tribute to dead majesty.

After the funeral, Constantius was detailed to watch field punishments of those who had 'failed to rescue the Emperor'. In icy paralysis he saw them digging their graves, then lined up on the edges, to be stabbed. Manilius had died silently, Ammas weeping and screaming, Ammas whom he taught the precept of Marcus Aurelius, that a man should be upright, not kept upright.

Later, he met Gavian, also promoted, eyes still fresh in untroubled blue. They had said little, parted quickly, gravely wishing each other well.

A new group was assigned Constantius, a personal retinue, to whom he had nothing to say. He was summoned to a few meetings but never consulted, and spent long days in idleness. At Probus's accession he heard that Gaius Valerius was in high favour. Whether he had been involved in the conspiracy was another secret.

New orders were issued, signed with Probus's florid, even ornate signature, and Constantius was consigned to the Rhine frontier, doubtless intended to meet death there, certainly oblivion. He would welcome both. The pain within him denoted a spirit already rotting.

The complicity of each general, the deepest motives of the conspiracy, he would never know, such affairs are seldom revealed. To mention the killing was forbidden; *Aurelian* had relapsed into *former*. His own guilt, behind his breaking pledges, was his insufficiency, his need to play second, to follow as he might rhetoric or trumpets, his inability to step forward alone.

The breath of a murderer darkens the air, and he was left much alone, to ponder the nature of guilt, will, being. Some held that all human blood was contaminated by descent from pack-animals, or from Titans, abnormal half-men who had slaughtered Zagreus, child of Jupiter, reborn only by a miracle from Redeemer Dionysos. Were this so, Fate ruled all, as he had long suspected, despite Julian's shrugs. Fate, forcing submission, conditioning the failure of integrity.

Whatever the truth, the New Rome would be far from what he had taught Gulls who had trusted him and trusted too well.

Lucretius had written that violence and injury cast their net over those who commit evils, and generally retaliate on the guilty.

XXII

Many years had passed. A prematurely aged man, gold threads woven into his dark silks, sat alone in his gardens, surrounded by hedges cut into camel-heads, ships' prows, square and circular shields. For two decades he had ruled the Empire, then he had awed the world by relinquishing power and retiring for ever.

The Salona Palace, of his own making, backed by Dalmatian mountains, overlooked the bay where an armed galley lay anchored, and fishing-craft bobbed and turned. The sprawling, powerful edifices, columns and sharp roofs aching against the sky, the colonnaded courts and shaded arcades, were enclosed by ramparts packed between massive towers. The white central complex lacked windows, the blankness yet suggesting a despotic nerve resting within. Level with the towers were trees, black and white obelisks, the famed Golden Gate, the spires of the octagonal temple of Jupiter, and the lofty peristyle of the House of Aesculapius the Healer, near the black granite sphinx, whose slumbrous inertness collected shadows throughout the day until, swollen in twilight, it crouched as though massed to swallow the entire square.

He sat on a wide stone seat, its base carved with lions' feet. He was proud, he would say, of his roses and cabbages, and was now staring before him as if envisaging behind the hedges the long ranks of rose deployed before the starry marigolds and Persian zinnias, the sweet aspalatons from which the region was named, the moon daisies and strong hyacinths in the crescents and rectangles he had designed, the fountains he had requisitioned, the lawns where, on days which, his chamberlains purred, he had ordered to be windless, he would laboriously pace, brooding, still upright. For flattery, for epics, comedies, rhetoric, music, he cared nothing, no more than for dancers and catamites. When he finally learned their story, he dismissed Antony and Cleopatra as irresponsible buffoons, and queried the strategic abilities even of the pious Aeneas, wondering whether great Virgil had ever seen battle. Here, with grass, leaf, butterfly and the guardian sun, he could gaze back on his crowded life: infancy in a peasant's hut, enlistment, wounds and promotion under Aurelian, his own crushing of invaders and of his rival Carinus, of Galileans, of great Persia; his untiring reforms, domestic sadness, illness, withdrawal to long, settled afternoons of sunlight, and longer evenings of darkness and chill. Prisca, his Empress, was dead; their daughter Valeria, married off to a Caesar, then tormented and exiled, might now be dead. Traps were laid for him, dagger and poison threatened, but he lived on, abjuring power, contemplating suicide, but prepared to commission an altar to Jupiter at Pergamum, a marble Triumph of Neptune for himself.

Ghosts might gossip until dawn, but he had few self-reproaches. Philosophers were do-nothing fools in their belief that by opposing violence a ruler must become criminally maniacal. His reign, hailed as the envy of gods, had begun when, in public view, he had killed a murderer with his own hands – Aper, Praetorian Prefect; a deed prompt, merciless, and saving the bacon of *Roma Aeterna*.

Unseen guards roamed the great gardens. A peculiar hush always surrounded him as if the very birds recognized the depleted face, the unwavering eyes and mouth, of him who had been Augustus, Father of Peoples. Even the furrows and pouches of that visage remained firm, like the folded hands, their huge, solitary emerald almost sunk into flesh tired but unshaking.

On the low table before him, enamelled blue and golden, shone a cup of filigreed silver, gift of the Senate, a body he had methodically ignored, and from which he occasionally remembered to sip, consenting to accept advice at least on matters of health.

222

Parting the foliage a woman, grey wigged, blue robed, moved briskly towards him. He remained still but for a small nod; she knelt, head bowed, until his sleeves rustled and he signed for her to join him on the seat.

She was Clodia, mistress of the library which he never consulted, though he welcomed her presence here in the hour of kingfisher and dragonfly. Later they would walk, saying little, towards gardens yet remoter where, constant as glass, wide strips of water flowed down strictly cut marble cubes and, from kennels under apricot trees, dogs old but still valued, painfully stirred, then rose to lick their master's hand.

Clodia too was at peace, here in green spaces lit by aster, lily and rose. Obeying Domitia, she had married early into a senatorial family, her husband perishing in the tumults following the murder of the divine Probus. Her second husband, an Official, died of plague. Her lack of children she regretted just as she might lost trinkets of charm but small value, or that sister so long ago drowned or strangled by those who had created her.

For years she had been pledged utterly to the man beside her, who needed not her body, very seldom her counsel, but her resolution. Agonies of fatigue, betrayal and forebodings had been his daily lot.

'Marianna' never returned. Occasionally the Lady Clodia looked up from her rolls, documents and missives, and murmured, 'Where is that girl now?'

In palace, in camp, on the road, she had known fear, sometimes panic like that when a bird, trapped in her room, had swept frantically between the walls, darting, falling inert, then flying up as though aiming at her eyes. Fear, though, was a constant companion, one of the pains that struck, receded, struck again, throughout life.

Domitia had never left the Villa until imprisoned for her Galilean beliefs, dying during the purge decreed by the lord of these gardens, protector of rose, marigold, cabbage. Mother's cold smile and superior style would not have been disturbed by death.

223

Probus, in the style of Aurelian, had ruled energetically for six years, beloved of armies, saving Gaul from wild Teutons, completing the Wall, repelling treachery from his old associate Saturninus, until victimized by his hatred of inaction. Moving against Persia, he had halted near his birthplace, Sirmium, to await supplies. One sultry afternoon, irritated by the sight of idle soldiers, he impulsively had ordered the army to start at once draining the marsh for a canal. The men were still weary from marching, and the over-peremptory command incited an angry squad to waylay the Emperor, always trusting his popularity, then, after fierce complaints, to chase him into a tower and, in mindless fury, kill him. Contrition at once overwhelmed them; throughout the night, wails rose from all ranks, ultimately spreading as far as Britain. They erected a huge memorial cairn in his house, loaded with inscriptions so that, though he had joined the gods, his mortal name would endure for ever.

Carus, the Praetorian, succeeded, governed well enough until dying on a campaign, from, Rome was informed, a lightning flash, though actually from common fever. Illegally he left the throne to two young sons. Carinus died fighting the builder of this palace, who had accompanied the father on his last campaign, while the elder brother, Numerian, was murdered by his son-in-law, Aper, soon victim of this man whose reforms at last stabilized the Empire. The final outcome Clodia would not live to see. She was determined not to survive her companion.

Constantius's letters had dwindled, then ceased, years back. He had been removed from active service by her exalted patron who, while never uttering his name, seemed to know something of him, granting him not formal disgrace but a nominal governorship of a territory far away and desolate. She had never seen him since that departure with Aurelian. He was probably dead. Whether or not the Emperor had realized that he was her brother, she might never know.

There would never have been a Constantius Soter aloft in a roaring Triumph. His letters after the indistinct circumstances of Aurelian's death had been despondent, then hopeless. The last had described with dull, repetitive bitterness an incident he had heard from Africa. Roman troops had crossed for water into independent tribal territory. The local chieftain advanced with his people and, having smiled a greeting at the general, had solemnly spat in his face. Outraged, the imperial representative ordered an instant massacre, learning too late that the dead chief's apparent insolence had actually signified welcome and trust. The tribe believed that all possessions were vulnerable to enemy magic; footprints, shoes, hair, dung, even names. Thus, by entrusting his saliva to a stranger, the chief displayed extraordinary confidence in the general's aura and goodwill.

This tragedy Constantius had associated with the Wall that, for him, as for Julian, had sagged into an image of division and futility, despite the high intentions of one whom he could never bring himself to mention.

His final letters were abrupt, disjointed, often senseless, fixed on the twitters of birds, habits of snakes, the benevolence of horses. He fancied he had conversed with a centaur.

Julian she saw very rarely, though his gifts arrived from luxuriant cities: a roll of Chinese silk, a necklace of green glass, a golden torque from Britain, a Rhenish jet bracelet. His messages, short and elegant, usually reached her when she most needed them. At home, he wrote, we were lonelier than we realized.

He had always belittled politics, found brilliance in trifles, ignoring a Triumph but commending an ash hissing in the wind or a tortoise credited with the gift of tongues. A blob of ink creates a world. He was glad to encounter a Pisan gentleman who, to outwit ill-luck, never closed a door, a precaution unavailing against robbers. Unconcerned with a Probus or Numerian, he minutely described a grand Palatine lady endowed with millions, startling all by her beauty, also with her webbed feet. He referred to a statesman not for his professional achievements but for knowing the best way to evaluate a puppy: place the new litter in a circle of fire and note which the mother rescues first. He

225

named the three Armenian astrologers dispatched to discover the infant Chrestus's horoscope. The Emperor's distaste for Galileans, he had continued, was a public service, Chrestus having castigated law, family, temple, wealth, all the ingredients of the ancient Republic. 'Very plausible, of course, but perhaps not what's really needed. You can reassure Majesty that he has my passive support.'

Latterly he had reported seas still rising, drowning low-lying provinces. His tone was always ironic, unenthusiastic, faintly amused yet, withal, serious, more concerned than he would ever admit. The Officialdom – she could hear his sigh – was introducing a new road tax, though roads were vanishing beneath weed; also a new hospital levy – but where, my dear sister, are the hospitals?

Used to his manner, she learned with equanimity that Isis, Mourning Lady of her childhood, had once been a bee, then, believe me, a palm tree. 'Sons of space wed daughters of time.'

Julian himself, neither bee nor palm, was a notable, a personage of fashion and opulence, allowing his repartee considerable risks, and one whom her Emperor considered impudent, though refraining from doing more. The gods must love those who so casually dissected them, in ways so perplexing to poor Constantius.

Of the stupendous imperial reforms Julian was sceptical, gibing that they were an etherealized replica of old what's-his-name's Wall, striving to arrest history. The State was the omnipresent physician condemning patients not only to drink poison but to be grateful for it.

Nevertheless, Julian enjoyed boasting that, one of the most successful men of the day, he was invariably mistaken.

In her way, Clodia was as experienced as he. She believed the reforms would endure, they must endure, or the Empire would sink beneath waves, not of the sea, not primarily of the Goths and Teutons, but of the slaves, the debt-ridden and mortgaged, the frustrated and the indifferent.

Convinced that the Empire was too large and unwieldy for a single government, her monarch had imperiously divided it.

He himself, endlessly improvising against monstrous odds and implacable necessity, ruled as Augustus of the East, appointing as co-emperor a fellow Illyrian, to rule the West, both assisted by a Caesar, vice-emperor, the four linked by marriages, each with his own capital. Milan effectively replaced Rome, the eastern emperor was installed at Nicomedia. Only once, after almost two decades, did he visit the City, disdaining to celebrate the Triumph to which he was unreservedly entitled. Hearing grumbles about the cost of the Wall's upkeep, he swiftly withdrew its garrisons, advising the populace to keep their lamps oiled and their knives sharp and to reduce their own flabbiness, though, loving to build, he provided a fine set of baths.

He never returned. Despite his ignorance of history, he too may have known those words of Jugurtha, before his ignoble death, that Rome was for sale, doomed to perish when she found a buyer.

Enforced by grades of Officialdom radiating from both wings of the State, imperial Edicts thudded out so constantly that Julian complained that he risked his health dodging them. Emblazoned on innumerable market stones, irrespective of local conditions, were the maximum prices permitted by the State, deviation from which was a capital crime for customer and trader alike, at the mercy of informers and the Silent Ones, formerly the Gentlemen of Supplies. Maximum wages and incomes were also promulgated, trade fluctuations grandly prohibited, inflation pronounced treasonable. Certain professions, particularly the menial and agrarian, were made hereditary even for freedmen, against desertion from the soil, itself suffering widespread erosion, for which landowners were consistently fined, or had their lands absorbed into State farms. Inheritance laws were revised, favouring the productive citizens. For almost all, choices were constricted, lives were mapped by the Officialdom. Taxes for defence, schools and postal services were ruthlessly extended, to be paid in cash, goods and labour. An 'Expression of Gratitude' was levied in the wake of further currency reform.

Though the Empress and the unlucky Princess were Galileans, hundreds of their co-religionists were executed for civic apathy. Not only did they refuse their dues, but with phrases resounding if meaningless they denied the validity of dues themselves. Factions and sects were forbidden, unity was all, State power must be undisputed in a crumbling world. The Throne, courtiers enthused, had never been so overwhelming. Conspiracies were said to be officially fabricated, to allow the decimation of patrician families, senatorial cliques, Equestrian associations. Workmen's guilds and fraternities were prosecuted.

The Emperor had toiled unremittingly, grasping every expedient, manipulating law like a whip; he was an Atlas bearing the world, a dyke master daily withstanding great seas and darkening winds. Such centres as Antioch, Syracuse and Alexandria he transformed into arsenals piled with arms to be rushed to wherever danger loomed. Camps and barracks were reorganized, citadels repaired, barns stuffed with requisitioned grain, wine and provender from the State farms. The bloody Praetorian Guards were methodically weakened, the most suspect dispatched to frontier service. Much traditional administration was removed from generals, who henceforward were confined to duties exclusively military. Magistrates and landowners were strapped more inflexibly to their posts as unpaid State accountants and tax-gatherers, their estates resurveyed for further demands. The Aurelian Wall, Julian repeated, was inescapable, blocked every channel, stifling challenge, adventure, momentum. To exist for the Officialdom was more futile than to exist for oneself. The Galilean Kingdom itself might prove more enticing, if less tangible.

Though the Emperor had settled restless Egypt and frivolous Alexandria, then the Great King, he was foremost a man of prudence, disliking heroics, giving no attention to poets and shallow annalists. Merciless when situations demanded it, he took no pleasure in pain and battle. To reduce military expenses, he set barbarian tribes and confederations against each other, extracting advantage from confusion. More barbarians were incorporated within the Empire, swearing loyalty to the emperors alone. They were planted as frontier colonies, on ravaged countrysides, on estates usurped by the irresistible, mechanical State, as woodmen, shepherds, labourers, local police and militia.

All this, though, Julian noted, inflation, trade returns, bizarre cults, despite the Edicts, remained disobedient. Production still lapsed, confiscation was more sterile than equable taxes on capital more or less honestly earned, by such as himself. Merchant ships requisitioned for military transport left essentials to rot on the quay. 'Clever ones will one day need only three words to sum up the god-smitten Empire: *Survival, Conquest, Retribution.*'

'Darling Clodia,' Julian wrote, 'Do you remember Father telling us that King Romulus, in the beginning, saw twelve vultures, a prophecy that Rome would endure twelve centuries? Watch, for twelve centuries are almost completed.'

This reminded her that Constantius had once told her of an oracle vouchsafing to Emperor Aurelian a vision of nineteen careless heads melting with the sun. A soothsayer eventually disclosed that, from Gallienus to Probus, nineteen claimants to the throne had perished.

In old age she discerned that much which was seemingly wayward, devious and ambiguous could be part of a design. The children's taunt, 'accidentally on purpose', contained substance. Long despising Domitia for subservience and chilliness, she now recognized these in herself; also, some traits of Constantius – acceptance of Fate, dedication to another, a sort of courage.

Here, isolated by the sea, she was content. The Imperial Court had repelled her. The Great King, that brocaded idol so long haunting the West, might now allow a smile to flit over his stiff, painted features, for the Roman Emperor, the man asleep at her side, had transformed his regime into Persian theatre. He had withdrawn deep into his palace, with access to the Presence determined by a hierarchy of stately eunuchs, confidential advisers, State councillors, Officials, secretaries, chamberlains, ennobled porters, gilded doormen and, in shadows, the Silent Ones. In a vast hall the Lord and Augustus sat in robes sumptuous, bejewelled, himself silent and still as granite, the glittering Diadem, a cluster of sharp, iridescent hues, suspended above him. He was enthroned far above the embassies, diplomats, courtiers, petitioners and commanders, all of whom must prostrate to kiss his hem, purple on gold and crimson.

Such magnificence was yet another Wall, an exquisite refinement of authority, exorcising familiarity, even any hint of mortality. Robes, formal music, studied movements and inclinations, the abnormal stillness of that face afloat in rare, toxic air, made even attendants outsize and extraordinary to those waiting or toiling beyond the Sacred Enclosure. Against such majesty, a dazzle made flesh, none would raise his hand. No weapon would flash against eternity.

Today, several years after his abdication, the Emperor still received messages, pleas and warnings, offers reverently delivered by the Grand Chamberlain, dignified and fastidious as a crane, from Nicomedia, Sirmium, Trier, Strasbourg, Antioch, Milan. The new rulers were quarrelling instead of uniting against foreign conspiracy and internal fissures. Unknowns begged him to appeal to the armies and resume power but, encased in his gloomy vaults, he ignored them, glad to re-enter the gardens, once muttering that he had shown all the world how to manage its affairs, let the world take heed.

Occasionally he would talk, the masklike face crinkling into live fragments, the voice as if still giving orders, confiding what none but she would ever know. It would die with her.

The afternoon was very slow, golden at all levels. Leaning back, worn, his breathing inaudible, he might still be sleeping or vigorously, suspiciously alert.

Closing her eyes, Clodia saw cobwebs of peacock colours, transporting her to childhood. Father could control the weather – that he did not always do so, was aggrieved by a frosty wind or a thunderstorm – and eventually taught her the perverse complexity of power. Thinking herself too fat, she blamed the

230

moon, recalling Julian's strange joke about girls climbing there. In sleep a naked hunter pursued her with a blood-tipped spear, her body tightening with unseen knots. The yellow god faded to a quiet glow, Father complained of dishonesty, flowers bloomed on the sea, murky Rome thrilled to a Triumph she would soon forget.

At any instant Julian might enter, his small, slanted smile unchanging. A spry old man, still gratified that he had never been a child.

These drowsy, bee-haunted lawns and glades refreshed Clodia's cravings for life, though stories had wilted with the necessity to avoid Bran. The covert leer, insinuating offers, the wink. She became her own story, the words, colours, moods, proportions open to herself alone. She was proud, then, as if noosed, apathetic. A hero waited to deliver her; heroes no longer existed. The day after Father's death pains began, the red spear pierced her, girlhood died. She knew from slaves the significance but not the facts. She was a toy, probed by others. Mother would tell her to pray only to Minerva. Isis made no sign. She touched a beloved vase and at once it shattered. She sailed between islands in a leaky bowl, sometimes convinced that she was a witch blighted by an Isis not wrathful but disappointed. The goddess herself had slowly dwindled to a nostalgia of griefs, still stirred by a crescent moon or a star over the black sea.

Thereafter she had depended on herself alone, the vaunted Family and its descent from Mars were, as Julian put it, tarnished assets impossible to exchange for hard currency. For herself, little essential would come from the Wall, the State, from husbands, scores of deities, Chrestus's magic cross, from *Roma Aeterna*.

Summer, summer murmured and rustled under the sad stare of the dead. She awaited her companion to rise, take her hand, perhaps talk as they paced slowly through green air, always discovering a newly opened flower, a forgotten arbour. Their story could be related in ways very different, even conflicting, but might never be told by anyone.

231

Clodia looked at him, still undecided whether he was awake. A shadow closed his face like a shutter. An old man who had ruled the world, the very great lord, 'General Docles', Gaius Valerius Diocletian.